Blessed Are the Peacekeepers

Tom Donnelly
and
Mike Munger

Savant Books
Honolulu, HI, USA
2013

Published in the USA by Savant Books and Publications
2630 Kapiolani Blvd #1601
Honolulu, HI 96826
http://www.savantbooksandpublications.com

Printed in the USA

Edited by Zachary M. Oliver
Cover by Dennis Krull

13 digit ISBN: 9780988664005
10-digit ISBN: 0988664003

Elizabeth;
Thank you for your leadership at NSCC
And for your patience with me as Adjusted
To the Instructor position. You are an outstanding leader.

Michel Murpu
Bravo-one

Dedication

For all who risk their lives to keep the peace.

Acknowledgements

We would like to thank our families for providing the support and patience during the time it took to bring this book to publication. We also wish to thank: Tim, our original literary adviser; Leslie, our proof reader; Scott, who recommended Savant Publishing; Zach, our editor; Dan, the editor-in-chief; the real members of Bravo Team who gave their permission to write this story; and those who assisted in obtaining the security clearances necessary to publish the book.

Blessed are the Peacekeepers

Chapter 1

Someone once told me that I was born to be a cop, though I never really saw this in myself. I have never been very aggressive, or athletic, or prone to chasing after the high of an adrenaline rush. By nature, I was more the social creature, the storyteller, the joker, and the party animal. The only cop-like quality was my sense of curiosity. I've always had a need to know all the answers. Police detectives get to find out whodunit, to solve mysteries. So, after college, a stint in the Marine Corps, and several years as a patrolman, I became one in the small city in southern New Hampshire where I grew up. Mid-life boredom set in, however, so I applied and was accepted for a 13-month temporary assignment with the United Nations—UN—Police overseas.

How such a decision took me to the middle of the former Yugoslavia in the aftermath of its civil war is another matter entirely. But there I was in the parking lot of the UN Police headquarters in Peja, Kosovo, waiting for my new civilian translator to arrive. He appeared beside my patrol car ten minutes late, out of breath and carrying a backpack filled with college text books. I pointed to my watch, but when I saw how young he was and that he looked embarrassed I held out my hand as a peace offering.

"I'm Officer Mike Granger. What's your name?"

"My name is Jak," he replied. "You can call me Johnny, though. That's what the soldiers call me."

Seemed kind of backwards, but I shrugged and said, "Okay, Johnny."

I turned to my team of Kosovo Police Service—the local acronym being KPS—officers, and said, "Introduce yourselves quickly and let's get rolling."

A minute later, we piled into our SUVs. I had Johnny sit in the back seat out of concern for his safety and also to show the senior KPS officer some respect by letting him sit up front with me in the command vehicle.

I was pissed off at Johnny for being late, but I made myself get past it. He radiated honesty and intelligence, tempered with a hefty dose of humility. Besides, how could I not like a kid who was willing to go unarmed on patrol with us in one of the most heavily-armed and dangerous post-war countries that you could find.

Finally ready to roll, I saw Commander Tony Achebe at the doorway of the station, signaling me to come to him. He was a stern, six-and-a-half-foot-tall Nigerian officer with tribal scars under each eye and numerous police international actions under his belt. I assumed that he was going to chew me out for being so late to leave. When I got to him he was not angry, but he was in a serious mood.

"Mike," he said, "a construction crew was just fired on with a rocket near a village called Nashi. I want you to meet up with Willy's team and investigate. If you need more men or other resources, or North Atlantic Treaty Organization—NATO—troops, call them in."

With that he went back into the building, promising to pass along any new details by radio. I knew he would be busy for the next hour or so getting a full sit-rep of the incident so I jogged back to the car to get the map. I yelled to my patrol team on the way, "Does anybody know where the hell Nashi village is?"

No one answered.

The other team leader, Willy Steinhardt, was a highly decorated German police officer. He was also my friend, roommate and mentor. I contacted him on the radio using my team designation, Tiger Six.

Right away, he replied, "Tiger Five to Tiger Six, are you still in the damned parking lot?"

"No," I lied. "I'm on the way to Nashi. Where do you want to meet me?"

"Meet four clicks east of Vitomirica, on Route 1, over."

Moments later, we were on the road. The sun was climbing and it was getting hotter; my stomach was empty and now I had to figure out what four clicks meant. I had been out of the military for over twenty years and since then, had only worked with miles, feet and yards. After a bit of thought, I recalled how to make the conversion: One click was one thousand meters, a little more than half a mile.

About two and a half miles east of Vitomirica, we spotted Willy's vehicles parked on the side of the road. I pulled over behind them, got out with NATO map in hand, and walked to him. The KPS officers mingled with their companions. Johnny followed behind me. I thought that some of the KPS officers appeared nervous and mentioned it to Willy.

"One of my team has been to this village before," Willy said. "Alex, tell Officer Mike what you told me."

The KPS man shook his head slowly. "This place is bad news," he said. "These are rough people and they do not like outsiders. The Nashi clan fought the Serbs and they are well armed. We must be careful."

I rubbed my chin as I processed what he said. I asked him, "What is the terrain like? How is the village set up?"

Willy answered for him. "I already asked that, Mike. It is a cluster of small homes on the side of a small mountain with many trees for hiding. There is a dirt road leading to the main house complex, where the Nashi clan lives. It is surrounded by a wall. When the Serbs attacked the village, the Nashis beat them back from behind that wall."

"Okay, Willy," I said. "You're in charge. What do you want to do?"

He took the map from my hand and spread it out on the hood of his SUV. It showed our regional center, Peja, and the twenty-six villages surrounding the city. Ours was the Italian sector, a large rural zone the size of an average county back home. A Stateside Sheriff's Department might patrol it with five hundred police officers. The UN only had one hundred and fifty, of which only forty at a time were ever on duty. Our backup, besides the other group of UN cops on duty, was an Italian parachute battalion at a base ten miles away.

I pointed to Nashi village at the far limit of our area of responsibility—AOR—about twenty miles from our location. That meant about another hour or more of driving. The roads were not dependable: crumbling asphalt, hard packed dirt roads, loose dirt roadways, farm tracts and goat trails. There were more of the latter than the former, so the driving was going to be time consuming. There also appeared to be a stream crossing, with a blown up bridge in the way.

The distance and time required to get there meant that any significant backup force was two to three hours away. In Kosovo, people who lived out in the middle of nowhere lived by their own rules. Apparently, the rocket attack on the workers repairing a nearby roadway was a statement that someone wanted it kept in disrepair.

We were still one click—slightly over a half-mile—from the village at mid-morning. It was at the end of the road system that terminated at a goat path wide enough for a wagon, but not our SUVs.

We contacted headquarters by radio to see if there was any additional information. There was nothing new except a report that the rocket attack had produced no injuries to the work crew. That was good news because it would give us some negotiation room with the headman of the village. We began to think that this would be a simple job. When we arrived, we would just talk the tribal leader into giving us the village's weapons with a promise of no arrest. Then, after a proper UN scolding, we would hike back to our vehicles, drive to the nearest town with a café and get something to eat. What could be easier?

It was getting warmer and we wanted to get it over with before it became too hot. We picked a KPS officer from each patrol team to sit in the vehicles and man the car radios while Willy's team set off for the village that we figured was about a kilometer away. My team followed about fifty meters behind.

It made tactical sense to divide up that way. If things went south quickly, then my team would be in a position to execute a rescue. It also gave some protection from ambush. Police work in Kosovo was often paramilitary. The people we were there to police were tough bastards, and in many cases resented any kind of authority—never mind one that wore a UN emblem. They were all armed and knew how to do damage.

Halfway to the village, Willy called me on my mobile radio.

"Mike, I hear a vehicle coming down the road. I am going to stop it."

"Roger that," I said. "I've got your back."

I hustled my team nearer his location and found that he had stopped a beat-up older model Mercedes sedan. It was filled with hairy, angry-looking village men. I had half the combined team take up perimeter security in a semicircle, facing away from the car. I didn't want anybody sneaking up on us.

Willy and I both had our weapons in our hands, pointed at the ground. I motioned to Johnny, my interpreter, to come. He beamed, finally finding himself of value. The three of us approached the driver and the question and answer games began.

Using an interpreter was always tricky in the beginning. Except when there was an obvious display of emotion on one side, you couldn't really be sure if you were getting the message across the way you wanted to or not. It could be unsettling when you ask a short simple question, and your guy "interprets" what you said into a speech that goes on for over a minute. Johnny wasn't like that, though. He was sharp and direct.

The five men in the car said that they were going to a nearby town, but they were unclear about the reason. We searched them and the interior of the car, but found no weapons.

When questioned further, they told us that the village was aware of our approach, but it was a peaceful place and we should expect no problems. The main spokesman was calm when talking with Johnny. To Willy and me, the rest appeared hardcore, though. All of them were stocky in build, with rough-bearded faces.

I was getting a bad vibe. I pulled Willy aside and said, "I think these guys were trying to get out of Dodge before we arrived. I'll bet some of them are wanted."

Willy nodded. "Possibly, but we have no reason to arrest them. They are unarmed."

I had always been cautious, some might say paranoid, in situations like this. I asked, "What if they are just trying to get behind us? What if they have hidden a stash of AKs and grenades somewhere down the road?"

Willy did not say if he bought into that idea or not, but I could see that he was considering it. He looked at Johnny and said, "Ask them where the guns are."

Johnny complied and, when finished, relayed what they had told him, "Only a few old guns, for protection, in the village."

I don't know what the men in the car actually said in reply since I knew very few words of Albanian. Like I said, an interpreter can't tell you everything, especially when people are talking over each other. But something was said in that encounter that spooked the KPS, even if Johnny didn't catch it.

Willy decided to let them go. The old Mercedes, all dented and scratched on the sides from numerous previous trips up and down the overgrown path continued on its way. Willy had two KPS officers follow fifty meters behind the rest of us just to make sure that they did not stop and turn back on us.

We could see that the KPS officers were acting differently. They were exchanging glances with each other and appeared to be reluctant to re-holster their side arms even after Willy and I had done so.

I thought about it and then dismissed it all as normal caution on their part. What was there to worry about? We were trained and confident. It was a beautiful day, sunny and warm. We were up in some pretty mountains, a UN peacekeeping patrol doing its business to repair a broken country. We were there to help people and to put an end to the violence that had plagued the region for almost a decade. We were doing good stuff. All we had to do was convince the good people of Nashi village to stop shooting rockets at strangers.

Willy and I led the team for the last few moments on the trail before we walked into the clearing to the village. We waited for the two trailing KPS men to catch up and the twelve of us marched into Nashi.

There were maybe a dozen houses in total, three within a semi-enclosed broken down wall. It looks like there was an old barn in the back, built against one side of the wall. The villagers at this time were standing in their doorways, women and kids pretty much out of sight. They stared at us as if we were aliens from space who had just landed. While scanning the village for threats I saw the village elder come out of a house on the right and approach to greet us. He was dressed in cultural pants and a shirt-dress garment, and was not smiling.

While Willy tried to communicate with the old man through his interpreter I stood several meters away, providing security. It appeared that this tribal elder didn't want any part of our visit. There was no offer of tea or any other traditional gestures of greeting like I had experienced on other patrols. The conversation between Willy, his interpreter, and the old man was rapid-paced and tense. Johnny, who was at my right shoulder as always, leaned over and whispered, "They don't want us here. He is demanding that we leave."

I moved closer to Willy, who turned to me and said, "The old man denies there are any weapons at all in the village, and says that we should leave now."

Willy remained cool. Despite the rising heat, he did not have so much as a bead of sweat on his forehead. He explained again that we represented the United Nations, that we must complete a search of the village. He told him that we wanted no trouble and that we had no plans to take any of his villagers away. We just wanted to disarm them of any explosives or rockets so no one could get hurt. The tribal head wasn't getting it, though, and neither were the forty or so other village men who had quietly gathered in a semi-circle in front of us. They were only about thirty yards away. Some began talking loudly and aggressively, and appeared to be encouraging the old man to remain firm.

Willy stepped back beside me.

"Mike, this is not going any place," he noted.

I looked at the fired-up crowd and could not miss the hatred in their faces. Naively, I wondered what I had ever done to them to get them so pissed at me.

I said, "What do you want to do, Boss?"

"We will stand our ground."

The village men were grouped in front of us. Women and kids were watching from the doorways and windows. I glanced back and found that there were now only *three* KPS officers covering our back. I was alarmed, but could hardly blame the others for using discretion and backing away from the confrontation. Whereas Willy and I had a combined forty or so years convincing people to comply with the law, most of them had a year or less of police experience. With the defections, the numbers had just dramatically turned against us.

Willy and I conferred again. We decided the best option was to continue the Mexican stand-off and negotiate until reason came to this clan leader and he gave up, allowing us to do our search. After that, we would shake hands and leave.

The headman, however, was still not getting it from the way he continued to defiantly glare at Willy. On the far side of the semi-circle of male villagers in front of us, one worked-up young man began pointing and yelling at us. He was immediately restrained by two companions. I tried to watch him over the heads of the men assembled in front of us, but he was visible for only brief moments, obscured by the movements of the others. From what I could see, he looked to be about twenty-five years old, taller than the two that were straining to hold him back. They seemed to be telling him to knock off his shouting.

I was starting to get nervous. I looked behind me to make sure the remaining men of our patrol were in position, and saw only two KPS. Another had disappeared.

Willy and his interpreter still were making no headway with the old man. The other men of the village, who were becoming more confident by the minute, began edging nearer to us. I moved closer to Willy, and he said to me, "The old man will not admit that there are weapons in the village. He is still demanding that we leave now."

I looked behind one more time and saw that the last two KPS officers were now gone. I told Willy, "The KPS bolted on us. I think that discretion is the better part..."

"Steady, Mike."

I noticed now that our interpreters, normally loyal as guard dogs, were back-stepping their way towards the goat trail.

I also saw that the young out-of-control man was now holding a large ax. I had no clue who had handed it to him, or why. His two friends were still trying to restrain him, but he was getting more and more frantic. The old man started backing away from us toward his house, motioning for his family to get inside. I was starting to get tunnel vision on the man with the ax. My hand, almost on its own unsnapped my weapon holster. I then realized that he was not the only one in the crowd holding something. There were several men holding sharp farm tools. It had turned to shit real fast.

In some circumstances there is little difference between a human and a wild animal, and this was one of them. If we tried to run, we would be set upon and ripped to shreds by the mob. No doubt about it.

I could feel my heart beating. Sweat coated the palms of my hand were I gripped my weapon and held onto it. The man with the ax suddenly broke away from his friends. He was screaming nonsense. A gaping hole opened up in the crowd in front of us to let him pass.

"Mike, we stand our ground," Willy hissed.

Ax Man raised the weapon over his head, let out a bloodcurdling howl, and charged right at us from about thirty yards away. I was so tunneled on him I could count the holes in the buttons on his ripped farmer's shirt. I saw his dirty fingers strangling the ax handle and his face contorting in rage at Willy and me. All the time I was thinking, *what the hell is he doing—we're the good guys!*

I knew if I turned to run, the ax would be buried in my back before I got ten feet away. Instead, my training kicked in, over powering the fight or flight adrenaline. Finding myself looking down the sights of my firearm, I centered on Ax Man's chest. I don't even remember drawing my weapon. It was all business.

I yelled, "Stop!"

At the same moment, Willy shouted, "Halt!"

Ax Man had gotten dangerously close now, but both of us still held our fire. He wasn't stopping, and he was not just show-boating for his buddies, either. He was plain nuts.

There was an explosion of joint gunfire, and Ax Man went sliding on his face fifteen yards in front of us. It was nothing like the movies. He dropped his ax and fell flat on his face into the dirt like he had tripped. He didn't make a sound.

It was all a fucking waste.

The gunshots caused the rest of the crowd to scatter. I imagined that they saw us like a couple of Serbs bent on a massacre and instinctively ran to protect their families. In less than a minute, they were all in their homes, doors shut, peaking out at us through the windows.

I was surprised that I wasn't shaking. Shaking is the body's natural reaction to a powerful adrenaline surge. Together, we approached the body to check for vitals.

I hoped that he was alive, but I doubted it. He hadn't moved even a twitch since he dropped.

We never got to him, though. Angry and threatening voices came pouring from the windows. I began hearing sharp metallic noises. We were in the middle of an open courtyard street, in a village with at least one rocket launcher—and who knew what other kinds of weapons— and we just dropped a village alpha male.

We backed out of the village to the goat trail where the two interpreters were waiting at the trail head. Johnny was holding a short tree limb like a club. I said to him, "I'm going to have to write you up. You're not allowed to carry a weapon."

He smiled and dropped the stick.

"Did you shoot someone?"

I didn't respond to his question, except to say, "Let's get moving."

Chapter 2

We hiked double-time down to the vehicles. When we arrived there, Willy got on the radio to call in the shooting. He was told by Commander Tony to leave. Italian NATO troops would be sent the next day to clear the village.

I told Johnny to have my KPS team mount up; we were moving out. I had been shocked by the actions of the KPS. Before entering the vehicle, I made a show of taking out my blue beret and putting it on. The significance of that action was not lost on the others—we were playing for different teams now.

I was lost in my thoughts as I drove the SUV. I had been starving before we went into the village, but food was suddenly the last thing on my mind. I reviewed the incident over and over in my head, trying to figure what we could have done better. In the end, I decided that we could not have done anything to prevent what happened. It was in the hands of a stubborn old man and an impulsive young lunatic. We had done everything by the book. Willy was the consummate professional and never once raised his voice or did anything to inflame the situation. He was younger than me, but impressed me to the point that I aspired to be as cool as he was under that kind of pressure. I wondered what thoughts were going through *his* mind as he drove the lead car of our small convoy back to the station.

On the way back, I also thought of the States and my perfect life there. Why did I change all that to come to one of the most dangerous spots on the planet? I still had over ten months left on my deployment. For the first time, I realized that I might never get back to New Hampshire—that the next lunatic might be shouldering an assault rifle or an RPG instead of a damned ax.

Commander Tony was waiting at his desk in the Peja Station when Willy and I returned from Nashi village. He asked us to come in and closed the door behind us. He wasn't smiling as usual, and was all professional as he listened to our version of the events leading up to the shooting.

When we had finished, he asked, "Where were the KPS officers when you opened fire?"

Willy hesitated before replying, "They were in defensive positions behind us."

The commander's eyes widened for an instant, then he nodded. I could tell he had more questions on his mind, but he held back. "Okay," he said. "Tomorrow give me your reports. Take your time. I want to know what the NATO troops find in the village. Now, you've put in a good day's work. I will talk to you again about this when we have more information."

Willy and I collected our gear for the long walk home, but decided to go instead into another room at the station to discuss what had happened. As soon we both were seated, I said, "Do you think Tony believes that we fucked up?"

He sighed and said, "Mike, it is up to us to fix this. We were too focused on the threat and we forgot to give our men proper instructions —to maintain control. We should make a draft of our reports together. We need to learn from this."

Willy was right, and his point hit me right between the eyes. I had stood my ground because of the confidence I had in him. The KPS did not have that same confidence in us. We had failed in our leadership and could have been killed because of it. I vowed that I would not let it happen again.

We decided that we would include in our reports that the KPS took a defensive position behind us on the goat path like we had told Tony. It was technically true because they *were* behind us on the goat path. It was just that they were a long, long way back. We thought it best to concentrate on our own actions.

The KPS force was brand new and its reputation was fragile. There seemed to be no good reason to throw them under the bus and create a scandal. More important, though, was Willy's point that the failure was not with the KPS, but with us. It hurt to have to acknowledge that we had not provided the leadership or confidence that the KPS needed to stand with us.

We each wrote up short reports that played down the conduct of the KPS officers. Willy and I signed them. I left the station feeling that I had done the right thing.

The next morning, Willy and I got up a little earlier than normal and completed our morning routine, including the long walk to the Peja police station. When we arrived, we turned in our reports of the Nashi village shooting incident to Commander Tony. He had specifically instructed us to keep our reports to two pages maximum. I had submitted longer reports back in New Hampshire for housebreaks, but if that's what he wanted, that's what he would get.

The reception that we received from the officers that day was dramatically different from before. The other UN officers greeted us with back-slaps and congratulations. They asked questions about our encounter at Nashi, looking for details. We told them that we couldn't talk freely about it yet.

The KPS officers kept their distance, though some nodded

greetings in the usual manner, pleasant but reserved. Still, there was a sense of tension among them that both Willy and I could feel.

After the morning briefing by Commander Tony, we were instructed to gather our teams from the day before, go out on a short patrol and return at noon. At that time, Willy and I would meet with investigators from Pristina Headquarters. Tony had told us that by that time the NATO troops would have completed their sweep of the village and he would have their faxed report on his desk. He said that Italian soldiers had surrounded and entered the village just after dawn.

Normally, the KPS officers assigned to us were changed each shift so that the maximum number of KPS could learn from each UN officer assigned to our platoon. This day, we kept the same members as the day before because of the shooting.

Something had to be done to dampen the tension within our group. Willy and I took our teams to a large grass parking lot next to a marketplace and sat with them.

Willy started first.

"Mike and I apologize for failing to properly organize our approach and positions in Nashi village yesterday. We should have given you clearer instructions. None of you KPS officers did anything wrong."

He paused while his interpreter translated.

Willy then asked if any KPS had been questioned or asked to write reports. They answered no.

He continued, "Mike and I have received years of training on how to deal with situations similar to Nashi village. In our reports, we mentioned the defensive positions that you KPS officers took during the encounter because our focus was on the attacker. We did not see where you were. That is what is in the reports. It is true and those were the facts given to Commander Tony."

16

After the translator finished, the KPS officers began to chatter amongst themselves. Their previously dour expressions appeared to lighten.

Willy concluded with, "Mike and I are honored to work with the KPS and with each of you officers. We promise that our failure to provide you good leadership in such a serious situation will not happen again."

I had never seen a more relieved or excited group of cops once that last piece was translated. Willy, in my mind, was a genius. He should have been a politician. No, he was better than a politician. He was a real leader.

As a group, the KPS officers got up from their sitting positions and gave each of us hugs and handshakes. They asked a lot of questions about what they could have done, and we drew in the dirt, an alternative approach to the village. Willy had turned the whole situation into a learning experience. After the briefing, we broke into our two teams and went on patrol.

I took my KPS team out into the countryside and held a similar discussion. We sat on picnic tables at a small café, along a river about ten miles outside of Peja while we awaited the call back to headquarters. I explained to my men that I was still new in their country and would need their help. They asked a lot of questions about the shooting and asked if I was scared.

I told them, "Hell, yes."

I had vowed to be a better leader and being honest with them would be part of that vow. It was no time for false bravado.

Our openness and honesty worked like magic. They told me that they thought Willy and I were the bravest officers that had served under during their year on the force.

Now, to be honest, this was not a reputation I wanted to belittle.

A good reputation is important in police work. I ended the lesson with an old nugget that cops and military men have known for centuries. "There is nothing wrong with being afraid in a fight," I said. "It is completely natural. It is what you do when you are scared that counts. Doing your job, even when scared to death is what real courage is all about."

I had heard that said a million times in various forms, but the KPS officers were hearing it for the first time. They looked at me like I was Plato or some prophet speaking wisdom from a mountain top. I felt good, flattered even, by the way they hung onto every word. At that moment, I knew that I had made the right choice on coming to Kosovo. Maybe, I could actually do something good there.

At twelve noon, Willy and I were sitting stone-faced in the interview room at Peja Station with Commander Tony awaiting the UN superior officers from Pristina. We were expecting a three hour post-shooting briefing and all sorts of additional paperwork. Back in the U.S., that would be standard procedure, as well as a full month-long investigation. It was expected even though we were confident in the actions that we had been forced to take.

After introductions, the most senior officer began to speak.

"NATO troops have completed their sweep of the village and found nothing," he said. "No one wounded, no body, no shell casings. If you fatally shot him, he was probably buried at nightfall, before dawn, as is the tradition up there. The Italians looked for a fresh grave and couldn't find one. If you fatally wounded the suspect, his body could be anywhere in the forests surrounding the village."

That was unexpected, but good news. The other commander explained that after the sweep UN Police investigators interviewed numerous villagers, all of whom denied that anything had happened. No one saw or heard anything, according to the village headman. We were told that a lack of cooperation with authorities was normal in the remote villages.

The investigators did not dispute our accounts of the confrontation. The senior supervisor stated that the matter was closed and then asked how the KPS had acted during the altercation.

Willy said one word: "Good."

There were no follow up questions.

The senior UN Supervisor then said, "It is normal procedure to transfer an officer who has been involved in a shooting to another region for his own safety."

Willy and I exchanged glances.

He continued, "Since your commander has requested that you be allowed to stay, and because of the fact that Nashi village is so far from Peja, we will leave the transfer issue to the three of you."

Shit, I thought. *I just got here. It's a great place to live after spending a couple of weeks in the dreary cement apartment block used to house UN officers. I like my KPS officers and I like Peja. I'm just getting settled, and I still have a lot to learn from Willy. I don't want to go anywhere.*

Willy must have been thinking the same thing, because we both answered, "No, thanks," at the same time.

After barely forty-five minutes, the interview was over. There would be no further investigation, no additional paperwork, no suspension without pay, and no second guessing from Headquarters. The supervisors got up and headed back for Pristina, the Land of OZ, with its electricity, water, and diplomatic parties.

We remained in the room with Tony. He appeared concerned.

"Look," he said, "I do not know exactly what happened in Nashi, but whatever it was, it is done. You two are good officers, and I want you here in Peja. You're good for my team. The other UN officers like you and the KPS have a lot of respect for you now. But, please remember that this is Kosovo. Those clan members in Nashi will probably want blood revenge, so be *very* careful for the next month or two."

He had a point. Blood revenge was taken seriously in the Muslim Albanian culture. I had heard of numerous examples in Peja. If a man lost face or was wronged, he would vow blood revenge. He had no choice, really. Not only could he and everyone around him be satisfied until he had exacted revenge, but he would not be respected in the village until he regained his and his family's honor.

During my first in Kosovo, my KPS team and I found the body of a fourteen-year-old boy on the side of a road that ran between two villages. He got up one morning and rode his bike to a small farm stand to get some fruit. Unfortunately, it was in the territory of another village, one that had declared blood revenge against his village a few miles away. I found out from one of my KPS officers that the feud had been going on for over twenty years. Someone had seen the boy bicycling away from the fruit stand and alerted the locals. It appeared that a group of men drove up beside him and just blasted away with a shotgun. The poor kid was dead because of some stupid slight that had happened before he was born.

I remember seeing one KPS officer at the scene nod and say the kid should have known better—as if it were the boy's fault that he was dead. Blood revenge, to that cop, was an accepted, even justifiable form of behavior. Some of the cultural peculiarities of Kosovo, like arranged marriages and blood killings, were new to me and would take some time to accept.

"I am going to temporarily re-assign you both to other duties for the next week," Tony said. "I want you to keep a low profile. Some Egyptian officers are going home for seven days of R&R—rest and relaxation. I need you to fill their posts."

In addition to Peja Station, there were a number of smaller permanent posts that required UN officer presence: three substations out in the countryside, one border crossing, and a local courthouse detail. For the next week, Willy would be the security director of the courthouse and the eight KPS officers assigned there.

Me? I drew the short straw. I was ordered to spend the week at the remote mountain pass border crossing. Commander Tony said it was the best way to keep me out of harm's way and out of trouble.

After Tony informed Willy and me of our temporary transfers, he gave us the rest of the day off. We hiked through town to our new home, and relaxed for a while before getting our gear in order for our new assignments. I knew that the border station area had a heavy Arab influence, so I brushed up on a few words of Arabic and some cultural mannerisms I had already picked up.

I had been friendly with the Arab officers assigned to Peja Station. Whenever I arrived early for a shift, I would have coffee with them across the street from the station, though "coffee" was a loose description of what was served, as there was nothing even remotely resembling the western version of the drink in Kosovo. I had gotten used to a coffee-like drink, strong and flavorful, called Macchiato, while sitting with them in the morning.

Both Jordan and Egypt contributed large numbers of officers to the UN Mission in Kosovo. The Jordanians drifted to patrol assignments, and appeared interested in gaining experience in the paramilitary operations that Kosovo offered. The Egyptians, on the other hand, leaned towards more laid back assignments, like the courthouse and the border crossings. These posts were their little fiefdoms.

I had once gone to the courthouse on assignment, and at the

security checkpoint, the KPS officers stopped me and said that I must meet the courthouse commander. I was led to an office where the Egyptian UN officer was sitting at his desk. A female KPS officer hovered around him acting as his orderly. She prepared us tea and served him in an almost ceremonial fashion. I remember thinking that she was behaving more like a house servant than a cop—and he was behaving more like a pampered prince than a police commander.

The Egyptian courthouse commander then explained the way he had organized the KPS security detail, priding himself on how they jumped to his every wish and demand. He was also quite proud of how little actual work he had to do. Even so, he was friendly and I liked him well enough. He was personable, hospitable, and gregarious. However, I was impressed neither by his entitled behavior nor his subservient treatment of the KPS officers assigned to his detail.

I wondered how Willy would adapt to his new environment. I figured that he would fit right in and have a good week of relaxation. There was, however, a fringe benefit to his assignment: The courthouse detail officer had many female KPS officers to keep him distracted. I thought of my new post in the mountains, and wondered why I didn't insist that we at least flip a coin for who got to go where. My assignment required a ten mile drive to the base of a mountain followed by another harrowing five mile drive up the mountain to the border crossing at the top each day. I was told not to expect any women officers.

Chapter 3

The Peja region of Kosovo lies nestled against a rugged border range in the western edge of the province. This harsh landscape separates Kosovo from Albania on the west and Serbian Montenegro to the north. There is only one border crossing to Montenegro at a small pass on the top of Peja Mountain. I had been there once before after the KPS border guards and their UN commander had exchanged gunfire with the Montenegro military. Kosovo was not just a dangerous place, it was a place surrounded by other dangerous places.

On the first day of my temporary duty assignment, I walked to the Peja police station two hours early, signed out my UN vehicle and picked up Johnny. It was a forty-five minute drive to reach the base of the mountain. After that, it was another hour to crawl up a zigzagging mountain road. Mount Washington in central New Hampshire has a road that runs from the base to the summit with some hairpin turns. I had driven up it at least a half-dozen times. This mountain in Kosovo may not have been as high, but it was just as steep. The roadway, though paved, suffered from constant erosion and was peppered with potholes and washouts. The ascent would strain any vehicle's engine. There were no guardrails of any kind, so there was the constant danger of slipping off the mountain. The old wreckage of cars and trucks that failed to negotiate the many dangerous curves littered the mountainside. The ride scared the shit out of me.

When I arrived, I was met by the six KPS officers who would be working with me for the week. Two KPS officers had taken the week off because their boss, the Egyptian, was gone.

The border crossing at the top of the mountain consisted of a tollbooth-like checkpoint and two small aluminum trailer buildings. The UN had established a one-half mile DMZ—demilitarized zone—between our border post and that of a similar one operated by the Montenegro military, also on the top of this mountain. I was told that the guards on the Montenegro side hated us, though nobody seemed to know exactly why. Rumors were rampart throughout CIVPOL—the UN civilian police organization—of confrontations and armed assaults in the DMZ between the Montenegrins, and the UN and the KPS.

On top of that, the heavily pine-forested mountain range was a favorite hideaway for smugglers. A dangerous breed of criminal, they travelled the many tracks that marked the sides of multiple peaks much like the ski trails I remembered on the mountains where I often hiked in New Hampshire. I loved the White Mountains in the summer and autumn, and I thought that the assignment at the border crossing just might offer the chance to get in some hiking.

The crossing did not open until nine o'clock, so I had an hour to figure out what I was supposed to do up there, and get to know the men who I would lead for the next week. I found that they were a mix of old and new officers. They were all friendly and told me that they took their task of securing the border seriously. They also said that they liked working on the mountain because the temperature up there was ten to fifteen degrees cooler than the oppressive summer heat in most of the Peja region.

The senior KPS officer showed me to my office in one of the trailers and explained the paperwork that I needed to complete if contraband was found in any vehicle crossing the border. He also stated that normally four officers manned the crossing and searched the vehicles, while the remaining patrolled the roadway up and down the mountain on the lookout for smuggler's vehicles. The Egyptian Commander, he explained, usually just sat in his office in front of the UN computer and surfed the Internet all day. If contraband was found in a vehicle, or a suspicious car or truck was spotted on the mountain road, then the KPS would notify him and he would take action.

The senior KPS also told me that the men were all excited to have a new UN officer there for a week to break the monotony, especially when they heard it would be an American. For the rest of the hour before the crossing opened, the men peppered me with questions about the United States, Hollywood movies, TV, and why I came to Kosovo.

They also told me that they had heard about a shootout in Nashi through the KPS rumor grapevine, and that I had led an assault by the KPS that had experienced both rifle and rocket fire. According to the story, the KPS, led by American and German officers, had defeated the Nashis, and re-established law and order in that usually lawless region. That's the way they heard it, anyway.

I don't know if they confused the incident involving Willy and me with the NATO sweep the following day, but like all rumors, the story was taking on proportions that were larger than life. Johnny was no help, either. He seemed to enjoy his new status as one of the heroes of Nashi. I'm sure, despite his long-winded Albanian translations, he was not forthcoming with the details about what had really happened there.

One of the men asked me how brave the KPS were at Nashi—how did ten men take on an armed village of fifty and all escape alive, never mind unwounded? I tried to downplay the incident as much as possible because I really did not want to talk about it, but I did tell them that the KPS acted honorably. Hearing that was important to them. Honor was everything in Kosovo. I tried to explain that there was no armed resistance, and that there were actually two different incidents in Nashi, but they would not be swayed. They already had the "real" story they wanted to hear from their cousin's sister's brother's uncle's best friend, who, of course, saw it all.

I could sense excitement coming over this tiny remote mountain garrison. There to lead them, at least for a week, was one of the heroes of Nashi. To them, I had been sent not to hide out for a week, but to clean up a border smuggler's paradise. They told me of long mule trains crossing into Kosovo from Montenegro, carrying packs loaded with cigarettes, drugs, weapons, ammunition, and other contraband. They wanted me to do something about it.

To be honest, I didn't care what they expected or wanted. All *I* wanted to do was to go "Egyptian" and enjoy the break. I wanted to escape the heat below, sit in the trailer, and read, do crossword puzzles, and send out emails. I hoped to learn how to conduct a proper customs-like vehicle search when I felt more adventurous, but I reminded myself that I had been assigned there to chill out after a bad encounter.

If they were disappointed in my lack of enthusiasm, they didn't show it. They eagerly opened up the crossing and started the vehicle inspections. After the cars and trucks were inspected, they were directed to a chemical-filled splash pool, to drive through to disinfect the tires against agricultural contaminants. It was easy and routine. There were no seizures and no surprises. After all, why would the bad guys try to smuggle anything through the border post with its efficient KPS officers when it was apparent that the rest of the mountain was barely patrolled?

Commander Tony had told me to just lay back and relax, and I was the type of cop who followed orders. I stayed in the trailer working on my emails for two hours. Then, bored, I assisted with the vehicle searches, the KPS officers gladly showing me how it was done. The Egyptian had trained them well. No vehicle got by them with anything illegal.

By day two, I needed something more to break the monotony, so I went on the mountain road vehicle patrol with Johnny and one of the more eager-beaver KPS officers named Bekim. He showed me numerous turn offs on the mountain road where he said trucks would come up from the valley and meet the smugglers. We pulled into what looked like a small rest stop, just big enough for one vehicle, and checked the area out on foot. The turn offs led to numerous small foot paths that wound into the mountains.

On the way back to Peja that second night, I got an idea. I said to Johnny, "How would you feel about going on a foot patrol?"

He perked up. "When?"

"I don't know, maybe the day after tomorrow—whenever we can."

"I'd like that, Officer Mike. A mountain hike would be fun."

"Yeah, we could enjoy some fresh air and have a picnic in the woods."

Proving that he was just as bored as I was, he said, "It would break up the long week ahead."

I laughed. "Yeah, we definitely have to do this."

During day three's morning briefing at the crossing checkpoint, I met with the six KPS officers and explained that for the next few days I wanted them to wear hiking boots and battle dress uniform, called BDUs, instead of the dress uniforms that the Egyptian had them wear. Johnny and I had agreed to tell them that in three days (my next-to-last day there) we might do a short patrol on foot. Not that I didn't trust the KPS officers, but for security purposes I had Bekim tell them the foot patrol was in three days, though actually we planned it for the next morning.

Back in my house in Peja later that night, I shared my idea with Willy. I explained how the KPS told me that there had not been a foot patrol along the border all summer. Willy, who was fully enjoying his break at the courthouse, advised that I should not even consider undertaking anything remotely dangerous without him. He was my mentor, after all.

"Mike," he said. "We are supposed to use this week, as you American's say, to 'charge up the battery'."

"Yeah, but Willy," I replied, "I'm already charged up."

He didn't look convinced.

"Commander Tony told us to relax for the week," I said. "I know that. He didn't tell me to neglect my duty, though, and not do my job, and my job is to secure the border for at least four more days."

Willy shook his head. "Mike, I don't agree with you on this, but you must call the commander and ask his permission."

Willy was a superb officer, but, in my book, he was German, and Germans were anal about getting approvals and following instructions to the letter. So I called Commander Tony on my take-home radio. He said my idea was fine with him, no problem, but that he would have Willy and his team back in mobile patrol for tomorrow only, just in case I got lost in the mountains. He would also inform one other UN officer, an American who had extensive experience in that section of Peja.

Willy didn't like it, but it was a go.

The next morning, the three of us met early at Peja Station for a quick confidential briefing outside the eyes of the KPS.

Tony seemed happy. He said, "Mike, I think it is a good idea to have this patrol. It shows initiative."

"Thanks, Tony," I replied. Deciding that it was an opportune time to really kiss up, I added, "It seems like something that *you* would do."

He chuckled. "Yes, I would. I have to admit that I have not given the border station as much attention as I should. It is good for you two keep me on my toes." Then he turned to Willy. "Are you okay with this?"

Willy shrugged. "Sure. Mike knows what he is doing."

"Good. Then we are all agreed."

Tony was a former combat leader from a dangerous part of the world, so he was not going to let me on any mountain hike without backup. First, he issued us a shotgun to supplement our side arms. Then, he instructed Willy to have his team ready at the base of the mountain. Just in case.

While he was working on the details, an American officer entered the room. Commander Tony introduced us. "Mike, Willy, this is Officer Billy Ray."

Billy Ray was heavyset with military-cut short blonde hair. I shook his hand and Willy did the same.

Billy pointed at my American flag patch. "Where you from?" he asked. I caught a hint of southern accent.

"New Hampshire," I replied.

"Yankee, huh?"

"Yeah, live free or die. You?"

"South Carolina. I've only been in Kosovo a couple of weeks."

Tony interjected, "Billy has not been here very long, but he has spent all his time patrolling the larger area that includes the border station."

"I grew up near the Blue Ridge Mountains," Billy added. "I feel right at home here."

I liked Billy Ray immediately. He had an honest smile and

seemed eager to do a good job. He told me that we were lucky to be doing the patrol on this day because his friend and fellow South Carolina cop, Scott Michaels, was working the shift. I had met Scott before and knew that he was an excellent patrol officer. I could not have asked for better backup than Willy's team and these guys.

Commander Tony had one more surprise, though. He called out and another officer came into the room, a small, good-natured Filipino whom I had spoken with previously on the morning of the Nashi patrol. I recalled that his name was Rick. Tony said that Rick was a good officer and could be of help to me on the patrol. I could not see how. He was undersized and looked like he would buckle under the weight of a rifle, flack vest, and gun belt on a steep mountain trail. However, if Tony wanted him to go with me, then he was going. I wasn't about to object.

It seemed a lot of "support" for a walk in the woods in an area that hadn't reported any action in months. I had no plans to aggressively seek an encounter with bad guys. I basically just wanted to take a hike in the fresh mountain air to relieve some of the boredom up at the border crossing. The KPS border officers were expecting something different when I was assigned to the crossing and they were going to get it. I had hiked rigorous mountain trails my whole life and knew how not to get lost. A map, a compass, and a little common sense would do fine.

I told the group at Peja Station we would start at the turnout Bekim and I had scouted out halfway up the mountain at midmorning, and hike two hours into the mountains and two hours back to the vehicles looking for anything suspicious. It all seemed simple enough.

Tony, ever cautious, ordered a radio check-in every half hour with whomever we left at the turnout. Near the base of the mountain range, listening in, would be Willy's team. At the border checkpoint above would be a radio relay to all points beyond. It would be a fun day for everyone even if everyone was thrown together at the last minute.

Rick, Johnny and I left Peja Station at seven o'clock for the two-hour drive to the mountain top. During the ride, I learned that Rick's full formal moniker was Major Enrico Garcia Reyes of the Philippine National Police.

"How did you end up in Kosovo?" I asked.

"I was wounded on Basilan Island near Mindanao and almost died," he said. "This was a reward."

"Some reward. Where were you wounded?"

"I told you, Mike, Mindanao."

"I mean where on your body?"

"Oh, sorry." He pointed to his right side.

"Who shot you?"

"Muslims, *Abu Sayyaf*."

I shook my head. "So, what are you doing here with me, Rick? With all your experience, you should be leading your own team."

With an almost childlike smile, he replied, "I want to learn from you. You were at Nashi."

This was getting ridiculous. I thought, *here is this Filipino war veteran, a freakin' major, and he wants to ride with me? And he wants to learn from me, a cop?* Now, I didn't mind a little respect from the KPS, but Rick had it all wrong. If anyone needed to learn anything, it was me from him, and I told him so in no uncertain terms.

He just smiled, nodded, and said, "You do not need to be so modest, Mike."

When we arrived at the station, I assigned two older KPS officers to remain at the check point. I told them they were my best men and I trusted them to run the checkpoint without supervision. They were flattered by my compliment and seemed relieved that they would not have to do any hiking. I took the remaining four KPS officers, Johnny, and Rick with me. The young KPS were excited and pleased, but were also surprised we were going today. I apologized for misleading them about the date, and told them that I didn't want word to slip by accident that we would be in the mountains today.

At the turnoff halfway down the mountain, we dismounted, and I chose the KPS officer who I thought was in the worst physical shape to stand radio watch with the two vehicles. He was pissed, and I couldn't blame him. A big argument broke out between the KPS officers about leaving this guy at the cars, so I told everyone that if we had a good hike today, we would do it again in three days. That way everyone would get a chance to have a break from the checkpoint. Our radioman seemed satisfied, if not real happy, so off we went.

On the way into the woods, I loaded the shotgun. I put one round of buckshot in the barrel so that the first shot would be spray fire. Then, I loaded four slugs for long distance. The remaining rounds were buckshot. A shotgun is only good for short distance, unless you use a rifle slug. I would have preferred an assault rifle, but only Special Operations personnel had them available in their armories.

After a radio check-in with our KPS guard, Willy, and, via relay, Commander Tony, I figured we were good to go. I slung the shotgun across my chest and led my patrol off on my little hike, wondering how many miles it would take to find a good picnic spot. It was a leisurely walk on a beautiful mountain trail on a picture-perfect summer morning.

We wound our way through the woods and over cliff-edge goat trails until noon when I found a small pasture and stopped our patrol to have lunch. Rick had packed a rice pancake thing. Johnny and I had pastries we had purchased from the café across the street from Peja

Station. The three KPS brought their bag lunches they normally ate at the checkpoint.

Between bites of his rice cake, Rick asked, "Can I walk the point, Mike?" It was the second time he had mentioned it.

I didn't want to give up the position.

I figured that I was the grand leader, anointed by the KPS on this adventure, with a million years of experience in the mountains of New Hampshire, and replied dismissively, "Maybe on the way back, Rick."

A half hour after we finished lunch, we entered a small wooded area littered with trash. It looked to me like a spot where teenagers had gathered to drink liquor. I looked up in the trees and saw little white parachutes, old and toy-like, caught in the tree branches. I thought, *someone likes to come up here to party.*

"Stop, Mike! Now!" Rick yelled from behind.

We all instantly froze.

"Mike, this area was cluster bombed. Those are parachutes from the dropped ordinance, I have seen this before."

"Ah, okay," I answered. "What should we do?"

Rick quietly explained, "We need to back out of here. Many of the bombs do not explode, and can be set off if they are touched."

This was not at all what I wanted to hear.

Rick had us all do a quick about face and walk back following in our own footsteps with him now in the lead. As we exited the wooded area, I realized that what had looked to me like old rusted beer cans were old mostly expended explosives. The operative word here was "mostly."

I was mad at myself—and disappointed. I had led my patrol into a dangerous situation because of my ego, instead of listening to Rick's subtle suggestions that he be the point man. We sat in a small clearing fifty meters from the wood line where Rick explained that he had years of experience working with unexploded ordinance. To prove it he lifted his shirt and showed us the scars he had received from grenade shrapnel. There were no less than a dozen of them. I also noticed a larger purple scar on his right side where he had been shot. I was impressed to say the least.

Still acting way more humble than the situation called for, Rick said, "Mike, with your permission, I would like to take point. We are doing well so far, but I have seen some things that I would like to check out." He had a pained look like he had to say something more, but didn't want to undermine my authority.

I nodded in agreement. "What is it, Rick?"

He said, "Mike, if you don't mind me saying this, the patrol leader should never be in the point position. I suggest that you be in the middle. You can command better from that position. Also, may I carry the shotgun?"

I knew he was being way more than kind. I had fucked up. He was clearly way better at patrol tactics. He was being nice to me because I was formally in charge. I consoled myself with the knowledge that this kind of thing had happened millions of times before—the experienced non-com easing in the new untested officer. And I also knew he was absolutely right. I nodded and handed him the shotgun, explaining how I had loaded it.

"Yes, that is the correct way," he said. I felt a little better knowing I had at least gotten that much right.

I pulled out the NATO map and marked the area so that the NATO explosive ordinance teams could find it later and clear it. I called in to Commander Tony and reported the find, and that Rick wanted to check out a gully about one hundred meters away. Tony said fine and we clicked off.

The three KPS officers did not seem to understand what had

happened so Johnny gave them a quick update. Rick told Johnny, "Tell the KPS that Mike has asked me to take the point, but that he is still the commander of this patrol. We are going to check a gully just west of here where I smelled animals."

Shit, he was good. Rick informed me that while we were walking toward the woods he thought he heard a noise and stopped to check his senses. "Mike," he said, "I am certain that we will find something in the gully—maybe just some wild pigs."

Bekim, the young KPS officer who knew the trails, crawled over to Rick, Johnny and me, and in excellent English that I had never heard him speak before, said, "Officer Mike, the wash comes all the way from the top of the mountain and is filled with water all winter. In the summer, it dries out and is used by smugglers. I believe we may find a mule train there."

I turned to Johnny as I automatically did when speaking with KPS officers and he looked back at me, smirking. "Yeah, right," I said.

I turned back to Bekim. "Why didn't you tell us that before?"

He replied, very sincerely, "Officer Mike, I did not know if you really wanted to catch any smugglers today."

I tried to appear indignant. "Bekim, do you think we are here just to enjoy the scenery?"

I glanced at Rick who was smothering a laugh with his hand.

Bekim lowered his head and apologized.

"Never mind," I said. "Let's go look for the bad guys."

We all crawled to the lip of the ridge that overlooked the gully. Bekim, Rick and I poked our heads over the edge and looked down. Below us, about forty yards away, were twenty mules, all tied together in one long line. The mules were loaded down with large boxes strapped to their sides. They were standing still, and at the head was a gray-bearded man dressed like a farmer, trying to keep them quiet.

There were three younger males alongside the line of mules, all unarmed from what I could see.

We quietly backed away from the ridge top and made up a quick plan with the other team members. The smugglers had probably noticed us much earlier, and saw us go into the wooded area. They would assume that we would keep on going and not expect us to back track. If it wasn't for Rick and his spotting of the cluster bomb area, we would all be dead or, at best, still walking away from the area. These smugglers were apparently waiting for us to clear out before continuing on their journey.

I told the team I thought we could surprise and arrest them, but I would only authorize the action if they all agreed. I did not want any repeat of the Nashi incident. I told them Rick had the most combat patrol experience, so I wanted him with the shotgun on the ridge to cover our approach. Johnny would stay back until we had apprehended the four men with the mule train and the scene was declared safe.

We did not have a lot of time to waste. We outnumbered the bad guys and, at the moment, held the element of surprise. The three KPS officers and I, with weapons drawn, would descend from the ridge down the forty yards of grassy slope. Rick would angle off to the side so that he would not have to shoot over our heads, and would have a clear line of sight if things went sour. One KPS would confront the old man at the front. The other two KPS officers and I would approach the center of the mule train and grab the two suspects standing there. Rick would cover us and keep an eye on the guy at the tail of the mule train until we got to him. I asked if they had any questions and none did.

I turned to Rick and asked, "Anything?"

"Good plan, Boss," he said and smiled like a kid on a trip to an amusement park.

The three KPS were eager and appeared excited. Two of them

looked at Bekim, the English-speaking KPS. He nodded affirmatively, said to me, "We are ready. We want to do this!"

I called Commander Tony, informed him we had located a mule train in a gully, and were going to act before it moved.

Tony replied, "Go ahead, Mike, but be careful. I will send you help right now." With that the radio began chattering with radio calls from Willy, Billy Ray, Scott, and who knew how many others. I left the radio with Johnny and told him to keep in contact with Tony.

We lined up for the low crawl back to the ridge. Rick and I took our blue berets from our pockets and put them on. What the hell? I hadn't worn it in a while, and I wanted the smugglers to know that we weren't just local cops, hoping they would give up more quickly. With Rick lying down to the left of us on the ridge line, his blue beret and large shotgun clearly visible, the three KPS and I went over the lip of the ridge and down the steep grassy embankment.

I yelled, "Police! Stop!" and the four smugglers froze.

They looked startled and appeared as if none of them knew what to do while we quickly closed the distance. I figured it would all be over in a second. Hands up. We surrender. No problem.

Then, the old man did something that I couldn't at the time comprehend. He pulled a small knife from his belt and walked calmly to the rear of the second mule in line, and he did that with five weapons pointed at him. Back home, any bad guy surrounded by five armed cops would put his hands in the air and give up.

The old man looked me straight in the eye while he cut the line that held the mule train together. Then, he slapped the mule's ass and yelled. Pandemonium broke out. All the smugglers immediately copied him, slapping at the mules, and with a collective "hee-haw," the beasts reared and headed off down the mountainside.

While the KPS and I were midway down the embankment, the

last smuggler pulled an AK-47 off of a fleeing mule and pointed it in our direction, firing away on full automatic. He missed us only because Rick fired a load of buckshot at him before he had a chance to aim properly. At the same time, the old man, knife in hand, ran after the mule train.

In an instant, what by all rights should have been a picnic event became a shit storm.

The two other young men pulled pistols from their waistbands began firing while turning from us and running up the opposite bank of the gully towards an area thick with trees and shrubbery. There was nowhere for us to go except after them. We were too exposed down in the gully and would be easy targets for them if we tried to retreat up our side of the slope.

Rick suddenly appeared on my left, shotgun in hand, and motioned for the KPS officer closest to him to follow. Together, they went after the man with the AK-47, who was limping, apparently wounded by Rick's buckshot. Bekim and I chased the two armed with pistols. The third KPS took off after the old man with the knife.

Once into the woods and shrubs, Bekim hit the dirt like a trained soldier. I crawled up to Bekim and he pointed to some bushes ahead. I could see some bright clothing, but not the man.

"UN Police!" I called out. "Come out! You are under arrest!"

Bekim shouted something similar I assumed in Albanian.

No reply, but the shrubs moved and a shot rang out towards our direction. I held up two fingers to Bekim, and we both fired two shots into the bushes. The bushes yelped.

We waited while the wounded man continued hollering. I didn't want to move until we knew where the other pistol-packing guy had gone. Besides, the agony could be a feint to sucker us closer.

Suddenly, from our left, we heard the simultaneous blast of the shot gun and clack-clack-clack of the AK-47. I yelled as loud as I could for everyone to check in.

Rick responded first. "Rick. Okay. Suspect down and wounded. The KPS with me is okay, too."

I told them, "We have one of the guys with a pistol. I think he's wounded. We're going to move forward. Be careful, the other guy is unaccounted for."

Rick said he would leave the KPS with his wounded man and circle forward. As he flanked our position, Bekim and I crawled towards the bushes directly in front of us. As we approached, a pistol arced from the bushes through the air high above us. By the time we got to him, Rick was already on my left covering him with the shotgun. Damn, he was good.

The small wooded area was barely the size of an Olympic pool, so when we got to the suspect, we could see that the other guy was nowhere to be found. We checked the remaining cover and Rick found tracks indicating the second man had made his escape.

While Rick returned to examine his prisoner, I went over to my own wounded man to check his injuries. I found Bekim sitting on the prone teenager, slapping the kid's head, and screaming at him. I ran up and yelled, "What the fuck are you doing?"

Bekim explained that the boy was not wounded. We had shot off his tennis shoe. "He was faking, looking to draw us out in the open for a clean shot. I am teaching him that he should not point guns at police officers."

Bekim stood to the side, while I checked the kid over from head to toe. Like he'd said, the teen didn't have any wounds other than scratches from crawling around in the bushes. I wanted to smack the boy, too.

Rick's suspect actually *was* wounded, if only slightly, and we quickly bandaged his side. He was not a teenager. Up close we could see he was about twenty-five years old and had a tough hardened military face rather than the weathered face of a farmer.

Bekim pulled me aside and said in a very soft whisper, "Officer Mike, this man is not one of us—not Albanian, not Montenegrin, not Kosovar, not Serb. He's Russian."

Chapter 4

Down the valley, echoing up to our location, we heard a sudden cavalcade of distant gunfire. It was time to collect everyone and get the fuck out of there as we had at least an hour's march back to the mountain road. I still had to find the KPS who ran down the hill after the old man. We'd been out of radio communication for about fifteen minutes, except for Johnny who continued monitoring things from up on the ridge.

Back on the ridge, all hell was breaking loose on the airwaves. I tried to call Commander Tony, but couldn't get through to him for all the calls for backup. I could hear him giving instructions and positioning people in different areas. I heard the voice of Billy Ray reporting gunfire at his location, wherever that was, and Scott Michaels reporting that he was only two minutes out and would be there shortly to back him up. Then, we heard more live gunfire from below.

I did not want to interfere with these emergency calls, so I switched to an alternate regional channel, rather than the Peja Police station channel. That wave band was even worse. Regional headquarters, referred to as HQ, was several blocks from Peja Station. HQ contained the Regional Commander, UN administrative offices, a NATO liaison office, three special operations teams, and a UN legal office. They had their own radio band and it was going nuts.

While I was listening, the missing KPS reappeared in the gully. One called out to Johnny. "Officer Mike," Johnny translated, "the KPS say the old man outran him. He is very embarrassed."

I shrugged and said, "Tell him that he did a fine job. It's hard to run after someone when the person you're after is scared and running for his life, and you have all sorts of equipment weighing you down."

When Johnny finished, the KPS officer still looked disappointed, but somewhat relieved. What I really needed to find out was what the hell was going on down below us. I pulled Johnny to the side and was quickly joined by Rick and Bekim, while two KPS kept watch over the two handcuffed prisoners.

Johnny was very excited and blurted out the information that he had gathered while sitting on radio watch. Apparently, when the old man cut the mules loose and slapped them into a mini-stampede down the mountain, the mules headed into a village at the end of the trail. I don't know much about horses or mules, but I suspect after using the same trails for a long time, when cut loose, they head right back home.

With gunfire and chaos accelerating their flight they ran like hell, losing much of their valuable smugglers cargo on the way down the mountain. In the village where this smuggling operation was based, they heard the gunfire from our encounter and began to arm themselves, fearing that a rival gang was hijacking their mule train.

Johnny said that Billy Ray figured out from his map where the smuggler's village was and headed right there. He and his backup, Scott, got there just as the first panicked mule arrived. They were now exchanging gunfire with some village guards and calling for backup. Other teams were responding.

Commander Tony called and ordered us to stay put, as Willy's team was nearing our position. NATO had been activated when the KPS at border control at the top of the mountain relayed the incident.

An Italian Parachute battalion and its military police detachment were *en route*. My quiet mountain hike had turned into a military campaign.

On the radio, I could hear Billy Ray and Scott Michaels organizing a sweep of the village and describing the twenty frenzied mules running all over the place as the villagers and smugglers attempted to run, hide, or grab the remaining cargo. It sounded like bedlam, but I thought if anyone could get a grip on things, it was Scott and Billy.

Then I heard a pause in the radio chatter and called in, "Break, break. Tiger Six to Tiger One. Tiger Six to Tiger One."

Tony responded, all business "Tiger Six, go."

I told him, "Tiger Six, everything secure at my location. Two suspects in custody. No injuries to team. Suspects with minor injuries, but mobile. Can return to our vehicles."

Tony replied, "Negative, negative. Secure your team at ridge line. Tiger Five on foot will join you shortly. You can extract together."

"Roger."

"Tiger Six: Tiger Five team found the other suspect, and he is in custody."

I thought, typical Willy, always cleaning up after me.

Tony concluded with, "One more thing, Tiger Six. Teams Three and Four are encountering resistance at a village two clicks from your location. NATO and Spec-Ops backup will split between the village and your AOR."

There was a sudden burst of aerial noise as three military helicopters zoomed over us at treetop level, their rough chugging engines echoing in the mountain valley. They turned abruptly and headed over to the wooded area where we had captured the smugglers. We watched them land in a small meadow atop a hill on the far side of the woods. As soon as they touched down, Italian parachute soldiers in full military gear began tumbling out the side doors. Within seconds, three empty helicopters rose and headed down the mountain.

The presence of heavily-armed NATO troops made me nervous. I kept my team stationary, as ordered, to avoid an accidental encounter with these charged-up soldiers. Like paratroopers everywhere, they were aggressive and fast to fire. With so many armed people in our area, my team's safety had to become my primary responsibility.

From the chatter on the radio, I surmised that several hundred Italian paratroopers and some UN special operations teams had reached the village below us and were clearing it, collecting the smuggler's cargo, arresting suspicious villagers, and confiscating weaponry. It sounded like Tony was at the village, taking command of the situation.

We just sat and waited for things to quiet down. About five minutes later, from across the gully and out of the woods, marched a long line of paratroopers. There were about sixty of them, stretched out over a hundred meters. As they came into the gully, one group split off and headed down the trail in the direction of the mule stampede. The other group of about twenty climbed the embankment towards us. We were sitting on the ground as they approached. The troopers set up a protective circle around us while Rick and I greeted their commander.

The shorter of the two Italian officers offered me his hand. "I am Lieutenant Pugliese," he said, "and this is *Capitano* Rocca from the Twenty-Second Parachute Battalion. *Capitano* Rocca does not speak English well, so I will speak for him. We are pleased to come for your rescue. May I ask who is commander here?"

Rick replied before I could open my mouth, "We don't need rescue. Everything is under control. Officer Granger is in command."

Rick looked angry at what he considered an insult, though I knew it was just an unintentional language glitch. I waved him quiet and introduced myself to the Italians.

Lt. Pugliese figured out his gaff and said, "I apologize. Of course you do not need rescue. We were instructed to find and secure your group, then sweeping the trail back to the village. There, we meet the other men from our unit who are now securing the village."

Capt. Rocca spoke to his lieutenant in Italian. The lieutenant then informed us that Willy's team had been observed from the helicopters to be only a short distance away. He said that, once they arrived, his soldiers would head down the mountain to join their comrades.

I said that would be fine.

At 1400 hours, Willy and his team appeared on the trail, dragging the second of the gunmen as a prisoner. It was like a high school reunion as our two groups merged. The KPS were all hugging each other and chattering excitedly about the past hour's events. Bekim calmed them down and assigned some officers to watch the prisoners, while Willy, Rick and I caught up. I made a note to check up on Bekim at a later time. He was exhibiting strong effective leadership over the KPS, who were showing him a great amount of respect for such a young man.

Willy was wearing the happiest smile I had seen in a long time, and started on me in an animated fashion."Michael, Michael, Michael," he chided, "I cannot leave you alone for a moment."

"You got that right," I said, and we both laughed.

He pointed back to his prisoner now sitting with his comrades surrounded by KPS.

"We found this guy hiding in the woods on our way to meet you."

Willy explained that the moment we called in about spotting the mule train, Tony had jumped into action and began deploying his officers to the village that Billy reported. He sent Willy's team a click below my cut off in order to intercept any resulting foot traffic. That's what I call command leadership.

Tony also called Regional HQ and NATO, knowing he didn't have the manpower to handle all the emerging tasks. HQ mobilized to arrest anyone in the village who appeared connected to the smuggling operation and prepare for interrogation of our prisoners by UN Intelligence officers. NATO also wanted to sweep the valley and recover all contraband scattered on the trail. The Italian paratroopers were already finding boxes of automatic weapons, ammunition, cigarettes, pirated DVD's, and stolen vehicle parts in storage barns in the village and scattered along the trail behind the returning donkeys.

Our combined group of men and prisoners got up and started on foot back to the mountain road. As we lined up in single file, I called Tony on my radio: "Tiger Six to Tiger One. We are mobile and heading to our vehicles."

Tony replied, "Tiger One acknowledges. Will have Tiger Five vehicles meet you there. Good job, Mike."

His last words surprised me, because up until he'd said that, I didn't know if I was in trouble. I knew I had created a shit storm and still didn't know if my superiors would ultimately view things as good or bad.

I mentioned this to Willy.

"Mike, Tony is a little overwhelmed," he said, "but this is turning out to be unbelievably good."

He also said that NATO was planning to comb the mountains for the next few days, not only to search for additional suspects and contraband, but also to clear the cluster bomb area that, until I had called it in, had been unknown to the Explosives Ordnance Disposal Team. Most areas bombed during the war had been cleared, but occasionally a new one was located that required their attention.

By the late afternoon, we had arrived at our vehicles. Perhaps because it was already looking like a successful operation, everyone at HQ was trying to get in on the action. There were twenty to thirty police and military vehicles lining the roadway as we emerged from the woods, and an immediate buzz of excitement. The KPS there started clapping and greeting their friends. Rick, Willy, and I were greeted by the Regional Operations Chief, a Jordanian UN officer who outranked Commander Tony.

"Who is Tiger Six?" he asked. "I have a unit of *Carabenari* here to take the prisoners under guard in a NATO ambulance. I want the KPS assigned to the border to go back up there with one of my assistants to resume their shift and debrief."

"I'm Tiger Six. Officer Granger," I said. I was a little miffed by the Regional Operations Chief's superior attitude and added, "I report to Commander Tony. I'm awaiting his orders."

The Chief simply said, "Fine," and continued barking orders to everyone. Not having been dismissed, we waited. Turning his attention back to us, he said, as if we couldn't do anything without his direction, "You three go to the command post being set up at the base of this road and link up with your commander."

I could not tell if he was happy or mad. He turned and continued barking orders to others, so I left. I did not want to speak with anyone until I met with Tony. My little stroll in the trees to relieve my boredom had turned into a major military and police operation. I knew I was way out of my league.

We turned our prisoners over to the Italian MPs and watched the ambulance and escorting military vehicles race down the mountain, sirens blasting. The Regional Operations Commander, or ROC, mounted his UN Toyota SUV crowned with a forest of antennas, and followed.

I approached the KPS from the border crossing to say my farewells. I wanted a minute of alone-time with them, separate from the new UN officer assigned to take them back up the mountain. I knew I would never go back there. Willy was gathering his team to go down the mountain.

I looked for Rick and saw him off in the distance, acting like a teenager, flirting with a cute female KPS officer near one of the UN cars. He seemed to have a built-in off-and-on switch: One second he was a hardened warrior, the next a carefree laid-back gigolo.

When Johnny and Bekim had finished gathering up the border KPS, I addressed them. "Men," I said, "all of you acted bravely and professionally today. I was proud to be on this patrol with you. You did a good job for your country and your families should be proud of you. Officer Rick's experience and guidance today was invaluable. He also wants me to commend you. He said you did an *outstanding* job."

Johnny interpreted my words. The KPS were all smiles by the time he had finished.

As they loaded into their SUVs to return to the mountain border crossing, Bekim asked if he could speak with me. "Officer Mike, sir," he said. "I have a request: I have put in for a transfer from the border post to Peja Station many times. It is always denied by my Egyptian Commander, who wants to keep me there as long as he is there. I want to get off the mountain and serve my country better. I am wasted there. Officer Mike, you are a very good commander, but you are still learning about our country. If you help me transfer to Peja, I will help you. You will have much power after this day, and I think you can influence my transfer."

This kid was sharp. He was working me like a pro, like a hooker talking a john out his hard earned money. I was flattered; who wouldn't be? I had underestimated him that day, just as I had underestimated

48

Rick at the start of the patrol. It was starting to become a

"Bekim," I replied, "come to Peja Station next w
with me. If you are talking honest with me, then I'll see i
think there's more to you than you are telling me now."

He smiled at my last statement. With a handshake, we parted company.

Though I was basking in the glow of a success, I also felt uneasy. I had twice underestimated my partners and my enemies in the past week, with near fatal results. I thought the bad guys would give up in the face of superior firepower, but twice it hadn't happened. I realized that I had to start understanding the people in this foreign place better —or I might not live to regret it. Perhaps Bekim really could help.

At the bottom of the hill, we found a large command post set up in a field near the intersection of the mountain road and the trail that led to the smugglers' village. Army troops were putting up field tents and there were twenty or so UN and army vehicles scattered about. A helicopter rested in the adjacent field. Willy, Rick and I were directed to a tent that was still being erected. Outside, a handwritten sign read "UN Command Post."

Inside the tent, Commander Tony and the Jordanian ROC were standing bent over a large area map on a make-shift table. We were all wearing our blue berets because now we were working with military and ranking UN officials. We approached Tony and saluted him smartly. We used proper military protocol so there would be no confusion in the chain of command about us. Normally, in the field there was a "no salute" rule. You don't want the bad guys to identify the leaders. It was just like in the old war movies.

Tony and the ROC were directing patrols and setting up roadblocks on all the roads leading in and out of the area. They and the NATO Commander in the next tent were trying to lock down the ιole valley so they could round up as many bad guys as fast as they could. Additional military and police units were flooding into the area from all over Kosovo. A Spanish commando unit was coming in from Prizren, a Turkish armored unit was coming in from the south, and more UN Police were coming from Pristina.

Tony returned our salute and motioned towards a couple of seats. He would speak to us shortly he said. The tent was buzzing with UN officers from Peja being directed to move their teams to different locations.

Tony eventually approached us and told Willy, "Tiger Five, go back to Peja. Get the night shift out and working, but keep them away from this area. We have enough help coming. And, Willy, the press is coming from Pristina to follow the convoys. We will block them from this area, so, if they come to Peja Station looking for information, don't give them any. Just tell them there will be a press conference in the morning."

Willy, in full obedient German mode, answered, "Yes, sir," and was gone in a flash.

Though he was all business, Tony seemed in a great mood as he refocused his attention on the remaining two of us. "Mike and Rick," he said. "I want you here with me. I need some extra hands."

Tony then pulled me to a quiet corner of the tent, and said "Mike, I did not expect this to happen, but we have interrupted a major smuggling operation here. We will be here for the rest of the night. Regional HQ and Pristina Command are giving us anything we want or need. They are very happy." He gave me a broad smile. "NATO is here to assist us, they will follow our lead. For now, you are my number two. Regional HQ gave me command of this operation, but they will supervise what we do."

Tony explained that Scott and Billy were directing the sweep of the village and would document all the evidence collected from there. All the confiscated material will be transported to the Italian Parachute base, because they had the large trucks needed, and they could guard the illegal cargo, worth millions, more efficiently than the UN Police or the KPS. He added with a chuckle, "The mules will be shipped to a farm."

"Too bad about the mules," I said. "They should get a reward, not end up pulling a plow. After all, they led us to the pot of gold."

Tony was doing a great job, and I chose the moment to tell him so. I also apologized for creating the whole mess. I felt bad it had blown up the way it had.

He listened, then said, "Mike, you did well. I am very capable of directing my forces. I know my men and their capabilities. Did you think I assigned Officer Rick to work with you for no reason?" Tony then told me to get some food next door, and gave Rick the keys to my SUV to go back to Peja with Johnny, where he was to secure the firearms that we had taken from the prisoners. I could see Tony's political wheels turning. "We will need to notify everyone that this was all planned, so think of a name to call this mission."

It wasn't my forte, but I gave it a shot. "Okay, How about Operation Mountain Fury?"

He shook his head. "That may be over the top. Please go get some food, and think of something more realistic."

A half hour later, after stuffing myself with excellent Italian food the paratrooper cooks were offering in the food tent, I was back with Tony. Standing with him were a NATO colonel, the ROC, and the ROC's boss, the Regional Commander. I had never met the RC, even though his headquarters were in Peja. He had the equivalent rank of Colonel in the UN Police. He was large, Russian, and looked like he took no bullshit whatsoever.

The RC spoke first. "Commander Tony and I have locked down the entire valley. I am pleased that together we have been able to stop this terrible smuggling ring. Commander Tony said that the operation was preplanned, but was kept secret, so that the KPS would not leak the information. Is this correct?"

I looked over at Tony and saw him give me a slight nod.

"Ah...yes. That is correct, sir."

"What is the name of this operation, Officer Granger?"

I stammered, "Sir, ah, the operation is called...ah...Operation White Mountains."

Well there it was. My native New Hampshire mountains had just popped into my head and I went with them. The RC looked pleased. I had almost blurted out "Operation Mount Washington," after the largest peak in the chain, which, with him being a Russian, might not have been so well received.

He finished by saying, "At zero-nine-hundred, Commander Tony and you will be in my office at Regional HQ. There will be press conference on the HQ steps at ten hundred hours. The UN Ambassador to Kosovo, the UN CIVPOL Commander, and I will issue a joint statement, then Commander Tony will take questions from the press. All officers are to be in dress uniform, of course."

With a quick salute, the RC, his assistants, and bodyguards left the tent, disappearing into the quickly fading afternoon sun. Tony and I were busy for the rest of the day and well into the night.

I did not get back to my villa until after two in the morning. Willy was waiting up for me, even though we were required to be at Regional HQ in seven hours. He handed me a warm beer when I arrived and said, "Mike, I had much fun today. Thank you."

That was a nice intro, but we quickly got down to the more serious business. He asked, "Mike, what the fuck really happened up there?"

I couldn't lie to Willy. In every incident there are three stories: the official story, the story, and the real fucking story. The public and some bosses get the "official story." Your comrades and friends get "the story." Only your most trusted inner circle gets "the RF story."

For the next hour, I told him about my screw up in the cluster bomb area and how Rick hauled my ass out of that fire. I told him that Rick was also the one who found the mule train. I told him about me coordinating the approach to the mule train and how it went to shit so fast. I also told Willy that I did not care that I shot at the teenager, and I wished that I did hit him because he and his buddies would have been happy to kill us. I poured it all out for an hour. Willy just listened and took it in.

After I had finished, he said, "We must get some sleep, Mike. It's three in the morning. You did a good job and led the patrol well. You made some mistakes, but only because you are new here. Your decision to patrol the smuggling routes was a good one and had a successful outcome. It is time for us to get rest."

I felt better after our talk, and surprisingly, I had a peaceful sleep that night.

We all met in the RC's office at 0900 hours. Tony, Willy, Scott, Billy Ray, Rick, and I sat and waited in our dress uniforms, namely, clean BDUs and our blue berets. The ROC and apparently his boss from Pristina were always encouraging us to wear the berets, but most of us, as I mentioned before, ignored the rule whenever possible.

The RC started off in a tone that suggested there would be no questions afterwards.

"The first national elections are to be held in three weeks. There have been an increase of political assassination all across Kosovo. It is important to assure the public and all countries involved in this peacekeeping effort that we are doing all that is necessary to prevent such violence. You all here will agree with the press information given out today." He gave everyone the traditional three-second Russian stare down before continuing, "You have done an excellent job, and we shall strive to improve lines of communication! Understood?" The Russian seemed pissed that he was caught off-guard by the mountain patrol.

All answered, "Yes, sir."

Then, he put the sugar on top. "You will all receive UN commendation medals for your actions in the mountains yesterday. Dismissed."

We left the office and walked downstairs to the front steps of the building where the international press had been gathering since early morning. The press were already pumping everyone they could find for side stories. They had only received bits of information, so they were eager for the "real scoop."

The UN Administrator for Kosovo, a stately gray-haired diplomat, took the rostrum. He was flanked by the NATO Commander for Kosovo, a one-star French army general, the UN CIVPOL Commander, a British general, and a Kosevo Police Service senior commander from Pristina.

The rest of us stood on the stairs behind these four big wigs, with the Russian RC and Jordanian ROC in front. I was thinking: *This is cool. I hope this gets on the TV so that the family back home can see me.*

The UN Administrator started. "We are here to announce the completion of a joint military and police operation in the mountains east of here on the border with Montenegro. The operation resulted in the arrest of twenty-three persons involved in the smuggling of millions of dollars of contraband, including a large number of automatic weapons. Two suspects were wounded during their apprehension. No casualties were received by the one hundred UN and KPS police officers and three hundred Italian paratroopers involved in the mission.

"Several weeks ago, information was received by UN Intelligence specialists in Pristina that smuggled weapons were crossing the border from Montenegro, and a plan was developed at UN CIVPOL and NATO Command to put an end to this criminal activity. Under the direction of UN Police Regional Commander Colonel Alexi, Operation White Mountains was implemented yesterday morning which resulted in immediate success."

He paused for effect and looked across the group of journalists standing there, "Because of the dedication of the brave men and women standing behind me, the UN Peacekeeping Forces, in partnership with the Kosovo Police Service, have put a major dent in the criminal elements who seek to undermine the stability of this region..."

While this guy was giving out the "official story," and, seemingly giving himself and his buddies all the credit, we had content ourselves with trying to look stern and cool for the cameras that were clicking away. The press were eating it up, hook, line, and sinker. Of the cops on the stairs, most still did not know what had really happened. They just knew they had been called in to help, and had had to work their asses off all night.

I was tired, and getting even more tired trying to look professional for the cameras. Rick, behind me, kept poking me in the back, and smothering laughs.

"Rick," I whispered. "Knock that shit off," but he just kept it up. He was finding the whole press conference ridiculous and funny. I couldn't blame him. I desperately wanted the picture-taking to end before the sweat soaked through my shirt.

Then, I saw her—the stunning CNN reporter from California I had met at a party at the Grand Hotel in Pristina. I remember her touching my arm and her sweet voice whispering in my ear, "You're an American, right?"

"What gave me away?" I asked.

"I'd like to say it was the style of your tuxedo, but I can't. I think it has something to do with you and your friend's 'I-don't-really-belong-here' look. Only Americans would show up at a formal European embassy party dressed like they are going to a sports bar. By the way, I'm Cara Sanchez."

Cara Sanchez. I could never forget that name. She still looked great dressed in khaki pants and one of those jacket vest things with tons of pockets and shoulder epaulettes that war correspondents like to wear when they are where the action is.

She had pushed to the front of the crowd and fired off a question to Tony and the Russian RC, as they now had the podium. For the next ten minutes, Tony and the Russian fielded questions. The rest of us began visibly sweating in our hot uniforms and berets; all we wanted to do was get off the hot steps and into some shade. I neither knew what else was said to the press nor did I care. When the conference ended, we all ran for the nearest tree, stuffing the berets into our cargo pockets faster than shoplifters on a spree.

While I searched the vanishing crowd for California Girl, Tony came up from behind me with her in tow. "Officer Granger," he said. "This is Miss Cara Sanchez from CNN. She has a question for you."

"You look familiar, Ms. Sanchez," I said. "Have we met before?"

She grinned. "Possibly. I meet a lot of men in uniform, but I tend to better remember those wearing a nice pair of tan Dockers."

I smiled. She remembered. I said, "Okay, Ms. Sanchez, what

questions do you have for me? But I have to caution you that I can only answer if Commander Tony, my boss, here, agrees."

"Great," she replied. "Officer Granger, my sources tell me you led the patrol that found the smugglers. Can you give me some details on what led you to that particular site?"

"Ah…ah…," I looked behind her at Tony, who was shaking his head from side to side. "Sorry, Ms. Sanchez," I finished, "I can't do that."

She looked disappointed, but I could tell she knew how the game was played. Given that, I figured she just wanted to let me know she was in the area and remembered me. The curious thing was how she knew about my role in the bust. While Tony took over and physically steered her away, I called after her, "Ms. Sanchez, I hope you get to spend some time in Peja."

She gave me the same sexy look she gave me that night at the party. "I'd really like to, Officer Granger. Right now I have to leave for Pristina, again, but maybe sometime soon?"

Tony kept looking back and forth between us as we spoke. I could tell he smelled that something was up, but it would have to wait. He took her arm and I watched as the two of them disappeared into a crowd.

I was exhausted and hot in more ways than one, so I went home to get some much needed rest.

Blessed are the Peacekeepers

Chapter 5

The instructors had drummed it into us during the UN training in Pristina to expect things to change quickly and often in Kosovo. A week after the press conference in Peja, shift commander Tony was promoted to Peja Station Commander. He was now responsible for all three shifts working out of our police station, several sub-stations, and the border crossing. He was also the number three police official in the entire Peja region, subservient only to the Russian Regional Commander and the Jordanian Regional Operations Commander.

As chief, Tony replaced an American female officer who left Kosovo to begin a startup mission in a place called Darfur-Sudan, in northeastern Africa. My roommate, Willy, with just five months left in his mission, took Tony's place as Tiger One, the shift commander. The changes turned out great for me because now my best friend was my boss. It was a position I would not take advantage of, but it did give me some peace of mind because he knew my strengths and weaknesses.

I was offered a promotion as a shift commander on another team, but I declined. Every month, four or five UN officers would finish up their missions and new officers would arrive to fill the ranks. The shift commander in the other platoon had rotated home and, being an American, I was well-positioned to take over the spot. As I may have already mentioned, it was assumed that Americans, being among the best trained officers, could more easily move into leadership positions than those from many other countries. I knew, however, that I did not yet have the experience in country to handle the responsibility. I was still relatively new in Kosovo, and, besides, I did not want to leave Willy, Rick the Filipino, or the Tiger Team. Billy Ray, the good old Southern boy, gladly took the Team Leader position I turned down.

I took my job as a mentor seriously. I wanted to pass on to my team members in the KPS as much information and training as I could in the months I had left. On each patrol, I instructed them on the basics of American police procedure, like making safe car stops and vehicle searches. We conducted crime scene searches and handled car accidents. It was a good time for me.

There was a change in patrol procedures at this time because we were no longer in two vehicle patrols. The second follow-on vehicle, filled with KPS, could now operate independently as long as they stayed in Peja City. I was still responsible for them, but they only called if they got jammed up and needed help. There was little violence during this period and the days flew by.

I had not forgotten Bekim, the razor sharp KPS officer from the border crossing. I went to Tony and asked if he could be transferred from his mountain post to Peja patrol and Tony was fine with it. Now that he was in command of both locations, it was an easy change to make. The transfer was accomplished in a day and, since Bekim was very popular, it endeared me even more with the KPS.

I felt I was at the top of my form and I believed I was becoming the leader I thought I should be. I did continue to make mistakes, though. One day, while driving down the street, I observed an older man walking on the sidewalk. I could tell from his clothing that he was from a village outside of the city. His wife was walking several steps behind him as is the practice in most Muslim cultures. When he stopped to speak with another man, the woman, whose head was down, caught up to him. For a city dweller and a modern Muslim this would not be a big deal, but to this guy it was an insult and he got completely bent out of shape. He turned to yell at her and then suddenly backhanded her across the face, knocking her to the ground.

I slammed on the brakes of the Toyota police vehicle and jumped out to confront the backwards fool even as Johnny and Bekim yelled to me, "No, no, Officer Mike."

I picked the bleeding woman up off the ground and hollered at the old man as Bekim and Johnny tried to pull me back to the patrol vehicle. I told them to back off and ordered Johnny to interpret for me. Johnny tried to explain to me that the old man was justified in what he did and that I was making matters worse.

I was truly pissed off, both at the old man and my team members for interfering. I hissed, "Johnny, just follow orders and tell this guy what I say—exactly. Tell this guy that I don't care what he does with his family when he is at home, but when he is in the city and he sees my UN patrol car, he'd better keep his hands to himself or I'll break his fucking nose."

Johnny interpreted and the old man looked like he was going to have a heart attack there in the street. A crowd started to gather quietly on the sidelines. By their faces, it was clear that they were sympathetic to the batterer.

Having vented my anger, I walked with Johnny and Bekim back to my vehicle. We had driven about a block when they asked to stop and talk about what happened. Both were upset and told me that I had made a big mistake. I really did not want to hear it, but out of respect I let them have their say.

Johnny gave it to me straight. He said, "Officer Mike, you have caused that elder to lose face with his friend and his woman. You also touched her without his permission. He will take her back to his village and beat her every day for the next week. She will suffer greatly. You do not understand many things about this place yet. You thought you were doing a good thing, but you did not help that woman. You made it worse for her."

There it was. In my effort to inject some good old American cop justice in that foreign world, I ended up doing just the opposite. I should have felt worse after Johnny explained to me my mistake, but I didn't. I knew that he was right in *his* world; still, I hoped he would tell all his friends what I did. He and his buddies needed to get the message, that if I ever saw that kind of behavior again, I would intervene even more aggressively.

Johnny and Bekim in the meantime had a frank talk about my deficiencies, and decided that it was time to educate me about Kosovo. Soon after that incident, they began teaching me as much as they could about their culture. Johnny taught me about the *kanuns*, or codes, that had served as the guidelines for their culture for a millennium. I began to learn the Albanian dialect used in that part of Kosovo. They taught me about Muslim law and social customs. They took me to their homes in Peja. I learned to greet the men with "*Ah Salam Salekim*" in the home and not to address the women. I removed my shoes upon entering their homes being careful not to step on their prayer rugs.

I was learning and growing. The KPS began to trust and confide in me. Some older KPS, who had been policemen before the war, told me that, when the Serbs occupied the region, all the Muslim officers were fired. They did however continue to meet once a month at their union hall, and eventually became the intelligence agents of the UCK, or the KLA, passing information to the guerrillas in the mountains west of Peja in the Rogova Valley.

These older officers gave me their version of the KLA, the

Kosovo Liberation Army, and told me there were really three groups of former KLA fighters. The UCK fought the Serb military during the occupation. Other KLA members came into the area after NATO intervened simply for payback and to slaughter any Serb they could find. The third group that called themselves the KLA was made up of criminals who took advantage of the war to make money.

When NATO came in and took over the occupation of Kosovo most UCK members joined the police or joined the newly formed Kosovo Defense Force. Colin Powell had been successful in every conflict that he was asked to lead, from Grenada, Panama, Haiti, to the First Gulf War. He had always disarmed the enemy military and kept them under control. They turned in their weapons, reported to their bases and, most importantly, were paid. They were kept in authority, but under control.

He did the same thing in Kosovo. The fighters were disarmed and given uniforms and paychecks. They reported each weekend to a base on the outskirts of Peja. Their weapons were locked up in an armory and sealed by the UN. Only the front gate guard carried a weapon. On weekends, they formed up in construction companies and repaired the war damage. Often, on my patrols, I would stop at their base, have tea with the men on duty and check that the all-important UN armory seal was intact.

There were still KLA members acting as revenge killers and criminals in the Peja area and in the cities to the south like Junik and Djacovica. But there were also UCK guerillas in the mountains around Peja, keeping low in case the UN and NATO pulled out and left their fates to the Serbs. They were under the command of a mythical leader, who reportedly still had his fingers in all that happened in Peja. I asked Bekim about this and he just said it was a fairytale told by the people of Peja to make them feel safe, and I believed him.

Blessed are the Peacekeepers

Chapter 6

Willy and I arrived at work an hour early for the night roll call at Peja Station as was our practice. Billy Ray, commander of the day shift, called us into the office and told us that someone had found the body of a young girl in a village just south of Peja City. He wanted to know if Willy could send a team out there because his men would soon be off duty. Everyone shifted nervously, knowing that a dead body call alone would take up the remainder of the night.

There were only a few night-shift KPS at the station because of the two-hour journey between their home villages and Peja Station, and I was the only UN officer available.

Willy told Billy, "This will not be a problem. Michael will form a team and go there now."

Then Willy turned to me. "Michael, please collect the team. I will try to get out there later, if you need me."

"I should be okay," I replied confidently. I had handled similar calls in Kosovo, and investigated homicides as a detective back in the States. I went over to gather the KPS who had gathered the a café across the street, making sure that one of them spoke English well enough to act as an interpreter.

On the way to the village, I told them that all we knew was that someone had reported finding a girl's body. We did not know if it was an accidental death or a homicide, so I emphasized that I wanted them to follow my instructions carefully and without question. They all nodded okay.

An old farmer waved at us to a stop as we entered the dirt roadway that cut through the center of a small collection of homes and a single café/store building. He took off his old weather-beaten cap, bowed and greeted me with hand over heart, and explained that he was the one who discovered the body.

We followed him a short distance into the woods to a clearing that looked like a small trash dump used by the villagers to discard old appliances and other rubbish that they could not burn. The body was on the edge of this area. I told the KPS and the farmer to stay back while I approached the victim.

She was lying in the grass, face down, fully clothed, with blood spatter near her head. I tried to shoo away the flies that were swarming over the corpse but quickly gave it up as a waste of time. I noted that the body had no foul odor yet.

I planned to use the event to train the KPS officers, so I went back and explained step-by-step everything I was going to do. I asked the farmer to get me a long rope, some of which I would use to block off the area from bystanders. I would use the rest of it to mark a single path in and out of the crime scene.

Then it hit me. Where the hell *were* all the bystanders? I had never before been at a dead body scene where there was a complete absence of any curious people. I asked the farmer where everyone was. He did not reply, but looked at the ground in a manner that I can only describe as shame.

A KPS officer leaned towards me and said quietly, "This may be an honor killing, Officer Mike."

Shit, I thought, *I really hate this kind of stuff.*

I sent the farmer off for some rope, and he returned quickly. We set up the boundary area, and I slowly walked to the body again, laying down a length of rope that I had cut from the larger rope coil, trying not to step on anything important, and did a pre-investigator examination, meaning I did not touch the body, move anything, or pick up any evidence.

I had already decided on a full-scale investigation. I would call Willy and request UN investigators there ASAP, along with crime scene photographers, and a forensic team from Pristina. The whole nine yards.

I looked at the girl. She was short and quite young, probably a teenager. She lay with her right cheek in the dirt. She was wearing traditional Albanian farm-girl garments, undisturbed, not ripped or damaged, which probably ruled out sexual assault. Her jet black hair was matted down with congealed blood. A small bullet entry wound was apparent in the back of her head. Her left cheek was grossly disfigured by the exit wound, and flies were already depositing eggs in the opening.

I squatted and checked her vital signs, just for the record. No surprise there. It looked like she had fallen forward from a keeling position after being shot. I figured the KPS officer was right: She had been executed—killed by someone seeking what passed for "honor" among the old-line Albanians. But where the hell was her family? Why weren't they there to mourn her and swear revenge? I was resolute that this crime would go neither unsolved nor unpunished, and walked my way back out to the boundary rope to make my call to Willy.

When I turned to the English-speaking KPS, he had a sad look on his face. "Officer Mike," he said, "the old man has told me that the dead girl was nineteen years old. She had just returned here from a failed marriage to a man in another village not far from here. The farmer says that the family home of the dead girl is close and he would take us there. The farmer thinks that she was killed by her family."

Which explained no family at the crime scene.

The farmer pointed out the girl's family home from a distance, and then disappeared. I could understand that he didn't want to get involved any deeper, but this was murder. I instructed a KPS officer to go find him and have him write a witness statement.

The English-speaking KPS officer and I approached the home of the girl's family. I put on my UN beret so everyone would know that I was not the local police. We found three males sitting at a table in the front yard of a rundown cottage—an old man, a twenty-something man and a young boy. They were drinking tea and smoking, pretending not to notice our approach. There were no women in sight.

I unsnapped my holster as we walked up to them. They noticed, and appeared sad, but not in the least fearful. I gave a slight bow as a gesture of respect, but my right hand was not on my heart in the common fashion, it was on the grip of my handgun.

I said, "Good evening, I'm Officer Granger of the United Nations Police Force. I am here to find out what happened to the dead girl."

My KPS partner interpreted my words. He spoke to the old man in a respectful tone. The old man replied in a lengthy speech that appeared both remorseful and defiant.

When he finished, The KPS officer turned to me and said, "The old man is the girl's father. He said that he shot her because she brought shame to her family. She was recently returned to the family by her husband of one week—a husband of an arranged marriage. The one who sent her back said claimed the girl was not a virgin when given away by her father."

I said, "Not a virgin? So she gets a bullet in her head? He admitted that he is a murderer—so why is he acting so defiant?"

The KPS replied, "The father is angry that you are here. He does not want the UN to investigate the incident. He said that what happened was a justifiable act of honor, and that the case should be handled by a local or religious court."

The guy had a point. Given the situation, even if involved, the UN would likely hand off the man's trial as he said. A local court, if they convicted the man, would probably sentence him to about three to five years in prison, if they found he was justified in defending the family's honor. A religious court would likely be even more lenient, maybe doling out some meager punishment like asking Allah for forgiveness ten times a day and not eating goat for a month.

I tried to contain my rising sense of injustice and focus on my job. I got permission from the old man to enter his home and get the murder weapon. After the women inside were removed from my sight, the youngest son and I went in and he showed me the gun that the father had used to execute his daughter. It was an old barely-functional Russian-made handgun. I also noticed a beat-up Kalashnikov assault rifle and confiscated it as well.

I thanked the boy who really did seem sad. Maybe he had liked his sister. I took the weapons to my UN vehicle and secured them, then waited for backup from Peja. The KPS could do the customary welcome tea later. The father wasn't going anywhere. He had no reason to hide. It was simple: Anyone engaged in an honor killing would not deny it or run. That would defeat the whole purpose of the act, which, in the end was a show of resolution and pride in this theater of the bizarre.

Within the next few hours, uniformed UN and KPS investigators arrived from Peja Station and began examining the crime scene. They didn't touch anything, though. They left that task for the specialized UN forensic team and the UN judge who would arrive from Pristina later. The local guys quietly took the father into custody and drove him to Peja for interrogation and processing.

Willy showed up soon afterwards and listened calmly as I gave him the situation report. After I finished he shook his head and said, "Sometimes, I find it hard to believe that I am still in Europe."

He told me to stand by until everything was wrapped up, then left for Peja Station, having many other tasks to perform as the shift commander.

I returned to my car to wait for the two remaining teams to arrive, wondering if I'd made the right call. I was the one who ordered full scale UN involvement rather than allowing an unobtrusive local investigation to take place. I didn't care what anyone else thought, though. It wasn't as if I was trying to make a big deal out of nothing. I only wanted the dead girl to get the justice she deserved. Who else was going to do it?

The first of the two teams arrived within the hour. It was the UN judge and her security detail. The judge was an attractive dignified woman from Germany who lived in the Peja region. Her position was so sensitive in Kosovo that local police were not given the location of her villa.

She traveled in a heavily armed convoy that I had seen many times around Peja. The three or four vehicle escorts traveled at high speeds down the middle of the road, and everyone in the country knew to give them a wide berth. During my first week in Peja, I was on patrol when this convoy barreled down the street, coming right at me. I didn't know the protocol at that time, and pulled a little to the right. They of course headed right at my UN Police Toyota. At the last second, the KPS officer beside me grabbed the steering wheel and we ended up in a ditch on the side of the road.

After they had passed, the KPS officer told me, "Officer Mike, you must get out of their way when you see them. They will kill you, even if you are a policeman."

The convoys did not stop for anyone or anything, and their specialized teams, acting as bodyguards, had the authority to shoot anyone who posed a threat to their VIP. Since the UN police had diplomatic immunity and could not be prosecuted even for murder, they had huge intimidation factor working in their favor.

I watched in fascination as the vehicles from the UN Special Operations Protection Unit plowed down the roadway leading to the village. The moment they arrived, uniformed men poured out of every vehicle except for the armored car in the center and spread out, deploying around the vehicles and in front of the buildings in the village center. They didn't look like any UN officers I had encountered before. They were stern, tough and all business. They were dressed a variety of international uniforms like the UN guys in Peja, but were covered in black bulletproof vests and were festooned with all sorts of equipment. They had knives, flashlights, batons, flash grenades, high-end radios with ear pieces and all sorts of other exotic paraphernalia. All of them wore dark sunglasses, black shooting gloves and were heavily armed.

I didn't know how those guys earned their reputation, but the KPS clearly wanted no part of them, and backed away from me and the crime scene.

I had to admit that these men did look scary, and they maneuvered with deadly professionalism, but I had never seen that kind of thing before and my curiosity got the better of me. I walked towards the cars, relaxed in the thought that they knew I was a UN cop with my blue beret standing out amongst the KPS uniforms around me. When I was within three steps of the parked convoy, two members of the unit leveled their weapons at me. One said simply, "Stop or die."

Well, that put my pucker factor on level ten. I froze in my tracks while the other team member approached me with his MP5 pointed at my chest. He examined my uniform and asked me if I was in charge. I introduced myself, confident that being a fellow UN officer based in Peja, he would recognize my name. I was surprised that he not only acted like he'd never heard of me, but also took the time to make certain I really was a UN cop.

After I passed examination, the guy lowered his weapon and waved down his attack-dog comrades. Then he identified himself and offered me his hand.

"Hi, I'm Jim Durfer," he said, "team leader of this protection unit. I'm an American, too. From Virginia Beach. Sorry about the threat to shoot, but we need to be cautious."

Jim was tall, sandy-haired and extremely fit. I found out later that he had been a Navy flyer prior to being a cop. He explained that, only after they felt the area was secure, would they allow the UN judge to exit her protective armored car in order to examine the crime scene. It was standard operating procedure. He and his men obviously took no chances; I could only have respect for such professionalism.

Team Leader Durfer went over to the armored car and knocked on the door. It opened and the judge exited. Once out, two large Special Operations guys hovered about her while she put on a wide-brimmed straw hat. She was short and middle-aged, with slightly graying dark hair. She walked straight to the crime scene, her light summer dress flapping in the steady breeze. She followed my rope guides to the body and was careful not to disturb anything.

UN judges have a special role, much different from what I was familiar with in the States. In most of Europe and the rest of the world, the majority of criminal cases are heard by a tribunal. That means no jury, just three judges appointed by the government. In Kosovo "smaller cases," like the honor killing, are heard by one judge—either a local judge or, if called, a UN judge. Both the UN and local judges would often conduct a preliminary investigation before the case was placed before them for judgement.

Everyone here was playing by European rules. The special operators stood guard and deployed around the crime scene. These men were all UN cops, like me. There wasn't a KPS officer or interpreter in the group. I saw from the flags on their uniforms that the team was made up of cops from the USA, Canada, Germany, Denmark, the Netherlands, Russia, England, Ireland, and Jordan. There was also one woman. She was blond, British, and tough-looking. I was sure that if she wanted to, she could not only kick my ass, but would probably enjoy doing it.

While the UN judge did her thing, Jim and I talked. I offered him a cigarette, but he declined. I lit one, took a drag, then said, "Looks like a pretty nice gig, Jim. How did you get it?"

He smiled. "Simple. When I first arrived I applied for special operations—Spec Ops. I tested and got the job."

"Any regrets?"

"Not really. I like the travel and excitement, though I don't work with the KPS or locals as much as I would like."

"Is this all you guys do?"

"What? Guarding VIPs? Nope. We act as SWAT teams and sometimes go on classified missions. We also work closely with intelligence. I remember reading a report on a smuggling bust near the border recently. It was called Operation White Mountains. Heard of it? Some hotshot named Granger kicked it off. Sound familiar?"

I wanted to smack him on the side of the head. "Son-of-a-bitch," I said. "You knew who I was when you saw my name tag, but you still busted my balls?"

He grinned. "That's what we do, Mike. It's in our job description and nature."

The UN judge wrapped up her business and Jim escorted her back to the parked convoy. His men slowly withdrew to their vehicles, but only after the judge had been safely tucked away.

In a cloud of dust, the convoy sped away to whatever secret location they came from, only to be replaced minutes later by another group of UN specialists from Pristina.

The UN forensics team was equally impressive. Under the direction of the lead specialist, a British forensic scientist from Scotland Yard on loan to the UN, they literally left no stone unturned. The fifteen-person team worked under large lights that they had brought with them. They worked through the night, and, at daylight, combed over the scene again in case they'd missed anything in the darkness. The body was removed and everything wrapped up two hours after daybreak.

I finally left to return to Peja Station. Once there, I checked out and walked home, tired and bothered by the events of the past twenty-four hours. I felt drained, and dropped my uniform and gear as I walked into my room, confident the housekeeper would clean up the mess. Then, I slept well into the afternoon.

When Willy and I arrived at the station to start our shift, Station Commander Tony summoned us to his office to speak with the investigators. The autopsy results were already in. The nineteen-year-old farm girl was killed by one shot to the back of the head. Also, the coroner had confirmed that the farm girl was, in fact, a virgin.

The investigators went to the husband's village. The forty-five-year-old farmer, who had paid for the arranged marriage, confessed that he was so intimidated by the girl's beauty and sweetness that he was unable to get an erection. Because he was embarrassed, he sent her back to her father, making up the story of her lost virginity to get his money back. She died because he couldn't get it up. All I could do was shake my head.

They re-interviewed the father of the girl and confronted him with the medical report. He broke down and told them that his older son had helped to drag the protesting girl to the trash dump to be killed. The pair was locked up in the back cellblock at Peja Station where they would remain until transferred to Kosovo Prison for pre-trial detention.

I was royally pissed, and asked Tony if I could see the father one last time before he was taken away. Willy and Tony said it was not a good idea, but I was firm in my request. I wouldn't be able to sleep another night if I didn't get the last word in. I took Johnny with me with instructions to translate word for word, and not with the usual polite social banter. Johnny didn't look happy about handling the task or going with me into the dingy cellblock area, though, to his credit, he did willingly follow.

The old man—the girl's father—was sitting on his bunk crying. I should have felt sorry for him, and I think a part of me did, but I had to tell him how I felt. I said, "Johnny, remember, word for word."

The old man looked up. The defiance and justifiable pride he had shown at his home were gone from his face, replaced by sorrow and tears.

I know I shouldn't, but I laid into him without mercy. "The world is round, not flat you stupid old man. Your medieval thinking has brought shame and dishonor to your family. Your beautiful daughter is dead after spending her short life doing your bidding. You might still get off easy in this crazy place, but I hope you rot in hell for eternity!"

Johnny did as he was told and translated word for word. I am sure the old man did not understand everything I had said or meant, but I was sure that he got the gist of it. I didn't wait for a response. I left him sitting there bent over, head in hands. The important thing for me was that I'd gotten it off my chest, so now I could sleep at night.

And I did, until the nightmares caught up with me.

Chapter 7

It was still early September, and while the day were still hot, the nights were becoming noticeably cooler. Fall was around the corner, and, with the electricity rotation problem, I was concerned about keeping warm. We were now getting power about seven or eight hours a day in the city, but I wondered how Willy and I were going to manage once the cold winter weather set in. The locals warned us to be prepared for an early cold autumn because of Peja's altitude and the bone-chilling effect of the nearby mountains.

My patrols were becoming routine, and the KPS officers and I were closer. I felt I was accomplishing the UN mission of getting these young men and women trained in modern policing. They were responding with good will and loyalty.

Willy was doing an excellent job as Shift Commander. Before each day's pre-shift roll call, he gave us an idea of what was going on around the country. It was a blend of good, bad, and sometimes bizarre news, usually in that order.

One afternoon, Willy started with the bad news first. "Listen up, please, everyone. Two KPS officers were killed last night. While off duty in their village, they came upon and confronted armed thieves, stealing the village cattle. If you are interested in the details, see me after roll call."

He paused while the KPS murmured amongst themselves for a

minute, then, continued, "One American UN officer died in Pristina after suffering a heart attack yesterday, and two UN officers were seriously injured in Mitrovica when a hand grenade was tossed at them during rioting in that city."

Mitrovica was a bad place. There were constant riots and they were always violent, often deadly. My friends, Jack and Beth, were stationed there; I hoped they were safe. They were both savvy tough cops, but as we had all found out, it was easy to get hurt in Kosovo. Any mistake could be the last.

Willy then gave us the good news.

"We were informed today that a German company is beginning repairs on the broken generators at the electrical plant. It is expected that the repairs will be complete before the winter sets in, which means for us here in Peja at least three more hours of electricity each day." Then he added, with a grin and some obvious national pride, "Did I mention that it is a *German* company?"

Everyone clapped. Then he finished up with the bizarre.

"Traffic units in the larger cities are now being issued with radar guns donated by a company from Sweden. Yesterday, two UN officers were killed, and several KPS were seriously wounded when one police vehicle was destroyed while training with this new equipment. It is reported that the UN officers, out of curiosity, pointed the radar gun at a NATO warplane flying overhead to clock its speed. The aircraft mistook the radar lock-on as a threat from a ground anti-aircraft weapon. The aircraft fired a radar seeking missile, which struck the UN vehicle, causing the above damage. UN High Command recommends that this practice not be continued in the future."

No shit.

He finished roll call, adding his own words of advice: "Everyone, do not ever forget that this is a war zone."

Again, no shit!

My four-to-midnight patrol shift that day was uneventful. It was only after it had ended that things got interesting. I was returning my vehicle to Peja Station when I saw that pretty much everyone, UN and KPS, were outside in the parking lot. The KPS coming in for duty appeared to be having animated conversations with those just coming off their shift. I could tell that something unusual was up. Then, pandemonium broke out.

KPS officers were running out of the station's front door, jumping into their small Kia SUVs. The UN officers were standing around in confusion.

Willy came outside and grabbed me saying, "Mike, a KPS officer just called in from Junik and said that he had been shot. The KPS are headed to Junik. I can't raise the UN officers on the radio. Go with them and take command. I will stay here and get things organized, and let the other UN officers know what's happening. Go! Go! The KPS are leaving now!" He pointed at three Kias leaving the parking lot, and I ran for the last one in line. The KPS vehicles were full of nervous and angry officers. Like clown cars in a circus, nearly every inch of space was occupied. As I ran, I slipped on my UN beret.

I got to the last vehicle while it stopped at the main intersection and banged on the rear window. Bekim and a KPS officer named Jorgji were stuffed in the cargo area. They opened the rear cargo door and I jumped in. I landed on top of them, and rode the rest of the way on their laps.

The radio was blaring with KPS chatter, all in Albanian. The voices transmitted were full of panic. Jorgji spoke English and filled me in on what was happening as we sped out of Peja. Bekim jumped in and gave me what information he could gather from the radio traffic as well.

Junik was a small place about twenty clicks—ten miles—from Peja on the main road south. It was bigger than a village, but smaller than a European town. It had thirty houses, a couple of cafes, and was smack in the middle of bad guy territory.

Bekim continued with the background information: Earlier that night, there was a fight in one of the town's two cafés. A group of outside villagers got beat up and left town, returning later with friends to seek revenge on the townspeople of Junik. Two UN teams and two independent KPS vehicles had responded to the fight. The first two KPS were climbing the stairs to the second floor café when one was apparently shot and wounded. The wounded man was on the radio saying that the scene outside had turned into a major riot with some serious fighting going on.

A call came over the car radio from the senior UN Officer on scene. He said, "I am asking for you to lend some assistance to our location. It is very very bad here. Thank you for help."

I thought, what the hell was that about? This guy was definitely not European, and he sounded too calm for someone caught in the middle of a riot.

We rushed there as fast as we could, though "rushing" is an understatement. That ride from hell scared the shit out of me. I was bouncing around with two other guys in the unpadded cargo space of a vehicle, while the three KPS drivers were doing their best imitation of the final leg of the Indy 500. In a screech of tires, we arrived at Junik in twenty minutes flat. I nearly puked when I got out, but I recovered fast.

The scene that greeted us in Junik was straight out of Dante's Inferno. We were stopped about half a block from town center at the edge of the town square. The square consisted of a main street with a fountain in the middle surrounded by small shops and cafes. There was no electricity in Peja tonight, but Junik square was bright with light from an overturned and burning KPS vehicle. In the eerie pulsing glow, we could see bodies strewn along the street and sidewalks, and about a hundred men locked in serious hand-to-hand fighting with fists, pipes, clubs, or rocks. The fighters paid us absolutely no notice, even though we were clearly back-illuminated by the headlights of our cars.

I had taken all the riot training that my hometown police department offered, and I knew the proper protocols, but this was different. What I was looking at was a horde of crazed men trying to kill each other, not some civil demonstration gone ugly. And, somewhere in that mess was a wounded KPS officer who needed our help.

I looked around for the on-site UN people, as the twenty KPS officers of my ad-hoc rescue force exited their KPS cars. Then I spotted two UN vehicles parked in the darkness on a side street, the officers in their vehicles. I told Bekim and Jorgji to tell the KPS to stay where they were, and that I would be back in thirty seconds.

I ran up to the two UN cars parked next to each other. Inside the nearest car I saw an Indian UN officer, and in the second, an African UN officer. Also inside each car, there were two KPS officers looking very pissed off.

The Indian UN officer rolled down his window and said pleasantly, "Thank you for coming so quickly. I am pleased."

I couldn't believe it. I wanted to reach in and strangle him.

"What are you doing sitting here? Where is the wounded KPS officer?" I yelled.

The Indian shrugged his shoulders and looked at me as if I was speaking Chinese. I ordered the KPS out of the cars and to come with me. They responded in a heartbeat, relieved to finally be taking some action. The five of us ran back to the twenty KPS gathered in front of the rescue convoy. The two UN cops locked the doors and remained in their cars.

I put on my game face. I was apparently the only functioning UN cop. I had Bekim, my best KPS guy with me, and Jorgji seemed competent as well. It was time to put a stop to the madness.

I told Bekim and Jorgji to form the KPS behind me into a line stretching to my left and right. They executed it in seconds.

I took my baton out of its sheath and raised it above my head. The KPS all did the same.

Then, I swept my baton downward. The steel rod expanded to its full length with a loud metal snap. The twenty-four men and women behind me instantly followed suit. The sound of so many batons all opening at the same time in the narrow confines of the roadway echoed off the buildings and sounded like a hundred shotguns being loaded.

That, and only that, drew the attention of the people fighting in the town square. The crowd of bloodied men stood and stared, unsure what to make of us.

"Follow me," I shouted, and I started walking forward holding my baton in front of me with two hands. My "riot squad" did the same.

Some of the rioters got smart and took off. I hoped that as we got closer the others would think smart and do the same, so we could go find the wounded KPS.

That didn't happen, of course.

As we approached, the fifty men still standing looked at each other, picked up any weapon they could find from the scattered debris on the ground, and collected into a single group.

For a minute, we faced off like opposing football teams at kick off time. They outnumbered us two-to-one and knew it. They began to yell and taunt us, waving weapons made larger in the shadows cast forwards towards us from the light of the fire in the square. They seemed confident we would not advance any further. It made sense. The crowd had successfully intimidated the UN and KPS into their two cars. They had no fear. They were a mob and were ready to hurt us.

That was their mistake. They saw an undersized group of inexperienced cops standing there. What I saw were twenty-four steady KPS officers who had stormed out of Peja Station and headed to Junik on their own, rushing to save a comrade, without the need for UN leadership. They were the cream of the force—the youngest, fittest, toughest KPS in the area. Many had fought the Serbs as part of the UCK. They would stop at nothing to help their wounded friend.

I was ready for this fight. Willy and my backup were still at least fifteen minutes away, and I knew there was a bleeding, maybe dying KPS that needed immediate help. I was also angry. At Kosovo. At the UN cops hiding in their cars. At the fifty ignorant brutes in front of me who had no respect for the law, and who viewed us as flies they could just flick away.

I looked for the biggest of the fifty men. He was near their center, brandishing a club. I charged right at him at a full sprint, screaming as loudly as I could, with the KPS following on my heels, screaming as loudly as they could.

We hit the opposition like a tornado of whirling steel rods. A few feet short of my target, I jumped into the air to get height on the giant in front of me. I think he was in shock, our all-out attack catching him off guard. I swung my steel baton down and struck him from forehead to mid-chest. It split his face open and he fell like a rock, holding his bloody face in his hands.

I did not, however, see the guy right behind him. Big mistake.

The man, who could have been the twin brother of the one I had dropped, came down on my head with a piece of brick. I instinctively moved my head to the side just enough that the brick caught only my left ear and shoulder. I was stunned, but managed to side-step his next blow. As a cop, the first thing I'd learned about street fighting was to always stay on your feet. If you go down, you're probably done for. To stay up, keep moving, and live had been drilled in to me by my instructors. Before I could dodge a third swing, two of my KPS descended on him. In less than a second of flying steel, bad guy number two was also down.

I was so pumped I held my baton over my head, howled, and began striking at anyone wearing civilian clothes. So did the KPS. In two minutes, half of us had fought our way to the far end of the square. Then, it was over. Everyone not on the ground behind us was running away.

When I scanned the scene behind me, it looked like one of those paintings of the aftermath of an ancient battle. The ground was littered with bleeding bodies. Half of my KPS officers walked among them, checking them for weapons and IDs while the other half stood guard. It took several KPS officers holding my arm to bring me back to reality. Two and a half minutes of uncontrolled madness was over. Well, almost over.

The KPS officer said, "Sir, we need you. Now!" and dragged me over to where Bekim and Jorgji were standing at the bottom of an outside staircase leading up to a second floor café. They were covered in blood as were most of the other KPS gathering there.

Finally getting a grip on myself, I asked, "Bekim, are any of the KPS hurt?"

"Just bumps and scratches, sir."

The area where we were gathered was dark, but the lights inside the second floor café were on, shedding some light onto the landing. Bekim shined his flashlight up the staircase onto the landing, where I saw the wounded KPS officer who'd called for help holding a hand to his bleeding stomach. The KPS, firearm in his other hand, extended his trigger and second fingers upward, gestured smartly with the barrel towards the open café door, then shook his head. Jorgi translated: "There are two gunmen inside the café but no civilians. We must get to the second floor and pull the wounded officer down here."

I nodded and started up the staircase with six KPS behind me, moving in single file. I was still pumped up with adrenalin and had made it to the top of the landing before I knew it. I did not want to give the gunmen any chance to shoot at us, so I stuck my semi-automatic in the café doorway and blasted away with covering fire while two KPS officers pulled the wounded man down the stairs. I probably fired about ten times. The noise was deafening—like tossing a box of M-80 fireworks into a cement hallway and having them all go off at the same time. Bekim and Jorgji joined me and continued firing into the café.

When shell casings are expended they are burning hot for several seconds. So hot, as a matter of fact, that, if they touch skin, they not only sting like a bee, but stick to it and continue burning. As Jorgji and Bekim fired in to the room, the casings began flying wildly around. I was being pelted by hot brass. One stuck to my forehead until I swatted it off.

On top of that, the flashes from the gunfire made me lose whatever night vision I had. The blinding lights, deafening sounds, and the casing stings stunned me and I had to stop for a few seconds to reorient myself. I reloaded my nine millimeter, even though it was not empty. Better to reload and have a full weapon then to have to reload in the middle of another exchange.

The landing area filled with cordite smoke which added to the chaos. As my hearing slowly came back to normal, I could hear some moaning from inside the café.

I yelled, "Bekim! Take a couple of KPS and clear the café. I'm going down to check on the wounded guy," and ran down the stairs, confident that Bekim could finish the job without me.

At street level, things were getting organized. The KPS were gathering up the injured rioters and giving medical aid to those with serious wounds. I asked a KPS officer if any of the rioters had been killed, and she assured me no, none had. Some might still die before they got to a hospital, but at least there had been no deaths in the street, and would therefore be no justifications for revenge killings from the civilians. I heard several more shots from the open café behind me. The jury was still out on the suspects there.

I looked ahead at the surrounding hills and saw a convoy of blue flashing lights approaching. Willy and the cavalry were only about a minute away. I looked at my watch. The KPS and I had been in Junik only ten minutes.

I found the wounded KPS officer in the back seat of a KPS vehicle. I reached for a large sterile pad from the medical kit on my belt, and ripped his shirt open to find the wound. There was a small entrance hole that was longer bleeding.

"Does it hurt?" I asked.

He grimaced.

Dumb question. I held the bandage in position while I rolled him over to check for an exit wound. That's the one that will kill you. When the bullet hits the body it begins to tumble. If it exits, it usually rips open a large hole.

He was in luck. There was no exit wound. The KPS was conscious, alert, and not bleeding, with the bullet somewhere in his gut. Thankfully, there was no sign of shock.

This guy just might live, I thought. I needed to get him to the Italian NATO base in Peja quickly. The hospital at the base had the best medical staff in the region and they were trained to treat battle wounds so I jumped in the car and headed there. As I was racing out of Junik, I could see in the rearview mirrors Willy's rescue convoy driving into the mess I had left behind. As the moment, I no longer cared about the rioters or the gunmen I had left there. All I cared about was that none of my men and women were hurt or injured, and I had only one last mission to complete that night: keep the KPS officer lying in the back seat alive.

Then, Murphy's Law hit. I was informed by radio on the way to Peja that NATO does not treat wounded KPS, only UN or NATO troops. This surprised the hell out of me, but I changed direction and within minutes arrived at Peja Hospital. They do their best there, but to me the hospital looked like it was right out of the 1950s. The equipment inside looked old and battered. There was no nurse standing by to help. The hospital was clearly understaffed and underfunded.

The doctor and I carried the wounded KPS to a treatment table in the emergency room, where he began examining the wound. Slowly, the room filled up with KPS officers; even the hospital cleaning staff with mops in hand were there. The doctor, who spoke good English, was quick and efficient. "We need to open him up, find the bullet and see what damage it has caused."

It sounded like a good plan to me. The doctor washed his hands, picked up a scalpel and began to place it on the wound.

That's when I yelled, "What are you doing? Get him to a surgery room. There is no rush here. He's not bleeding that much."

He looked at me with exasperation in his eyes.

"Young man, we have only two treatment rooms. This is one of them." He eyed my waist kit. "We have run out of latex gloves, so if you really want to help give me a pair of yours from your medical kit."

I took out a pair and handed them to him. I felt like an idiot again. Willy's words from roll call rang in my head: "Always remember that you are in a war zone."

A middle-aged nurse gave the patient a shot of morphine and the doctor waited for it to take effect before digging away. I cleared the spectators out, concerned about infection and cleanliness in that dirty exam room, with its open window that lacked any screening. As I watched the doctor work, I kept half-expecting an alley cat to jump through the window and into the room, saunter over to the KPS officer on the gurney, and lick at the blood pouring all over the place. No IV, no plasma, no blood tranfusion, just cut and dice. Yup, it was very 1950.

In a few short minutes of what was actually a very professional surgery, the KPS rested quietly, a short line of stitches on his torso.

The doctor took off the gloves and me his prognosis: "He should live with no permanent disability if we can keep him here for a week or so. But that, of course, is up to you."

I wanted to say, "Okay, what is it I need to do, now?" Instead, I responded in polite cop-talk. "Please explain what you mean, sir."

The doctor, who I was beginning to like, explained that KPS have no insurance. The UN would not cover the cost of the care at that hospital. So, unless I could find enough money to cover his stay at the hospital, he would have to send the KPS officer home in the morning. To recover, he would need to stay at least week.

My mind was screaming, *You've got to be shitting me! No coverage, no backup plan, no nothing! This is ridiculous!* but I calmed myself and asked the doctor, "How much do you need?"

"Seven hundred Euros should cover the staff," he replied. "I'll throw in the surgery for free if you give me all the medical supplies from your kit. American bandages stick more efficiently others, and we are desperately short of supplies."

I couldn't believe what I was hearing. I was making a lot of Euros each month, and had spent very little. There were no banks in Peja, so I got paid in cash. Until a friend went to Switzerland and would make a deposit in my Swiss account for me, I kept the money on me. I was currently carrying four thousand Euros.

I pulled the doctor into another room, and dug out seven hundred Euros. He protested. "Maybe you could take up a collection from the other KPS or UN officers. It has been done before."

In the mood I was in, I didn't give a shit. The Euro in my hand looked like play money. I would have, at best, spent it on beer. If I gave it to the doctor, it became real life-saving money. So I gave it to him and told him not to tell anyone. I also gave him the contents of my medical kit. After today's firefight, they would replace everything at the Italian base. Free of charge.

I was tired, sweaty and hungry. I had been working for eleven hours straight. My clothing was ripped and bloodied. As I left the examination area, I saw injured rioters from Junik begin filling up the waiting area of the hospital. KPS and UN officers went from one rioter to another searching for details about the shooting of the police officer. The senior UN man came up to me and asked, "How is that KPS officer doing?"

The KPS in the room crowded around us.

"The surgery went well," I replied. "He should be okay."

The English-speaking KPS officers translated for the others and there were smiles all around.

"Is there anything we can do?" he asked.

I said, "Yeah, make sure that he is placed under guard so that none of these dirt bags from Junik bother him."

He said no problem. I thanked him, and asked if one of the KPS would drive me to Peja Station. Everyone volunteered, and after some discussion, one was selected to do the honor.

When I arrived, the station was humming with the kind of activity one would expect when an officer is shot. A lot of KPS were there, either processing prisoners or standing around waiting to hear how their friend was doing. As I walked in the front door, Tony, who had gotten out of bed and drove in from home, met me in the hallway along with Willy. Behind them were twenty or so KPS, who were looking at me strangely, almost fearfully. I couldn't understand the look until Willy, smiling broadly, said, "Michael, you look like shit. You are covered from head-to-toe in dirt and blood."

I stared at my reflection in a nearby doorway glass window. It was the first chance I'd taken to examine myself that night. My left ear had been cut by the brick and, like any head wound, had bled all over my left side. It had stopped bleeding earlier and just hurt now. I had been so hopped up on adrenaline from my hand-to-hand encounter in Junik, that up to now I hadn't noticed the blood or felt any pain.

Not realizing that I had been cut, I had unknowingly created a truly nightmarish look by spreading the blood all over my face each time I wiped what I had thought was sweat from my face or head. I was literally covered in what looked like red war paint.

Tony and Willy laughed. I laughed, too and wiped my face and licked my fingers, saying, "Uhm, good," in my best "Arnold the Terminator" imitation. We all laughed for a second, but the KPS hushed and backed away.

I went into the washroom and cleaned up. Then, I sat down with Willy and Tony and gave them a quick rundown on what had transpired at Junik. They didn't require that much information because they had already been briefed by the KPS. In fact, Tony had only two outstanding questions; First, why didn't I wait for backup to arrive? And second, did I want to take any action against the two UN officers who were already in Junik when I arrived.

"I know how it must look, but I'm not really a cowboy," I said. "To answer your first question, I didn't have the luxury of waiting. According to what I'd heard, a fellow officer was bleeding to death. As for number two, I don't give two shits about those UN officers. They will have to live with themselves. I'm not going to make a stink."

My two supervisors seemed okay with my answers, so I wrote my quick two-page report, providing few details and not mentioning at all the two UN cops. Tony pulled me aside, as I prepared to walk home with Willy. He put his arm on my shoulder in a fatherly manner and said, "Mike, you acted with quality leadership in Junik tonight. The KPS look to you with great respect. The KPS in Junik acted with courage and bravery. This was something they've needed to do for a long time. It will be important for the overall KPS organization and their success in Kosovo." Then, in a lower though still-fatherly voice he added, "I must caution you on two things, though. Do not go 'native' on me. Remember you are a UN officer first and foremost, not a KPS leader. Also, you are taking too many risks. You must use your head as well as your heart. Think about this."

Willy and I walked home together. About halfway, we were stalked by a pack of wild dogs, who growled constantly, but kept their distance after Willy threw a rock at them. On the way, I gave Willy the Real Fucking Story, including the hospital experience. Later that night, I quietly thought about my life in Kosovo. I was changing and I was not sure if it was for the better. The violence seemed to be rubbing off on me. I cared less and less about hurting bad guys. I was getting angrier quicker. I thought that maybe I needed some time off. Maybe I just needed the soft comfort of a woman to chill me out. I knew that I had been flirting with the KPS women more and more lately and that was a big red flag. I needed some R&R.

Tony and Willy gave me the next day off. Apparently they knew I needed some rest, too. I planned to sleep all day and maybe catch up on some reading in the evening. It was the second week of September and the weather was so fine, I easily convinced myself that things were not that bad. I just needed some sleep.

Chapter 8

The day after the Junik riot I got up at noontime and headed right for the kitchen. Willy and I both had our stashes of home food supplies that we pretty much lived on before and after our daily dinners in area cafes. Mine consisted of an industrial size bag of Animal Crackers, chocolate candy bars from Greece, and a bag of apples, all located in one cabinet. That stuff needed no refrigeration and could last all month, rain or shine. On the floor, I kept a case of warm Coca Cola from Czechoslovakia, a case of warm beer from Germany, and a case of bottled water.

Each day, I ate my main meals at a café, and for the most part they consisted of some type of chicken with either rice or pasta. There was not a lot of red meat available, and if there was I stayed away from it since there was little reliable refrigeration or electricity in Peja. My diet had no dairy products and little, if any, junk food. We UN officers walked everywhere when not on duty and I worked out religiously in my courtyard with makeshift weights and a pull up bar. I was in decent shape, but with my work schedule and odd diet I was tired a lot. Still, I was happy to have a day off to kick back and regain my energy. I felt it would be a great day.

I had just finished eating some of the cookies and a coke when Willy got up and filled me in on the parts of the Junik riot that I had missed.

"Michael, I cannot believe the damage that the rioters caused," he said. "There were many of them injured, but other than that wounded officer, the KPS had only a very few minor injuries. How did the KPS end the riot so quickly and efficiently?"

"They're better than we thought," I replied.

"Yes. I think so. I think we have done a good job here with them."

"So, what happened after I left Junik?"

"When you took away the wounded man, we gathered up the injured. But none of the KPS could identify who they fought with, so there were few arrests, maybe six in total. They are in the jail and will be charged today."

"Are there two big ugly guys among them?"

Willy shrugged. "They are all big and ugly."

We both laughed.

Willy went on to say that afterwards, my twenty-five KPS had the look and swagger of a soccer team that had just won the World Cup. They were physically a mess, but morale-wise they were on top of the world—jubilant, more like triumphant.

Like me, Willy thought that Bekim and Jorgji had shown themselves to be the leaders of the KPS in Peja. He said that he interviewed the two UN officers who had been on site when I got there, but he had little to say on that. There's never any need to expound on an embarrassment.

"What about the gunmen in the café who shot the KPS?" I asked.

"There were two. One did not make it to the hospital. The other survived."

"Who were they?"

"That's the sad story, Mike. The shooter was the owner of the café and he was only protecting his place from the villagers who attacked the town. He said he shot the KPS in the dark stairwell thinking he was one of the men from the mountains coming to harm him."

"Do you believe him?"

"Yes, I do. It does not take away from what you did. You did the right thing to save the KPS officer. Remember, this is Kosovo. Things like this happen a lot."

I understood what he meant. Officially, it was a clean shooting on our part. The real story was more nuanced than that. I did not feel at all bad. I just did my job. The gunmen could have surrendered at any time.

I was happy that the KPS were proud of their charge to break up the rioters as this was their first experience working together in a large group. Most riots or demonstrations in Kosovo were handled by UN Military Police, with the KPS serving basically as traffic control. It was important to them, because that action at Junik, and all the rumors that would spring from it, would spread through the entire country within a few days via the very efficient KPS word-of-mouth system. The story that resulted would probably be very different from the one that started, but to us that was fine. It was time that the populace and the UN both gave the KPS some respect.

Willy said that, not surprisingly, the KPS are very guarded about information they pass on to the UN supervisors, and that they were very guarded with him about my actions. "Mike, I know that you told me about the charge at the rioters, but the KPS at the scene spoke of you much like palace guards might speak of their king. Jorgji said to me, 'Officer Mike had blood on his face and in his heart.' This is good for morale right now, but we need to calm things down if we can. We need to get the KPS to trust all of us so we can trust them. We must not let them trust only one of us."

I got what he was saying—that it could not just be all about me. I

95

didn't want to tell him that I actually enjoyed the fighting. A good bar fight or riot creates a rush—a high that is hard to explain. The rush is only good if you win and are not physically messed up afterward, though. This fight met both criteria. I knew that Willy would not approve of my attitude, so I kept it to myself. He was a gentleman and a good guy. I wasn't sure what I was becoming.

I looked at him and did not say a word. Willy, in his wisdom just let it go. We talked for a couple of hours, then he left for work. I decided to stay home and rest some more.

Chapter 9

Despite my intention, I didn't get any more rest that day. It was September 11, 2001. At four p.m., I was picked up by some Russian soldiers who transported me to the American Support Compound on the outskirts of the town. There I was informed that New York and Washington had been attacked by terrorists. We were given the choice to stay on mission or go back to the USA. All thirty of us decided to stay and complete our mission, with a new, better understanding of where we were and what we were doing. It was better to be in Kosovo than in Manchester, New Hampshire. Here, I could continue to operate on the world stage and be part of the bigger picture.

Around seven a. m. the next day, Sept 12th, I heard voices by my front door. I remembered the United States flag was hanging from a pole on my balcony, and for a while I'd been thinking that maybe it wasn't a good idea to advertise exactly where an American lived. In fact, I was the only American who lived in that part of town. I had put it out the day I moved into the house out of a sense of pride and also because it irritated Willy. I had been considering taking it down, but decided that this was not the right time. As a matter of fact, I would have put out a bigger flag if I had one. I, got my gun and went to check on the noise outside.

I could not see the landing from my balcony, but someone was definitely there. I thought maybe it was maybe the landlord or his wife, our housekeeper, who could not find a key.

I opened the door and found two KPS officers sitting on the brick step wrapped in blankets. They had a make-shift tea heater with them and were sipping tea from ceramic cups.

Wondering if this had something to do with another emergency, I asked, "What are you guys doing? What's going on? How long have you been here?"

One answered in English, very respectfully, "Officer Mike, we have been here all night. We don't want anything to happen to you. Jorgji said you would sleep better if we were here."

I didn't know what to say. On their own, off duty, the KPS had set up a protective shield for me. The two officers stood and hugged me, almost crying. Thoroughly embarrassed, I tried to back away. They were genuinely concerned and asked me if my family was safe. I admit, my eyes watered a bit at the unexpected gesture of friendship.

The English-speaking officer continued: "Officer Mike, we must call Bekim and tell him that you are awake. He wanted to be told. Also, you must speak to the people at the gate."

"What people?" I asked.

The KPS officer said they had arrived an hour ago from Junik, but seemed friendly.

Seemed friendly? Right. I was in Kosovo. I tucked my gun into my waistband and walked to the front gate, my KPS escort in tow.

My courtyard had an eight-foot steel gate that was kept locked. I could hear some men talking on the other side, and even a few laughs, so I figured it was okay to take a peek. As I unlocked the gate, I realized that the two KPS had scaled the courtyard wall to get in. So much for security.

When I opened it, I faced thirty-five rural people who had gathered there in the early morning hours. The men instantly greeted me by removing their hats and bowing. The women offered flowers. One passed me a plate of chopped meat in pita bread with rice.

A spokesperson eventually emerged from the group. "We are shamed by fellow Muslims who attacked your cities," he said. "America is a great and good country. Clinton stopped the war, and you protected our town. America and you are good to our people— good to Muslims."

"Thank you," I said, "but there was no need for this. I know that the people of Kosovo are kind and loyal friends."

I could see that he wasn't going to stop no matter what I said. He raised his hand and added, "We know your heart. All the Kosovo police lead us here to where you live when we walked here from Junik."

Walked? I looked around and there were thirty men and five women, but only one car and a wagon. The wagon was pulled by a small motor on wheels. Many of these people had walked ten miles to pay their respects to an American for the tragedy of 9/11. It was hard not to be touched by that.

"I have brought my best carpenters from Junik," he continued. "They wish to go to America and repair your buildings."

I looked into the wagon and saw it was filled with old well-worn tools. I was frankly overwhelmed. I thanked them for the kind gesture. It took me another several minutes to convince them that America had all the carpenters it needed to rebuild.

It took twenty more minutes to convince them to leave. I thanked them liberally for the visit, their support and, of course, the flowers and food. Then I thanked the KPS and had them send everyone home, themselves as well. An hour later, after eating like a king, I went back to the gate to make certain I had re-locked it. The two KPS were still there, but now sitting outside the gate. I went out and pleaded, "Come on guys, really, you can go. I am fine. Willy will be back from Prizren shortly and I don't want him to see you here."

The senior KPS shook his head. "Bekim told us to stay until our relief arrives."

Sure, I was flattered, and got the message that they genuinely wanted to help the USA and me in return, but it was time for them to go. I put on stern face and said, "Okay, I outrank Bekim. It is time for you to go. By the way, why is Bekim telling you what to do?"

They just looked at each other, said nothing, hugged me once again, and walked down the dirt street toward Peja center.

I was deeply touched by all the affection and attention, but I kept wondering what Willy would say if he saw this. I had a pretty good idea. He would bust my chops for the next month over the fawning attention that I had been receiving from the Kosovars as of late. Then, he would warn me, again, not to get too big a head.

When Willy finally arrived, we exchanged information and agreed that there should be no real threat from any terrorists there in Kosovo, though we should keep alert. I told him that the neighbors brought some food "for the two of us, as a goodwill gesture." He dug into the half-mountain of food on the plate I had saved for him. I didn't tell him that the "neighbors" had walked ten miles to deliver it.

Chapter 10

We went to work the rest of the week on our normal four to twelve shifts, and nothing unusual happened. I was the only American on the Tiger Team shift, and I spent the first few days avoiding the many KPS who wanted to hug and comfort me—wanting to express their shock, sorrow and love of America.

While this was going on, I spent some time with the Egyptian and Jordanian UN officers, discussing politics and terrorism. These policemen were high-ranking men in their countries and well educated. They wanted my perspective on things. They also told me many things that I did not know. For example, Osama Bin-Laden had been wanted in Jordan for many years because he was behind an assassination plot against their king. The officer said that the Western powers did not assist them in hunting for Bin-Laden because he had helped the Americans fight the Russians in Afghanistan. The consensus among the Middle-Eastern cops was that America was naïve concerning Arab affairs.

The Russian UN peacekeepers were smug about the 9/11 attacks. Some of the older ones had served in Afghanistan in the 1980s and still held a grudge against us for our support of the rebels. Their take was that we had created the Mujahedeen and now it had come back to bite us on the ass. Welcome to the real world. They said that even now the Western powers were holding them back from wiping out the Islamic extremists in Chechnya, and America was wrong there, too.

I had heard that before from a college friend, Leo Pauli, who was a security agent at the Department of State. Leo was a patriot and a bona fide international man of mystery. He had talked me into applying for this temporary assignment with the UN Police. But, I wasn't sure if I was ready to thank him just yet.

It was Bekim, Jorgji, and the rest of the KPS who impacted me most during this time. The stories from Junik had spread across the province. They and the KPS had earned widespread respect, and I had been there with them. They were heroes to their kinsfolk, and in turn, my status had grown with KPS.

The UN officers as a whole had earned good reputations in Kosovo, except for a small minority, but the Americans were really shinning. Six-foot-seven-inch Rooftop Rob Smith was made the new shift commander of the Vitomirica sub-station. They even found an interpreter for him who had spent time in Alabama and could understand his southern drawl.

Scott Michaels was a star. He had led many successful operations, and now was the "go-to guy" in Peja, leading his own special task force. He had led a successful shootout in the mountains with a group of smugglers who he'd intercepted at a roadblock.

Billy Ray had been promoted to a shift commander position known as "Panther One." He had shut down some major crime rings and led a difficult recovery mission in the hills when a bus loaded with passengers tumbled off the Peja Mountain Road into a deep ravine.

But the KPS still wanted to ride with me. Bekim and Jorgji started to dress like me and walk like me. At the same time, the KPS were also a little afraid of me. I realized that this cult-like situation was getting out of hand, but I didn't know how to stop it. Maybe, unconsciously, I even encouraged it.

Strange and fantastic rumors as well as outright fabrications took hold like how I licked the blood of my enemies from my hands and howled at the moon. Or, how, at Junik, I cut my own ear and smeared bloody war-paint on my face like an Apache Indian before we charged.

Some rumors were embarrassing to the UN such as, "The doctor in Peja refused to operate on the KPS until Officer Mike pulled his gun and threatened to shoot him," or, "They would not let Officer Mike work for two days after Junik because he was going to shoot the UN officers that ran away."

Another rumor was personally embarrassing. It went, "Officer Granger cannot be harmed because he is a vampire."

That one was my own fault. One night on patrol with an older KPS officer, Johnny, and two young KPS, they asked me to stop driving so they could rest a while. It was late at night and very quiet, so I saw no harm. The older KPS officer really looked and acted like an old guy. When he patrolled with me before, he always carried himself and talked like a veteran cop. In his mind he *was* a veteran and he obviously had seen a lot of action in the war. Then he told me his age and it turned out that I was two years older than he was. I passed around my ID with the date of birth to the KPS and they were all surprised. They told me that I looked much younger than my age and asked how did I have the energy to patrol at night without getting tired?

I was bored so I raised a finger to my lips. "You must not tell the UN," I whispered, "but I am a vampire. I do not age. I do not sleep at night. My clan raised me to love people, not to eat them, so you have nothing to fear. That is why I came here. I am here to save Kosovo from evil."

The KPS looked at me and never said a word. I thought it was a funny skit, a joke, but after a half hour of complete silence, I asked them what was wrong. Trembling, the older guy asked, "Officer Mike, you are not really a vampire, are you?"

I then recalled that most of the KPS in my patrol vehicle were simple farmers. By culture, folklore and tradition they were a highly superstitious people. I remembered too late that the instructors had mentioned that during orientation training. I had once again overstepped my bounds. I apologized and assured them that it was a joke, that I was definitely human, and that my American sense of humor was different from theirs.

After the shift was completed, Johnny asked to speak with me alone. He said, "Officer Mike, many of the people here are raised in the small villages, and believe in many forms of magic and legends. To some of them, the vampire is very real. It was a mistake to say that to the KPS. I hope you do not think that all the people of Kosovo are backward."

I apologized profusely one more time and readily admitted that what I had done was stupid. After Junik, and my dumb blood-licking act at the Peja station, the vampire stories started up again. Some KPS laughed it off, some believed it completely, others just weren't sure what to think. Another lesson learned the hard way.

A week later, Willy came up to me at the end of a shift with a copy of a UN bulletin in his hand. He pulled me into the shift commander's office and showed it to me.

United Nations Special Operations Command is looking for UN officers to man Spec Ops units. Those selected will eventually be expected to assist in the efforts in Afghanistan. You must be an active duty UN Officer at the time of application.

The rest of the notice explained the requirements needed to pass the application process, and stated that selection testing would be in Pristina. Applicants could test for the positions regardless of current duty assignment.

Willy was the happiest I had seen him all week. "Mike," he said, "we get to go to Pristina in a UN vehicle and spend the day there after the test. I have been in patrol division since I arrived here nine months ago. I have only three months left to go here and need the change. I spend most of my nights at a desk now."

I looked at the test requirements. When I finished, I looked at him and said, "Willy, did you read all this? The first part is a two mile run in the shortest time I have ever seen. Then, we have to shoot while running and hit the targets every time. I have never done that! Look at this other stuff."

He just brushed me off, saying, "Not a problem, Michael."

Despite his continued enthusiasm, I wasn't at all convinced.

Nevertheless, for the next two days, Willy was relentless; he never let up on me. He wanted this badly, but we were a team and he didn't want us to break up. He eventually figured out that guilt was his best tactic, and said that I owed him—he had taken me under his wing and now I was loved by the KPS. He had listen to and laughed at all my stupid American jokes. He had live in a house with my stupid flag hanging from the balcony. If it wasn't for him, I would still be living in a concrete apartment block on a UN base. He said he was not going to go to Pristina and take the test unless I did it with him.

When guilt didn't work, he changed to a softer sell. "Michael, did you ever see those Special Operations teams? They go everywhere! They have the best equipment, and the use of all the vehicles off duty. I have seen them in Peja. You would be perfect for this job. Like you always say, it will be really cool."

I finally gave in. I just couldn't take it anymore. "Alright, I'll take the test and go with you, but you have to buy all our drinks in Pristina." Then I added, "Willy, you do know that I won't pass the test, right? We work out some, but I've not run more than a few steps since I got here. And don't forget I'm forty-six years old."

He grinned and gave a simple, confident German reply: "I will make you pass."

It was 0700 hours and I was standing in the pouring rain on a cold mountaintop five miles outside of Pristina, wearing a tee shirt and running shorts waiting with him for the "test." I was tired, freezing and wet. I was even more tired from having to get up in the middle of the night to drive all the way to that desolate spot near some forsaken KFOR military base (KFOR, for Kosovo Force, is the military designation for the NATO peacekeeping contingent in the province).

I was miserable; however, Willy was excited. He had tried to talk me up on the ride there, telling me about how great this would be. It was all fine for him. He had the longest legs I had ever seen. He was a stud and athlete, and was in great shape. He was also ten years younger than me.

We were met by a pair of muscle-bound Special Operations trainers and two other candidates. The trainers passed around binoculars and pointed out a small wooden shed at the bottom of the mountain. A narrow winding trail led there from where we were standing.

One of them said, "Run down there and then back up to here. The shed is roughly a mile away. That's it. That's all you have to do."

I looked at Willy with daggers in my eyes. The trail was wet and muddy, and it was easy to see that the shed was at least two miles distant. "Roughly one mile, my ass," I hissed.

The other trainer smiled, then gave us each a backpack filled with rocks, saying, "This is to make it more fun." Then he reached into his pocket and pulled out a stop watch. "Get going you idiots, I already started timing you."

Four soaked candidates bolted down the trail in the heavy rain. The downhill leg wasn't that bad, except for the poor footing and the sucking mud. Near the bottom, though, I was puffing. When we reached the shed, I told Willy I needed a minute to catch my breath. He looked at me with annoyance, but stopped and waited.

As the two other candidates approached, their feet suddenly entangled and they slid the rest of the way to the shed in the mud on their backsides. Before they could get up, Willy grabbed at my shirt and said, "Mike, we go."

As we started running back up, I knew it was impossible. I felt like despite all my efforts, I was barely moving.

About halfway up, I gave in and fell flat on my face. The two other candidates ran by us while Willy stood there, hands on hips, looking down at me with a combination of pity and exasperation. "Mike!" he yelled. "Stand up! Put one foot in front of the other. We pass together or we fail together."

I got up and restarted scrambling as fast as I could up the hill. From behind, he reached his right arm under my back pack and practically lifted me off the ground. "Run," he ordered, and I moved my feet as fast I could to keep up. Three quarters of the way up, he looked at his watch and declared, "We can still make it!"

We hit the finish line together, Willy ready to go again, and me looking like I had escaped from a prisoner-of-war camp. He slipped his hand from under my backpack and let me drop me in the mud, declaring to the instructors, "We both passed."

They didn't say a word.

We both passed the shooting part. It was hard, but I was a much better shot than I was a cross-country runner. Willy made bulls eyes on every shot. When all the phases of the test were completed, Willy and I were informed we had passed. The other two guys failed and were encouraged to try again another time.

The instructors congratulated us and said that we would receive orders in a week for Special Operations School. We were both wet, muddy and tired as we walked back to our UN Toyota. We toweled off and changed back into our BDU uniforms out in the open. No shower, nothing. I could barely talk, except to moan, "Willy, drive me back to Peja, now."

He did, and I slept like the dead whole way back.

Chapter 11

We finally received our orders to attend the Special Operations training course two weeks after the test. Tony looked surprised. While he said he respected our desire to attend the school, he had written a letter to UN Command asking them to deny our transfers. He explained, "I understand what you both want to do, but I want to let you know that I wish you to stop this. I would rather you stay with me. The KPS here would greatly miss you two men."

It was a reason, I suppose, but neither Willy nor I thought it was good enough. Two days later, UN Command sided with us and denied Tony's request. Special Operations School was back on. As I expected, the KPS were upset that Willy and I would be leaving patrol. We assured them that they no longer needed our direction—that they had become professional police officers through their own hard efforts.

After our announcement Bekim took me aside and said that he wanted me to meet his family. He asked if he could make arrangements for Jorgji to pick me up and drive me to the village where he grew up. I had become fond of Bekim so, of course, I accepted the invitation.

The next day Jorgji picked me up at sunrise for the four hour ride to Rogova Valley where Bekim's village was located. While he drove, he told me that there was a nice reception planned for me. First, though, we had to stop at a market and purchase two packs of cigarettes. He would not tell me why.

After about half-an-hour, we left the last Italian Army checkpoint on the one road in and out of the northern Albanian Alps. Rogova Valley plows into the Alps in an area that borders both Albania and Montenegro. It is stunning in its beauty.

After an hour on the road west, we passed by some Turkish ruins, marking the limits of the old Ottoman Empire. After another hour of driving, we passed Rogova village and the summer KPS sub-station. It had become a scenic drive and Jorgji passed the time talking with me about Kosovo, the KPS, the UCK, and the war years. When it was my turn, I asked a lot of questions about the war with the Serbs, mostly to understand what it was like to live under an occupation force.

Another hour of driving and we left the last area patrolled by anyone wearing a uniform. NATO did not go there. Neither did the UN, Montenegro, or Albania. The Rogova Road quickly deteriorated and headed uphill into stark mountainous terrain.

One last hour of driving and we peaked a ridge. Below us in a mountain glen right out of a Swiss Miss commercial was the neat little village. We followed a dirt road downward and entered a walled pasture and village of about fifteen houses and three or four vehicles. As we approached, forty men, women, and children ran toward our vehicle, lined up alongside the road, and waved us in.

I looked at my watch. Everything was right on schedule. It was a little before 1000 hours. If we stayed two hours, I could still drive back and make roll call for the night shift. I was already dressed in my uniform and had brought all my gear with me.

We came to a stop in front of the main house.

I didn't know what to expect. Reading my mind, Jorgji said, "Don't worry, Officer Mike. I will stay with you and guide you through the reception at the home of the village headman."

I stepped out of the vehicle and was swarmed by the crowd that had followed our car. Like munchkins guiding Dorothy down the yellow brick road. the children, blond and cute, grabbed my hands and pushed me toward the front door of the headman's home. Everyone was dressed in traditional clothing: the men in robes and white tribal headgear, the girls and women in long colorful dresses.

Inside, I was guided into a huge rectangular room where twenty men sat, leaning against the walls, on large pillows. I was ushered to a place against the far wall. Opposite me was the only chair in the room. It was empty; there was a pillow on the floor beside it. Jorgji sat on my right. There were no women in the room, but I could hear them, talking in side rooms. The open windows were filled with the faces of kids and old men who were apparently not allowed inside.

The headman, Jorgji told me, was Bekim's grandfather. After a minute, an old man, using a cane, came into the room, walked slowly with Bekim, and sat in the chair. Everyone stood when he appeared, so I followed suit. Bekim sat down on the pillow on the old man's right. I started to say hello, but Jorgji stopped me with a wave of his hand. We all sat down after the old man was seated. A pretty young woman came into the room and placed a cup of tea in front of each guest, then, giggling, exited quickly.

Everyone took a sip of tea and then each man in the room took something from his pocket and threw it into a pile in the center of the room. They were mostly small items like a candy bar, a pipe, or some trinket. When they finished, I felt all eyes turn to me. Jorgji softly said, "We throw the cigarette packs in now." We each tossed one and all the men in the room clapped and laughed.

A middle-aged man stood up and said in perfect English, "We will now introduce our honored guests."

Bekim's grandfather started to talk in Albanian. Jorgji softly interpreted for me: "We are honored to have an American representative of President Bush as a guest in our mountains. His name is Granger, and he is a friend of the freedom fighters of Kosovo, and of our KPS comrades. He has fought beside our brothers Bekim and Jorgji, and is a friend of all Muslim believers..."

He went on and on for over ten minutes. When he finally stopped it was my turn. Jorgji told me to stay seated, he would stand and translate. He told me, "Sir, you have to make the same type of speech."

Of course, I was caught off guard, but I understood the importance of participating, so I cleared my throat and began. "My friends. On behalf of my comrades in the United Nations and the United States of America, I thank you for welcoming me into your village. I have been honored to serve with your sons Bekim and Jorgji and the KPS. They are brave men who will help bring peace to Kosovo."

I noticed a few smiles and some positive nods, so I laid it on thick for another five more minutes. I guess it worked, because everyone cheered and clapped when it ended. Jorgji and Bekim looked at me and tried not to smirk.

I figured that the official welcome had ended, but the old man started again, only this time with questions. Is President Bush as good a friend to Kosovo as President Clinton? Will the United States abandon Kosovo and allow the Serbs back in? Will Kosovo ever become an independent country?

I answered as best I could and hoped that what I said would prove helpful in the years to come. I told him I did not personally know President Bush, but I did work for General Colin Powell. I said that Powell was a good and decent man, a warrior of experience and integrity. After listening to the translation, the old man told me that Bekim's family was killed in the war. I then told them about my father coming to Europe to fight in World War Two, and about my sons who now served in the United States military. During this time, the old man and I were the only ones allowed to speak.

Then, he dropped the bombshell.

"As tribal leaders, we, in this room, must decide if Commander Bekim should disband his guerilla UCK fighters that operate in Kosovo. If the United States will not abandon Kosovo, it is time for us to bring our sons down from the mountains and back into our homes."

Well kiss my ass! Bekim was the mysterious mountain guerilla leader whom I had heard so much about. I stared at Bekim for I don't know how long. He and I had spoken many times about the war, and the need for reconciliation and peace. He hated the criminal offshoot of the KLA, and he hated the Mujahedeen, who had allied with them. But I knew he hated the Serbs even more.

I gathered my wits and put together my response. "It is time for peace," I answered. "Your country has seen enough war and fighting. You are honorable men or you would not have confided this to me. My commander, General Colin Powell, is also an honorable man and will not allow the Serbs to make war against you. Your young men can best serve their country in the KPS or the new Kosovo Defense Forces."

There were many glances, long looks, and hushed murmurings amongst the tribal leaders. The headman seemed to be processing what I had said. I thought, *I'm just a freaking cop! Who do they think I am?* This whole thing was turning out to be way above my pay grade.

It was a long ride home with both "Commander" Bekim and Jorgji, and I had many questions for which I demanded answers. Most of their responses were cryptic, though. They dropped me off at the Peja Station just in time to make roll call. Before I got out of the car, Bekim called me his brother, and suggested that we may need each other soon.

113

I told no one at the station about the strange trip, not even Willy. Maybe I was becoming paranoid, but I could not get it out of my head that I may have just created some sort of international incident.

It was definitely time for me to go on R&R, but first, I wanted to find my State Department friend, Leo Pauli, to get his take on what the hell was going on. The next day, I went to the Peja American Support Compound to call Leo's number in Washington. I got a recording, so I left a callback message. He called back a minute later, saying that he was at Camp Bondsteel, the U.S. military base located in southern Kosovo.

"Hi, Mike," he said. "I told you I would be here often. How about we meet tomorrow at five? That's an hour into your shift, so you can check out a car and drive to the American Compound here. Leave your KPS in the car. See you tomorrow."

It was hard not to talk to anyone about my experience the whole next day. Willy knew I was on pins and needles, but he probably figured it was just excitement about my R&R trip to Switzerland scheduled to begin in two days.

An hour into my shift, I drove to the American Compound, leaving the KPS and Johnny in the Toyota as Leo had instructed, and practically ran from the car into the villa. I found Leo in the front room, wearing jeans and a tee shirt, sipping a beer, relaxing like he owned the place. He was square-jawed and solidly-built; sporting an army airborne tattoo and short military haircut—he was still tough looking even at forty-seven years of age. I was on duty and had to get back to my team, so we didn't have a lot of time to talk.

I wanted to tell Leo what had happened yesterday, but I was a little worried. I liked Bekim and Jorgji. I didn't want to rat them out, so Leo seemed the right guy to talk with since he was not involved with the UN police, at least at our level. I needed someone I trusted to hear everything. Someone with some State Department clout if it turned out that I needed help. Leo was that guy. He had the right connections.

He smiled when he saw me and said, "For crying out loud, sit down, Mike, and relax for a minute. You look like you need a drink."

"Leo, some strange shit has been happening lately."

"I know, Mike. I've been keeping tabs. Nice jobs at Nashi, Operation White Mountains and Junik. I'm impressed, really."

I sat down, wondering what he had heard.

"This place is like an alternate universe," I said. "Every time I screw up, it turns into a bigger success."

He laughed. "You only have to worry when the screw-ups stay screw-ups. Same as in college, right? Things don't change; they just get murkier." He then leaned forward, looked me dead in the eye and said, "So, Mike, do you think Bekim will work with us?"

I just stared at him like a dummy, a million thoughts racing through my head at once. It finally dawned on me that Leo and Bekim had both been playing me. They had been using me in some quaint Kosovo version of the great spy game. All the time I had no clue. I wasn't really mad. Both of them were like family to me, but this thing was out of my league and I knew it. Why didn't they know it?

"Uh, yeah. I think so," was all I could muster.

"Well, Mike, can you introduce us?"

"Yeah, sure. I think so. Why not?"

The next day, I arranged for the two of them to meet in a Peja café. I have no idea what transpired between them. I tried to forget the whole thing and concentrate on my trip to Switzerland.

I had booked a flight to Zurich, and the best hotel room in the best hotel in the city. I planned, or at least hoped, for three days and two nights of uninterrupted drunken debauchery, hopefully with a female. All I had needed was the female.

I contacted my old girlfriend, Erin, by email and tried my best to talk her into joining me there. I volunteered to pay for everything, and told her was a great time to see Europe. Nobody was traveling. She told me in no uncertain terms to forget it, reminding me that I had left her to go to Kosovo, remember? And how could I ask her to risk her life in terrorist-filled Europe only a few weeks after 9/11? I knew then our relationship was over. *C'est la vie!*

I had chosen Zurich for several reasons. On my flight from the U.S., I had flown over Switzerland and marveled at its postcard perfect landscape in the summer from above. As we descended into Zurich International Airport for a plane change, I noticed it was about five miles outside the city. Zurich was a mix of old and new architecture, bisected by a wide river that flowed into a gorgeous lake at the southern edge of the city. It was a big lake, with ferries and sailboats cruising lazily along. Fifteen miles further south the Swiss Alps, jutted sharply into the sky. During the layover, I deplaned and located a rack of tourist brochures. Zurich had everything I liked: exciting nightlife, good food, a large international population, and a low crime rate.

While waiting for the announcement of my flight to Kosovo, I went to one of the many bank branches in the airport and opened an account with the small amount of cash that I had on me. So, now, I had a real Swiss bank account, and too much cash on me in Kosovo. The UN paid us well, and I spent freely, but the money still piled up. I wanted to dump some of it into my Swiss account before a house fire, needy bad guy, or some other calamity in Kosovo took care of the cash surplus problem for me.

Willy drove me early as far as Pristina. He needed to make it back to Peja for his shift. Commander Tony loaned us his UN Toyota. It was the best one in the fleet. I had packed light—a gym bag with a few changes of clothes, a jacket, shoes, and a ton of freaking money. I planned to spend as much of it as I could in three days.

My initial goal was to get away from Kosovo. Then, Willy spoke, and I suddenly had a second goal: "Michael, here is a thousand Euros, please find and buy this watch for me. It is what I would like you to do." He handed me a computer printout showing some super duper Swiss watch that supposedly cost five thousand euros in Germany.

"Great, now I have to go shopping," I muttered. He asked me what I said and I replied, "I said I love to go shopping."

He grinned. "Good, that's what I thought you said."

After successfully passing through the numerous Russian and KFOR checkpoints on the way to the airport, I walked across the tarmac to the stairs of this beautiful Swiss Air jet. At the bottom of the ramp, a Swiss Air flight officer and flight attendant re-checked everyone's boarding pass. When it was my turn, the flight officer pulled me aside out of line, and with a serious expression, asked, "Sir, are you military or police?"

I figured my green gym bag with USMC stenciled on the side had given me away, and thought, *Shit, now what? Doesn't this guy know I'm going on vacation?* I said, "Yes, Captain. I'm a UN Police officer," figuring that, even though I could see the flight captain readying the plane in the open cockpit window, by promoting him I might gain his favor.

He replied, "Sir, we have no air security on this flight. Would you be willing to sit in first class close to the cockpit door?"

In my best official voice, I said, "I have no problem with that request, sir."

My compensatory time off, or CTO, was starting out on a good note. I had booked coach because the flight was short, just two hours, and I was planning on sleeping Now, I would have the best seat in the house with free drinks.

The flight officer and I returned to the bottom of the ramp and he told the flight attendant, "Please take this police officer aboard the aircraft and show him to his seat."

The flight attendant was slender, blond, and stunningly beautiful. She took my arm and escorted me to my seat in the first class section, and then went about her duties. I settled in and closed my eyes.

I opened them as the jet jerked and began to take off down the runway. Sitting in front of me, on a small jump seat pulled down from the cabin wall, was the flight attendant who had seated me. She was looking at me and smiling. "You are awake," she said. "You must be tired."

Her name was Greta, and during the next two hours, as her duties only involved the few of us in first class, we had plenty of time for small talk. Small talk is probably not the best choice of word, because, really, we were flirting with each other the whole time.

I told her that no, I was not going back to the United States, but to Zurich. Yes, I originally planned to meet a woman there, but she blew me off, and, yes, I was single and no, I had never visited the city. She told me she lived just outside Zurich and would love to show me the city if I wished.

If I wished? She was gorgeous, a wonderful conversationalist and a stewardess! Of course I wished! As I was deplaning, she slipped me her number and I promised to call her later for dinner. At least on my first night there, I would not be eating dinner alone. Maybe I would even take her dancing. Things were looking up.

When I reached the main terminal and shopping plaza, I went to my bank and made a hefty deposit. Then I located a high-end clothing store. Zurich is a classy place, and, like in New York City, people dressed up. I had packed light, but had money. If I was going to have fun, I would have to dress for it. The shop offered hand-tailored suits, shirts, and ties. I went on a spree.

My CTO plan was coming together nicely. Twenty minutes after entering the store, I had purchased a dark European-cut suit and slim white button-down shirt. It cost some bucks, but this was my James Bond outfit while I was in Zurich—Dockers wouldn't cut it here. No tie, though. I was going for the classy relaxed look. I left an extra big tip for the shopkeeper to deliver my purchase, fully tailored, to the hotel before sunset, shirt and pants pressed. I bought a pair of black Bally dress shoes and slipped them in my USMC bag. I was done shopping and it was only noon.

I hailed a taxi outside and gave the driver the flyer that Willy had given me. He nodded and off we went.

The driver found the watch store quickly, but, of course, they did not have the watch that Willy wanted. They had every other type of watch made. According to the pushy salesman, they even had one that he guaranteed would work in space even if hit by a meteorite. Wouldn't I prefer this one? But the gist of it was they didn't have Willy's watch. I tried four more shops, but without luck, and decided to screw it. It was time to ditch Willy's plan and implement my own. I had planned to be in a tub of hot water, drinking a cold beer, and eating a thick Swiss steak by then.

I had to wait until three o'clock when I arrived at the hotel. The Marriott was top notch, and my room was huge, with separate bedroom. As I planned, I settled into my warm bath, but instantly fell asleep.

I woke at six, feeling relaxed and rejuvinated. The hotel bell-hop brought my shop-delivered suit to my room, and helped me call Greta. She sounded excited when she answered, and said she would meet me in the hotel lounge at eight o'clock. I made dinner reservations, again with the help of the bellboy. The Marriott had a five-star rooftop restaurant overlooking the city. I sure wasn't in Kosovo anymore.

I met her in the lounge and thanked God that I had bought the suit. Greta looked stunning in her short black cocktail dress, a black shawl draped over her bare shoulders to keep the cool night air, and for the moment, me, at bay. She was cute enough in her flight attendant uniform, but dressed up, with her blonde hair down and a diamond necklace around her neck, she looked like a movie star.

Dinner was perfect: fillet mignon, French champagne, and conversation filled with delightful stories. Through the rooftop window, Zurich looked in on us, beautiful and romantic. After dinner, we walked to the old town section of this thousand-year-old city, and strolled the sidewalk banks of the Limmat River arm-in-arm. A couple of blocks later, in the direction of Lake Zurich, we came to the cobblestoned neighborhood of nightclubs, small cafes, and shops called Niederdorf. The old town. No automobile traffic was allowed, and the streets were filled with people and music.

Sometime around three in the morning, Greta said, "Michael, take me home."

I asked her where she lived, and she laughed. "You are a silly policeman. I meant *your* home."

We woke up around noon the next day and I ordered room service: a triple order of sausage and bacon, four glasses of milk and two glasses of orange juice. Greta had a bagel and coffee. I picked at my food so as not appear a slob, but the second she left to go home and change, I inhaled the entire breakfast.

Greta returned at three in the afternoon, and we went sightseeing across the river at the Swiss National Museum. Then, we took another walk down to Lake Zurich. She lectured me about the history of the city and of Switzerland. Not only was she beautiful, but she was well educated.

She spoke English, French, German, and Italian. She modestly explained that Switzerland borders so many countries that everyone speaks many languages. I modestly explained to her that I was a lingual idiot, and that I felt that everyone I had met since the beginning of my mission was smarter than me. She laughed and said that is because America is so American. Why should an American spend time learning all the other languages of the world when everyone in the USA speaks English? She was right, of course. Americans aren't stupid, just lucky.

We partied again that evening in Niederdorf and spent the night together. Our lovemaking the second night was more relaxed, like a couple of college kids. She asked me to keep on my dog tags while having sex. I said I would if she showed me in pantomime how to put on an airplane life jacket, like flight attendants do pre-flight. In truth, she was the only one close to college-age. I was the older man—way older.

In the morning, she left to continue her life, while I finished packing. I still had one more errand to do before leaving. I bought a large suitcase-sized duffle bag in the lobby of the hotel, and walked down the street to a pharmacy Greta and I had walked past the night before.

I went in with the empty giant duffle bag and walked out ten minutes later with it bursting at the seams with every kind of medical supply I could stuff into the damn thing. Then, I caught a taxi to the airport and flew back to Kosovo.

Blessed are the Peacekeepers

Chapter 12

I arrived back at Pristina Airport around noon, and had to fight my way through a crowded terminal and parking lot, both of which were teeming with civilians. UN soldiers and police were containing those inside the terminal, while those outside were being kept in line by armed Russian paratroopers. Only official vehicles were allowed anywhere near the airport for security reasons and all the civilian vehicles were directed to a large grass field four hundred yards from the small airport complex.

I had no doubt that Willy would be there in the official parking lot, on time, with a full tank of gas, and in a borrowed UN Toyota to drive me back to Peja. His German upbringing precluded any thing else. Back in the States there was always the lingering anxiety of a possible missed connection or a traffic-delayed pickup. In Kosovo, even in the middle of a war zone, I had no such worry with Willy as my driver. He would have rammed a Russian tank to get there on time.

I spotted him standing next to his red and white UN police Toyota in a line of military trucks and Humvees. We greeted each other with smiles and a quick handshake, then piled into the car and took off. While driving, Willy told me he had stopped on the way at the UN Post Exchange—PX—and bought supplies for the house. A couple minutes into the ride, Willy asked, "Do you have my watch?"

I returned his money and the computer printout, and explained in detail about my failed attempt to find one. He didn't say anything for the next five miles.

"Are you going to talk to me or what?" I finally asked.

After another minute of cold-shoulder treatment, he replied, "Mike, you tell so many tall tales all the time, I don't know whether to believe you or not. I see you brought back a large bag full of shopping for yourself."

I didn't want to talk about the medical supplies and why I'd brought them, so I stuck with the watch. "Hey, if you don't believe me check the back of your printout. I wrote notes with the addresses of all the stores I went to. It's all there."

While he was quietly processing my reply, I told him that I had a good time, and had been shown the city by an attractive blonde Swiss girl.

He didn't take the bait.

"Willy," I finally said. "You're being immature about the freaking watch."

His hands gripped the wheel so tightly that his knuckles turned white. "*I'm* immature?" Then, he unloaded. "Michael, I have had to put up with your American shit for so many months that I that don't know where to start. I suppose that the blonde girl was cute and young, too! Blond this, blonde that. Do you realize that you will not even talk about a woman unless she is blonde? And you know why? It is because *you* are the immature one. I bet you a million marks that your first wife had black hair, and you are too weak and stupid to get over it. Yeah, the girl in Switzerland was probably young, too, because you cannot handle a real relationship. It's always some young woman who doesn't want a real relationship."

Okay, he nailed me. My ex-wife did have raven black hair.

Willy was far from done, though, and followed the slap with a hard uppercut.

"Even your sense of humor is immature. Do you think I did not hear about the vampire story? What were you thinking? You tell tall tales because you think they are funny, but many of them are hurtful—and stupid. You got a 'Dear John' letter from a woman you cared about, and you did not even fight to keep her. Instead, you chase after young blonde girls—and you call *me* immature?"

That one hurt, but he wasn't finished with me yet. It was time for the knockout punch.

"I have been pulling you along since you got here, but it is time that you carry yourself. We'll see how much of a man you are in Special Ops training. From now on, Mike, you are on your own."

Of course, he was right about everything. He knew me like a brother, and like a brother, he overlooked my many quirks until the time came when it was necessary to confront me. He had conducted himself professionally and with spotless integrity at all times. I had nothing to throw back. The only weak counter-punch I had, I gave: "Fuck you."

"Well, fuck you too!"

We drove the remaining three more hours to Peja in total silence. The tall, reserved German, who I looked up to as a mentor had finally lost his cool and we'd had our first blow out. Maybe it was time. We'd been living and working together in close quarters, and had been through so many stressful times, that we were finally getting on each other's nerves. At least, that's what I told myself.

The next morning we got up and went through the normal morning routine. We spoke a bit but with none of the usual relaxed banter, just business topics in a cool, formal manner. We had a scheduled meeting with the Special Operations Commander from Peja Regional Headquarters at eight o'clock. There was a frost in the air and it had less to do with the approaching winter in Kosovo than with our fractured relationship. We walked together to the Commander's office, again, in dark silence. We were both still wounded and had our egos to protect.

In the past, I could fight with a guy and make up easily afterwards over a beer. That's what American men from New England do—identify the problem, deal with it, and move on. Germans, however, have an extra layer of stubbornness and vanity that gets in the way of easy reconciliation. I had never dealt with it before, and it worried me that I might not be able fix this problem with Willy.

We met the new commander and, of course, he was German. Like most officers in Kosovo Special Operations, he had never served in the patrol division. The majority of the Spec-Op guys had gone directly into the unit from the UN prep school in Pristina. It turned out to be unfortunate for relations with the local KPS. It was like if cops in America became detectives right out of the academy without serving a day in a patrol car. It didn't work well.

Two other UN officers were at the meeting: Another German and the American who had led the security detail for the judge at the site of the honor killing. We all shook hands and sat down. The Unit Commander welcomed us and told us, "If and when you complete Spec-Ops training, you will return to Peja and join one of two teams under my command. Your training starts tomorrow at the facility specified in your orders."

His manner of delivery was strict and autocratic. I watched Willy out of the corner of my eye for direction, to see if we were expected to jump up, click our heels and salute. He sat there like a concrete wall, as if I weren't even there. Our new boss then explained that Alpha Team was led by Commander Ernst, and Bravo Team by Commander Durfer. He explained that UN Special Operations was divided into several sections, though they numbered very few UN officers. There was CPU, the Close Protection Units, which were special operations teams based only in Pristina. There was the RPU, the Regional Protection Unit. One RPU unit was stationed in each of the five NATO sectors of Kosovo. There was also the strangely named Team Mike, a very small unit of specialized commandoes tasked with the most dangerous missions for the United Nations.

I didn't care for the RPU Commander from the start. He was stiff, pompous, and seemed to have an administrative pencil stuck up his ass. Willy and I just sat there and listened to him without saying a word. I wondered if Willy had the same thoughts as I did. But, then again, he was German, too. Maybe he was eating it all up.

"The two of you will be given one of our UN vehicles for your training," the commander continued. "It will be returned here in the same condition in which you have received it. Understood?"

Willy and I stood and responded in unison with a sharp, "Yes, sir!" minus a heel-click or salute, and left the room. We had been instructed to use the rest of the day to pick up our vehicle and get our affairs in order.

Team Leaders Durfer and Ernst walked us out to our assigned Toyota. They were both pretty good guys and put us a little more at ease. Durfer said with the slightest smile, "Gentlemen, we badly need more manpower in operations, so please try to pass. Get plenty of rest today and start early for the base tomorrow. It's a long drive. Good luck, guys. We'll see you when you get back." Then, they were gone.

We filled out the paperwork and picked up our vehicle. It was clean, sleek, white, and had large serious black UN letters on the side. It had none of the laughable red and white "fire chief car" look our previous car had.

Willy slipped into the driver's seat; I climbed into the passenger's and shut my mouth. I think he probably figured if I had the opportunity, I'd take the vehicle for myself for the rest of the day, so he wanted to keep tight control of it. Without acknowledging me, he turned the key in the ignition. The engine purred like a kitten. Then, he gave it some gas, and it roared like a lion.

"Whoa!" I yelled.

Willy looked over at me and grinned just before he pealed out of the parking lot.

Our old patrol SUVs had been driven twenty-four hours a day. Each team would park it at the end of the shift, and the next team would get in and drive off. Those vehicles took a real beating. The Spec-Ops SUV, however, had a modified engine, re-enforced frame, and thick hardened doors.

"What shall we do now, Mike?" Willy asked politely.

I answered, "I want to go back home and get that duffle bag I brought back from Switzerland. I have one quick errand, and you can have the SUV for the rest of the day. Okay?" I wanted to stay out of Willy's hair and let him continue to cool off. As for me, I wanted to run my errand, then relax for the rest of the day. To be honest, I had a lot of trepidation about the next few weeks.

We went back home, got the bag, and drove to Peja Hospital. At the hospital, I told him to park the car and come inside with me. I think at this point he suspected that my duffle bag was filled with cigarettes, Swiss watches, and silk stockings for the blonde nurses inside. He didn't say it aloud, but the surly look on his face made me suspect as much.

I found Dr. Meski in a small office. He had a look of pleasant shock on his face when he saw me enter. I smiled and held out my hand. "Hi, Doc," I said. "I don't know if you remember me."

"Of course I do, Officer Granger. You are not so forgettable."

I wasn't quite sure if that was a compliment or not, but I could see that Willy was intrigued by our informal interaction. "This is my partner, UN Officer Steinhardt," I said, sweeping my hand in Willy's direction.

Willy leaned forward, shook the doctor's hand, then stepped back out of the way.

"Maybe you can help me," I said to the doctor.

"I'll do what I can," he replied with a look of concern.

"You see, I've got this problem." I placed the overstuffed duffel bag on his desk. "I'm trying to clean up my house, and I have no room for these things anymore. I was wondering if you could take them off my hands."

Dr. Meski adjusted his glasses and unzipped the bag. I watched his eyes nearly pop out of his head. He pulled out bandages, medicines, antibiotics, sterilized surgical tools and other medical paraphernalia—all in original packaging.

He removed his glasses and wiped the tears from the corner of his eyes. "You didn't..."

"What? Steal it from the KFOR base? No. I bought all of it in Switzerland. Honest. The receipts are in the bag. It's all yours.

"I don't know what to say."

"'Thanks' works fine where I come from."

He shook my hand again, holding onto it for a long time. "Many, many thanks," he said.

"Just one thing, Doc. Please tell your staff that you got these from an anonymous benefactor." I looked over at Willy and added, "I have my reputation to protect."

Willy and I returned in silence to the car. After we got in, he turned to me and said, "Mike, I didn't know what was in the bag. Sorry. That was...cool."

So you finally got it, I thought. But I wasn't going to let him get off that easy. "Willy, everything you said about me was one hundred percent. I needed to hear it." Then I grinned and continued, "And I promise to work on *some* of my faults in the days ahead. By the way, did you see that beautiful young nurse at the station?"

"Ya, ya—the *blonde* one. When I die and go to heaven, I'm going to ask God why he thought it such a smart thing to make Americans."

"He'll tell you it seemed like a good idea at the time."

That was that. Our fight was over, never to be brought up again. Like every bad argument between siblings or close friends, though, the scar from the words we had exchanged in anger left its mark. It had changed the dynamic of the relationship, if only slightly. Willy was right: It was time for me, the baby bird, to leave the nest. I had to prove to myself and Willy that I belonged there among the Special Operations studs. What started as a reluctance to go on this quest for the winged dagger badge of special operations became resolute determination to pass the training course. And it was no simple desire to pass. I would pass, or I would die trying. It was that simple.

The next morning, after several hours driving, we were less than five miles away from the training base. It was only a little after seven. While Willy drove, I gazed out the side window, taking in the pretty countryside. Silhouetted against the sunrise, I spotted a small rural farm with a large haystack and small wooden hay wagon that I would have missed had I blinked. "Willy, stop!" I yelled.

"What the hell, Mike?" he yelled back, stepping hard on the brakes, the wheels squealing. He'd been in a sort of mental cruise control and I startled him.

"Go back to that farm we just passed. I need to take a picture."

Willy wasn't happy with altering our driving plan, but he gritted his teeth and did what I asked.

While in Kosovo, I always carried one of those small disposable cameras in a cargo pocket of my BDUs. Though taking pictures on military bases and on patrol were forbidden, there were always opportunities for tourist-type or group pictures. I would break the camera apart on the last picture, save the AA batteries for other important uses, and place the film cartridge in my pocket for safekeeping.

As we pulled into the farm, the owner came out and greeted us, offering us tea. I told him that we would be only a minute. With Willy beside me, I pulled out a photograph of my dad from World War Two. He was in uniform standing next to hay wagon somewhere in France. He had passed away the year before I left for Kosovo, and I kept the photo with me in his memory. I pointed to the farmer's haystack and wagon then showed the picture and camera to the farmer. That ended the old man's confusion and replaced it with relief. He smiled and nodded. This was a lot better than having to invite two strangers inside his house and serve them tea.

Willy rolled his eyes at my idea, but took the picture of me leaning against the wagon in the exact pose as my father. Mission completed, we thanked the farmer for his kindness and departed. Fifteen minutes later we passed a small UN helicopter airfield and we were at the front gate of the base.

The base was guarded by Jordanian Special Forces troops who checked our names on a roster and searched the undercarriage of our vehicle with a mirror. They looked serious. There was no simple wave and drive in as had been our experience at most checkpoints. Inside the base, we parked and formed up in the parking lot along with a dozen other UN officers. They were mostly well-built, stud-like Americans, Germans, Brits, and Scandinavians. One blatantly undersized officer stood out. It was our Filipino friend, Rick. He gave a shout and ran over to join Willy and me. He explained he'd heard that we had transferred and wanted to join us. He'd came from Pristina, where he had used CTO to visit friends before the training. We were happy to see each other. In spite of his small stature, Rick was special operations material if there was such a thing.

The lead instructor appeared and gruffly ordered us to form up and march to one of several Quonset huts on the base. As we entered the main classroom in the smallest of the hanger-like buildings, I looked above the entry door. There was a small sign that said, "Through these doors walk the bravest men in Kosovo."

That clinched it; I knew I was in the wrong place.

Inside, waiting, were the lead instructor and his six assistants. The Lead explained that the goal of the training was not to weed out the candidates, but to train us up to the qualifications needed to become a Spec-Ops "operator." I hoped that he was telling the truth. He outlined our rigorous training program for the weeks ahead, then dismissed us for lunch.

On the base there were two buildings that were not simple Quonset huts. One was a wood-log cafeteria that looked like it had been taken right out of a ski lodge pamphlet. The other was a sandbagged concerti-wired enclosure containing several square cement block buildings. Our guide explained that this last area and building were strictly forbidden, and housed Team Mike. He explained, "Like wild bulldogs, that is their area. You don't want to screw with those guys."

We entered the cafeteria and found ourselves in grub heaven. Before us was an all-you-can-eat buffet of "real" food: Milk, hamburgers, steak, milk, French fries, milk, spaghetti, bacon and eggs, milk—the place had everything. And did I mention it had cold fresh milk? I had not even seen any in Kosovo. If nothing else, we would eat well.

With our loaded trays in hand, we walked over to an empty table on an outside deck. After we were seated for a few seconds, we were approached by a team of four operators, who from the rumpled appearance of their BDUs had just came in from the field. One mean-looking bastard growled, "Move monkeys, this is *our* table." They had that grim surly look that said we would soon be dead or crippled if we didn't obey. They weren't all that much bigger than us, but they looked and acted dangerous. If they weren't from the sandbagged cement buildings, they sure acted like it.There are times when two male groups face off in the street just sizing each other up. Then comes a decision: "Is this worth the fight?"

Nope, it wasn't. Willy, Rick, and I all moved. Even if we had stood our ground and didn't get the crap kicked out of us, who do you think would be punished for the brawl? Not those guys. The UN had already invested a ton of time, money, and training in them. We, on the other hand, would be sent back to patrol with letters of reprimand and nobody here would miss us.

Ignoring the cafeteria bullies, we gorged ourselves, then returned to our classroom for the second block of instruction. The Lead informed us that UN Spec-Op teams were currently deploying to Afghanistan to guard food supplies and vehicles in support of Operation Enduring Freedom. Kosovo teams therefore needed replacement operators. "If you stay with the training and follow the instructors," he said, "all of you should pass. Your records were carefully reviewed by our instructors before letting you come here. You have all shown an ability to take risks and use deadly force when necessary. Find your quarters and review your training materials. Formation is at 0700 tomorrow. Dismissed!"

Willy, Rick, and I did exactly as told. At seven o'clock the next morning we were in formation with the twelve other candidates, all of us wearing BDUs, but with running shoes instead of combat boots. It was a cold late-fall morning. All seven instructors came out of Quonset Hut One and the Lead Instructor hollered, "Morning run!"

Off we went. During the morning runs, we went out into the woods and scampered up and down small mountains. Then, we performed countless sit-ups and pushups, sometimes under the boots of our instructors. After morning warm up, the classes began. It's how we started each day, and it was brutal. At the end of each morning warm up, I felt barely alive. One lesson I learned fast was not to eat a big meal in the morning.

Classes covered basic bodyguard positions and drills. We studied combat first aid, land navigation, hand-to-hand combat, and special mission planning. At noon, we had a quick lunch break where I always stuffed myself to regain as much energy as possible. Then we'd pile into our souped-up Toyotas for a trip to the shooting grounds.

The shooting exercises were the most dangerous thing I had ever experienced. Any sane firing range officer in the States would have had a heart attack watching us. We shot on the move getting in and out of vehicles, carrying a wounded comrade—even from inside passenger seats through the windshields of junk cars.

The instructors were demanding, but they gave us incredible lessons in controlled shooting. We were already pretty good but they made us experts. We fired semi-automatic handguns, H&K MP5 submachine guns, M4s, AK-47s and AK-74s. We shot moving forward in attack positions and moving to the rear in quick withdrawing movements. We learned to fire safely while operators in front of us withdrew to new positions. It was insane and I loved it.

We also learned to drive different kinds of vehicles, maneuvering in and out of various ambush scenarios. I was even given a UN armored car license to drive the large South African-made anti-mine vehicles.

Though all the instructors were incredibly proficient, three stood out. Robert, a tall, middle-aged American with silver hair, who resembled Clint Eastwood, was the chief hand-to-hand combat instructor. A Norwegian trainee told us one day at lunch that he volunteered for Spec-Ops specifically to learn from this American whom he had read about in a host of martial arts magazine articles.

Robert was indeed a world famous martial arts instructor. He had served on many previous UN missions, after spending nearly a decade in the U.S. Navy SEALs. He was retired from a police department in the mid-west and owned a string of dojos across the country. He taught us to be quick, deadly, and efficient. There was no time wasted on sport techniques. He had been trained for years to kill terrorists, Spetsnaz, even crazed North Koreans. He was the real deal. His fighting tactics were direct, nasty and effective.

The second instructor of note was also an American, a shooting expert. He was young, wore glasses and was very quiet. He could do almost anything with any weapon. He taught us to shoot in any position, to cut time off our re-loading procedures, and to always hit our targets in the head. With balloons taped to the top of target posts, we perfected our "head shots," even if when the head was flapping in the wind. He was a perfectionist and made us close to perfect with weapons.

The third one that stood out was the British lead instructor, a man who carefully built us up from good basic material into a great end product. As he said, he wasn't there to break us, or force a percentage of the trainees to give up and ask to DOR, drop on request. Instead, he repaired our bruised bodies, emphasized safety at all times, and kept us hopeful that we would pass the course.

Our instructors were the best commandoes the UN could find. They hailed from several different countries and some came from military and police units that were world famous. There was no bullshit in that training. The instructors tolerated no horseplay. They wanted us to meet their high standards and to finish. They wanted us to live up to the reputation and effectiveness of the units, teams, and special air regiments where they had learned their own deadly skills.

Willy, Rick, and I changed both physically and mentally during our training. We showed up the first day weary and underfed, trained only in the basics, and lacking confidence. Soon, because of the extreme physical training, I began to add on pounds, replacing body fat with hard muscle trained to react instantly to any threat or situation.

Our last days of training were devoted to field exercises where we had to combine and apply all the skills we had learned. We ended our final field exercise with a hike into the mountains, carrying our complete combat "kit" with us. For two grueling days we trekked snow-covered peaks, demonstrating our knowledge and skill in land navigation, escape and evasion, and ambush scenarios—ending with my final traditional collapse over the finish line. This time, though, Willy did not have to lend a hand. I finished Special Operations training on my own.

The night before graduation, we gorged ourselves with food for the last time. Our plates were overflowing, including mounds of ice cream for dessert. It was late evening and getting cold outside, so we picked the only table left inside the building. A few minutes later a group of veteran operators came over to our table and stood over us, waiting for us to move. This time we didn't. They looked at us and we looked at them until Willy put down his fork and said, "Fuck off."

They grumbled, then turned and left.

The following morning, we received our formal certificates, a hardy handshake from each of the instructors, and orders to report back to Peja. I was now an "operator"—a certified UN commando. I had earned my winged dagger patch. Just before disbursing us, the lead instructor gave us a last bit of direction: "We expect you to live up to the high standards we've demonstrated and taught you," he said. "Always protect your VIP. Accomplish successfully each special mission you are assigned. Keep yourself and your men alive." He hesitated, smiled, then added, "And remember, you are now killing machines."

We left the building and the base pumped up with confidence in our new warrior skills and talents. Willy, Rick, and I had done it. We were now super-bad-ass Spec-Op operators, and we had new UN identification cards to prove it. We were also given red NATO ID cards that allowed us entry into restricted military areas. Even the Russians respected our red ID cards. We drove in serious silence, contemplating our next step in our journey.

There we were, our heads filled with our own importance, when Rick spoke up from the back seat. In the funniest Polynesian-Asian accent I had ever heard, he mimicked the lead instructor, declaring, "*You are all now killing machines. Go forth and kill!*" and burst out laughing. We all started laughing, releasing at last the weeks of pent up stress. For the next three hours, we passed the time telling jokes and laughing about the many things that had happened during training which we couldn't dared laugh at when the events actually occurred.

By the time we pulled into Peja, we together concluded that while we may not be true killing machines, we had pulled off something pretty cool—something that we could each be proud of for the rest of our life.

That night in my room, I thought about my accomplishment, but also of something else. The next day would be the two-year anniversary of my father's death. I had never missed him any more than I did at that moment. Before I fell asleep, I pulled out the old photograph and said out loud, "I wish you could see me now, dad."

Chapter 13

It was our first day working on the UN CIVPOL Regional Protection Unit in Peja, so Willy and I woke up early to be sure that we were alert, refreshed and on time when we reached headquarters. It was located in the west side of the city, much closer to our villa than the Peja Police station had been. We had no personal vehicle, so we walked there on foot. In our new physical condition, the walk proved quicker than we anticipated.

RPU headquarters was in a five story, modern, steel and glass building, surrounded by a large fence and wall. One of only two modern buildings in Peja, it was once a Yugoslavian bank. There was a large parking lot next to it filled with various white UN vehicles including exotic armored cars alongside the regular red and white UN Police Toyotas.

Regional HQ housed other units besides the RPU. It also contained the Regional Commanders' suite, a Special Investigations unit, the Russian Task Force office, and the office of the KPS Commander. Each of the five sections occupied a floor.

On the RPU floor, Willy and I were stopped at a checkpoint, where an officer verified our IDs before allowing us entry. I found the additional security comforting. It also made me feel a part of something special. The RPU floor contained the RPU Commander's Office, Alpha and Bravo Team rooms, the office of the United Nations judge, and an open bay area that contained her staff. There was the judge's male interpreter and five women. Not just women, but non-Kosovar, non-Muslim women in civilian clothes. Willy winked at me and smiled at them as we were hustled into the RPU Commander's office. I knew just what he was thinking.

Rick was already in the room with Alpha Team Leader Ernst, Bravo Team Leader Durfer, and our new boss, the snooty German I disliked. The RPU commander was all business again: "Welcome back to RPU," he said, "and thank you for not wrecking my Toyota." It sounded like a joke, but the man wasn't smiling. Some of the driving in Spec-Op school had, in fact, been quite dangerous, especially during anti-ambush drills, so I now understood his initial concern. "We have recently lost some men to injuries and rotation home," he continued. "The three of you are assigned to Bravo Team. I have moved men around in this RPU, so that Alpha Team, under Captain Ernst, is made up of all German officers. Bravo Team, under Captain Durfer, has the remaining fourteen UN officers—my international team."

He explained that each team would have numerous, sometimes overlapping responsibilities during our tour. Our primary duty would be the protection of the UN judge and the UN prosecutor located in Peja Region; however, at any time, a team might be called on for other duties. If that happened, then the one left behind would assume the functions of both teams. The RPU Commander explained that we could be called on to act as a regional SWAT unit, or as backup for another region. We could also expect riot duties, including the rescue of UN personnel.

He told us that teams had been deployed to Afghanistan to guard UN supply convoys, and there could well be quick deployments to other areas outside Kosovo for "classified assignments."

"The work is both boring and exciting," he said. "Even when

things appear routine, they may be quite dangerous. You have trained for this, so you will begin today."

The RPU Commander and Alpha Team leader stood, nodded at us, and left. Jim Durfer stayed with us in the commander's office. He wanted to give us a further briefing before we moved to Bravo Team's squad room.

"No formalities with me," he said. "Just call me Jim. Welcome aboard. I know you guys will fit in fine. We've been a little understaffed. With you here, Bravo Team now has thirteen men and one woman.

"We have three vehicles assigned to Bravo Team. One is the armored car in which the 'principal' rides. The principal is the VIP. The 'package' we are assigned to protect. We have a 'soft-skinned' Toyota SUV, with no armored protection to lead the convoy and clear the road ahead, as you know from training. The lead Toyota is followed by the armored car with the VIP. The third car in the convoy is a 'hard skinned,' slightly heavier armored SUV that acts as security—a 'gun car'. The job is mostly fun. I think you guys will like it here."

He explained that we worked all day, from early morning until the assignment was over, but there were not many overnight assignments. That was good news to me.

Since there were three vehicles on a mission, each containing four operators, it meant that twelve operators rode a mission, leaving the rest to stay behind at RHQ. Most days it would be two to four persons left behind, because the UN VIP took up one seat, and sometimes an interpreter took up another. The special operators left behind stood radio watch.

Radio watch meant one person manned the radio and telephones in the Bravo Team squad room leaving the others do whatever the hell they wanted, so long as they could be reached on short notice and return to RHQ. It was a sort of day off. After checking in at 0800, those not standing radio watch could do anything in Peja. With fourteen operators in Bravo team, that meant each person got a day off a week or more.

I smiled at the thought. I was already liking it here. Then, Durfer gave us some even better news: "At the end of the team's assignment for the day, the hard skin and soft skin are available to team members for off-duty transportation."

I did a quick count. There were three vehicles assigned to each team, six vehicles in total, and a seventh soft-skinned vehicle that belonged to the RPU German Commander. Discounting the two enormous South African made anti-mine armored cars, that meant five vehicles would be available for off-duty rides. Life just got even easier.

"Most of our escorts are simple in tactical terms, like transporting the UN judge or prosecutor to the day's assignments. But the special missions can be challenging. Let's go meet the team."

Hmmm, challenging. If I thought I was in heaven, then I just took one step back from the Pearly Gates. I liked challenging. But something in the back of my head was telling me that challenging in this case was a euphemism for something else—maybe dangerous as hell?

We went into Bravo Team's room and met the team members assembled there who were preparing for the first run of the day. They didn't appear impressed by us. Willy, Rick and I were clearly "new guys" in their minds, and would have to be tested before we were accepted. I knew that. I'd been a rookie many times in my career: for the feds, when working for them in college, in the police department, then again when I joined the detectives, and finally at Peja Station. No big deal. I was probably the world's most experienced rookie.

The principle rules of being a rookie are to keep your mouth shut, learn the job, and stay out of everyone's hair. It was simple in concept, but not always so easy in practice.

Jim Durfer gave a quick introduction and brief bios on the three of us. First was Willy the accomplished team leader of Tiger Team-Peja Station. Next was me, Willy's number two, not much else to say. Then, he introduced Rick, the new token minority to the primarily German-American-British-Scandinavian Spec-Op team. Introductions were swift and short on praise. It pretty much told us where we stood, at least for now.

Jim then introduced us to his number two, saying, "Meet Jack Kendrick, Royal Canadian Mounted Police. He's Bravo Two. You don't have to get to know him too well because this prick is going home to his bull moose and Canadian geese shit in a month."

Jack looked like a capable man, though he wasn't as big as some of the others in the room. He had that easy smile and strong handshake that I liked in a person."You'll learn about the others as we go along," Jim said.

I had seen this team in action at the honor killing crime scene. Two were big, perfect physical specimens. Both Germans and very dangerous looking. Officer Conrad "Hammer" Mauer was twenty-six years old, six-foot-two and built like a professional wrestler. The other was Officer Gebhard Nagle whom they all called, "Nails." Willy whispered to me, "Nagle means nail in German." Nails was not quite as tall as Hammer, but just as well-built. Peas in a pod, was my first impression. So the first team within the team was comprised of these two hulks.

Willy explained to me later that Germany, similar to the U.S.A., was divided culturally into the north and south. The southern Bavarian people came from agricultural stock. Hiking in the mountains and other outdoor type of living, was their common link. Of course, they had big cities, like Munich, but they were landlocked and there were probably those who had never hiked or seen a tree.

Northern Germany, especially Hamburg where Willy grew up, was heavily urban industrial. Many of largest cities bordered on water. Education was everything.

The southern Germans thought of the northerners as eggheads or fish heads, and themselves as honest meat eaters. I know this sounds kind of ridiculous, but so is the Mason-Dixon divide in the U.S. So, I just accepted it.

Willy, always blunt, said, "Mike, you should know that Hammer and Nails will think alike, move alike, and probably won't have a high opinion of you or Rick."

It was something to think about.

The third operator who stuck out was Inspector Sandra Wright. Sandy was a London Metropolitan Police detective. She was twenty-seven, about five-foot-eight, and probably about 140 pounds, though it was hard to gauge her weight in the full combat kit of a special operator. The standard operator kit consisted of the regular police outfit and gun belt get up, but also a medium weight bulletproof vest, and a "carry all" vest over that with a million extra pockets and zips packed with additional gear. It held bigger more efficient radios with earplugs, extra ammunition, weaponry, and all sorts of cool gear.

Sandy looked just as dangerous as Hammer and Nails, and she had attitude. Her face was attractive but she moved with a little too much swagger and masculinity for my taste. She gave us a slight— make that, *very* slight—smile, unlike Hammer and Nails who looked right through us and grunted.

Jim Durfer, Bravo One, showed us the work board. It outlined the next few days' assignments. It appeared that the current week was pretty much filled with escorting the UN judge back and forth from her protected villa to RHQ and the Peja Courthouse.

On the board was a list of the team members and their daily assignments within Bravo team, as well as a second weekly listing of each high-risk escort and everyone's pre-assigned positions. For escorts, there were always two operators assigned to bodyguard the VIP, three drivers who never left their vehicles, always keeping them running and accessible, and an escort commander, usually Bravo One or Bravo Two, Jim or Jack. The remainder of the team provided security for the convoy and bodyguard team. They were the shooters if things went bad.

We had all been trained for this work so there was nothing new for us to learn except what our specific assignments were for each day. When I examined the weekly assignment sheet, I noticed that Willy, Rick, and I would be rotating through the different escort positions during the week to gain experience.

It soon became clear that some team members favored certain positions. Hammer and Nails were almost always bodyguards. A Jordanian, "Mo" Mohammed Mayoff, who was a major in the Jordanian Special Forces, and Officer Darren Post, called "D-Train," an American from the Detroit Police Department, seemed to be in the driver seat on most runs.

My role the first day was to ride shotgun in Security Vehicle One, with D-Train as the driver. It should be a good day, I figured. No driving for me so I couldn't get lost leading the convoy, which, being a professional rookie was my greatest fear. All I'd have to do was get out at each stop and try to look bad-ass mean. Security, as we had been taught, was a "fun" position. You jumped out at each stop, scanned for threats, established perimeter security for the convoy and bodyguard team, then signaled to the Escort Commander the "all clear." As soon as Bravo One or Two got the "all clear" from the security team, he signaled the armored car and the bodyguard team exited the vehicle with their VIP. Security operators were the grunts. They would go in and out of a building, or wherever the principal was going, first, ready to deal with any threat.

The drivers were the technicians—they'd drive like hell, force people off the road and out of the way, and run over anything that presented a threat. The real positions of authority were the escort commander and the bodyguards. Both positions require a high degree of intelligence and savvy.

The escort commander's job was overall command. He called all the shots, but the bodyguards had to decide if a threat was present. The bodyguard was responsible for the close protection of the VIP, and had to be willing to lay down his life, if necessary. Is the argument that the judge is having with a lawyer just a professional disagreement, or is the judge in physical danger? Is the person approaching hurriedly a grateful victim of a crime, or a disgruntled criminal looking for revenge? Hammer and Nails may have looked like a couple of scary brutes, but they had to be both intelligent and experienced to be assigned that position on a regular basis as the job involved constant life and death decisions.

There were a lot of UN bigwigs in Kosovo. They had many jobs and positions under the umbrella of UNMIK, or, if you like long titles, the United Nations Interim Administration Mission in Kosovo. Each UN high official received a threat assessment report from UN Intelligence. Most of them received a low or no threat assessment since they were primarily administrators—paper pushers. UN high officials with risky jobs sometimes had one or two of their own bodyguards from the Close Protection Unit, or CPU, in Pristina. Most had no bodyguards, though.

Some jobs were truly dangerous and the person doing the job

required our protection. A UN judge and a UN prosecutor made a lot of enemies. They were under a high threat of assassination at all times. It takes a pretty courageous man or woman to go into a war zone, unarmed, and trust his or her life to a team of strangers. Obviously, all our principals were rated at a high threat level.

Jim gave the word for everyone to saddle up. I jumped in the front passenger seat of the lead vehicle. It had been warming up for a while. All the convoy vehicles were diesel-fueled, and it was best to let them warm up in the cold weather to ensure that their performance was at peak.

The driver was a large black guy wearing an American flag patch on his BDU sleeve. He grinned and nodded at me, but was unable to talk, having to listen to his radio. About ten seconds after I got in, two security operators slid into the backseat of our vehicle. One was Sandy, the Brit, the other was Constable Patrick Burke, an Irishman called, of course, Paddy.

The operators assigned to the other vehicles were all getting into their positions as well. My driver, still busy with the radio and without looking, stuck an oversized right hand in front of me and said simply, "D-Train."

I shook it and replied, "Mike."

From the back seat, Paddy said, "Bit of a chill in the air this morning, don't you think?

Sandy snarled, "Go gnaw on a potato."

I looked at D-Train. He leaned over and whispered, "They don't like each other. We'll talk later."

Everything got quiet and in my earpiece I heard Jim Durfer announce, "Bravo One. We're clear, so let's get going."

We raced out of the parking lot headed for a villa that belonged to the UN judge for the Peja area. Once the vehicles started moving each operator became switched on. There was no idle chatter. Everyone scanned the roadway for potential threats. It wasn't just the road that concerned us. We watched the house windows, rooftops—anywhere a crazy militant or KLA-trained criminal with a grudge might try to pull off an ambush.

As we moved, each team member was responsible for a certain area in his field of vision. Since I was in the front seat of the lead vehicle, I had a lot of area to scrutinize. While D-Train drove, he spoke little, mainly explaining his job which required his full concentration. If a vehicle was moving too slowly ahead of him, he would give them a beep, then a quick hit of the air horn. If the driver did not pull over, he'd tap the vehicle in the rear. If all that didn't work, he'd make full contact with the car's bumper and gun the SUV's powerful engine, forcing the slowpoke off the road. Most of the locals learned to move aside immediately after the first friendly beep.

D-Train wouldn't hit the brake for a pedestrian, either. If one were foolish enough to walk in front of his convoy, he got one blast from the air horn, and hopefully would jump out of the way in time. If not, they became part of the fender or grille. Nobody wanted that because it meant filling out paperwork for security, filing a KPS accident report for D-Train, and an unscheduled visit to the hospital or morgue for the unlucky jaywalker.

D-Train had to watch the cars parked along the side of the street for anything out of the ordinary as he drove. He kept an eye out for a fresh pothole or pile of trash in the street, or any suspicious pedestrian standing on the sidewalk, maybe paying us too much attention. Confrontations with remote-controlled improvised explosive devices, or IEDs, almost never ended well for the target. There were no Mulligans or do-overs if you made a mistake in judgment or missed a big red flag. You either spotted the threat in time or you ate it. It was a serious business.

About six minutes into the drive D-Train asked, "Mike, does that car look okay to you?" He pointed to a parked VW Golf, about fifty yards ahead. I saw nothing wrong.

He got on the radio and said, "Bravo One, I have a VW fifty meters on right. Looks parked at a funny angle."

I couldn't see what was raising the hairs on the back of D-Train's neck. He slowed the convoy to a crawl, and then made his decision.

"Bravo One, we're good."

He gunned the engine and sped by the Volkswagen. The convoy followed his lead, never more than three quarters of a car length behind. I figured it must be even more difficult to drive the follow-on vehicles than the lead. They could never leave enough room for a car to get between them and the vehicle ahead. With D-Train driving all over the road, fast then slow, it had to be hard to maintain that tight interval. We did it in training but they were a little forgiving then. If you failed and separated too far during a real run you might never drive again. Everything in Spec-Ops was a matter of survival of the fittest.

We turned onto a small side street just before Peja broke into open countryside. D-Train drove through the front gate of a small well-maintained villa, then parked the Toyota at a forty-five degree angle to block the street. Sandy, Paddy and I took our perimeter security positions even before the vehicle came to rest.

Everyone "un-assed"—dismounted—their vehicles, the rear gun car blocking access from behind.

I never even saw Hammer and Nails exit their vehicle and go into the villa courtyard to get the judge. I thought, Whoa! They were not only huge, but fast, too.

On the radio, I heard Hammer say, "Bravo Three ready." Then

Jim replied, "Bravo Team, we clear?"

Silence, then Jim said, "Bravo Three go."

In less than twenty seconds, Hammer and Nails had the judge in the armored car and the convoy started to move away. D-Train had the lead car heading for the courthouse with the doors still open and me hanging onto the roof with one hand and only my left leg in the car trying to hook the front seat. He reached and grabbed my free arm with a huge paw and hauled me inside, saying, "Gotta hustle there, Mike."

I made a quick mental note to move my ass quicker or, next time, I might find myself left behind or run over trying to get into the moving lead car.

There was a small patch of straightaway road before we hit the courthouse square. All three drivers floored their gas pedals through that area. I would have loved to be buckled up, but only the VIP principal and the three drivers were allowed to. The rest of us potential car accident victims had to have unlimited freedom of movement, 360-degree vision, and gun sight. We also needed to have immediate access to the weaponry that we carried on us or mounted in the Toyotas.

It was an exciting ride and definitely not for the fainthearted. As we dismounted in front of the courthouse, we did the same drill as before, except I blocked the sidewalk. All the pedestrians had seen this a million times, and patiently waited as we took over the sidewalk, front stairs, and doorway to the courthouse. After the all clear, Hammer and Nails hustled the judge up the stairs to the safety of the building. While the judge did her stuff inside, we mounted back up, and turned the cars in the direction that we would be going when it was time to leave the courthouse. D-Train and the other drivers parked in the middle of the street so that civilian cars could pass on either side.

Jim Durfer had told me that I was to follow D-Train's instructions to the letter.

"What's next?" I asked him.

D-Train told me we'd partner up for the rest of our stay at the courthouse. One of us would stay with the vehicle. The other could take a break, then we'd switch off for a while, maybe go next door and get a cup of tea. We'd just hang out until Bravo One gave us the ten-minute warning. Then we'd get ready for the trip back.

"It's a milk run today, mainly for you new guys," he said, then stuck out his hand one more time and introduced himself formally. "I'm D-Train from the fabulous Motor City, De-e-troit, Michigan."

"Okay. D-Train from Detroit. I can remember that. I'm Mike Granger from Manchester, New Hampshire."

He scratched his head like he was confused, playing with me a bit. "New Hampshire? I've heard of the place, but never knew anybody from there. They got any black people in New Hampshire?"

I was on to him. I replied, "Not a lot of black people. We've got black bears though, plenty of them, if that helps."

He laughed and slapped his knee. "Black bears, shit! I think we're going to get along fine. Hey, you were in patrol, right? Do you know my roommate, Rooftop Rob from Atlanta? We have a place on the other side of Peja."

Yeah, I knew Rooftop. He was on a different shift from mine, but we met up now and then. He was a good cop and was popular with the locals. We had shared a ride to the American compound courtesy of the Russians on 9/11. Rooftop once mentioned that his roommate was in Special Operations.

I learned about D-Train while we chilled. His real name was Darren Post. I could see right away that it would take a lot to rattle him. He told me that he had played college football at the University of Michigan where he was a starting defensive end. He said he'd made it to the training camp of the Minnesota Vikings, but was eventually cut for being too small. Too small? He was at least six-foot-two and a good two hundred-forty pounds. In my world view that was huge.

Later, he joined the Detroit Police Department where he served twelve years on the force, five of them on SWAT, before volunteering for the UN Police. He left a wife and three kids at home. He didn't say how they felt about his excursion to Kosovo. It was long way from Manchester, even longer from Detroit.

D-Train told me that he had majored in philosophy at Michigan and drove a city bus during the summers to help pay for his tuition. When I told him that I drove a taxi to help pay for UNH, we developed an immediate bond. He said he'd let me in on some of the tricks to driving the soft skin and staying alive—like what to do when approaching a culvert beneath the road. Culverts were a prime location for bad guys to plant explosives. He mentioned an incident where a bus loaded with Serbs—men, women, and kids—had been destroyed by such a bomb back in February. I had heard about it during our basic training in Pristina, but he was able to point out the technical mistakes that had been made and how he would have handled that convoy.

We pretty much spent our whole day in that fashion, making small talk, taking coffee and lunch breaks, and relieving each team member in turn. Then I asked D-Train what the deal was with Sandy and Paddy.

He smiled, "You know that Sandy is English and Paddy is Irish, right? So there's that whole Northern Ireland thing going on. It's more than that, though. Paddy is an intelligent dude. He was a Rhodes Scholar and has a Master's Degree in ancient history. He speaks Greek and Latin. Hell, we've discussed Socrates, Aristotle, Kant, and Nietzsche for hours at a time. He's a real smart dude."

I began to think that D-Train was no dummy, either.

"Sandy? Well, let's just say she's a bit earthier," he continued. "She's not like most ladies. She's not afraid to speak her mind. A little thin-skinned sometimes, though. They call her 'Sandy Wright—Can Never Be Wrong.' She's damn good at her job, but try to stay on her good side—when you can find it."

It would have been naïve to expect that there would be no personal tensions already at work in the group; however, I didn't want to add to any that existed or start any new ones. Since three of us had joined the team at once and we were already friends, it was a natural clique scenario. I wanted to avoid that by opening up to the others early on.

I had a chance to catch up with Willy before we took the judge home. He said he was partnered with Jim Durfer, Bravo One, and had talked mostly about the changes coming up in a month when Jack the RCMP guy rotated home. Jim was bouncing ideas around, as one team leader to another, even though Willy was a patrol team leader—considered second string by most Spec-Ops guys.

The German Regional Protective Unit Commander was to leave for home at around the same time, so there would be two positions opening up soon. Jim would be asked to recommend a replacement if he got promoted.

Willy asked me, "What were you and D-Train talking about?"

"Blondes," I said.

He gave me that look of disapproval I had seen countless times.

I shrugged and said, "Hey, we're Americans."

A few minutes later, we got the word to get ready for the return trip.

At the end of the day, Willy, Rick and I were issued our full load of Spec-Ops equipment and we checked our schedules for the rest of the week. We were scheduled to rotate through all the positions:

security, bodyguard, even driver. There was only one exception. On Friday, Willy was temporarily assigned to be Bravo Two—second-in-command of the team.

"Willy, you hot shit, you!" I said, congratulating him on the incredible political coup. One day on the job and he was already on the move. But it made sense, even if it seemed a bit quick. It looked like he was already being groomed for promotion and, in the end, that would only help me. Like they told us in Pristina, things change fast in Kosovo. Me? I was just happy to be on the team.

The first week in Spec-Ops went by without any big problems. Willy was planning to go back to Germany soon for his first CTO in many months to spend an entire week with his family. Like me, he had been in-country too long and needed the break.

When the weekend came, the court system was closed so the judge and prosecutor only had minor trips around the city, mostly for shopping or dinner at the homes of other UN bigwigs. That did not mean that we had extra time off, though. There was always radio watch duty and other special assignments. They could be fun tasks like conducting a recce, pronounced "wreck-kee," a British term for doing a reconnaissance mission to a location we planned to go in the near future. If in three weeks' time we needed to transport someone to another city court, or we would have to escort a principal to a border post, a recce had to be completed first.

Willy and I took a Toyota for a recce on Saturday morning to Border Crossing Post Macedonia. Our German RPU Commander thought this the most tedious and most distant one, so he assigned it to us, the rookies. Willy and I loved it, though. It took us across the whole length of the country through areas we had never seen—rolling hills, pastures, pine forests and rivers. Take away the violence, the destruction, and the poverty, Kosovo was really a nice place.

It was not just a sightseeing trip, though. We had serious business to perform. All along the route, we marked on our NATO maps any potential road obstacles, ambush areas, traffic jam sites, and convoy danger points. We also entered all these potential problem spots in our GPS locator. We took digital pictures of hazardous areas with our UN-issued camera. We located all the NATO military hospitals, and UN and KPS Police stations along the route, and noted their radio frequencies and telephone numbers. This was all necessary in case the high-risk escort got ambushed in the middle of nowhere.

Because the recce was not an escort we left our combat loads at home. It was a relaxing way to spend the day before Willy's trip to Germany. I dropped him off in Pristina on our way back from the Macedonian border, as he planned to crash there for the night at an old pal's apartment. That way he wouldn't have to get up early and drive half the morning to catch his flight. The next four hours, I drove alone with the radio cranked up, singing American oldie tunes. In the middle of a song, I realized that, for the first time since I'd settled in Kosovo, I would have the whole house just to myself for a week. Things were looking up.

Bravo Team had easy milk runs the entire next week, with one exception. We had to take an old woman to the dentist one day. Alpha Team took over our duties transporting the UN judge as well as their own principal, the UN prosecutor, that day. They managed it with a borrowed armored car from Pristina, dispensing with the front lead vehicle. The armored car would function as a ram vehicle with no problem—physics was definitely on the side of that heavy vehicle.

We had our morning briefing and, on the surface, the trip looked easy enough. A Serb-Christian woman had an appointment with a Muslim dentist in Peja who had been ordered by the UN to treat her. The UN order to the dentist was probably just a formality so that his fellow Muslims would not go after him for treating a Serb. Just in case, though, Hammer and Nails would sit with him until our convoy showed up. There was no radio watch that day.

The dentist's old Russian-made dental equipment was too large and bulky to be moved. The NATO base could not treat a civilian, and we had been briefed that the UN wanted to make steps toward reconciling the locals. At this time, the few remaining Kosovar Serbs were like prisoners in their own land. They lived in enclaves surrounded and protected by KFOR troops to prevent the KLA from killing them.

Jim Durfer told us, "You can be sure the KLA will make a point of trying to stop this trip. It will probably be only be a token attempt—it *is* just an old lady after all—but I want everyone to be specially alert."

While Hammer and Nails waited with the dentist, I was assigned the bodyguard position with UN Officer Igor Pavlov, from Mother Russia. As he would point out over and over to me later, he was a "real" Russian, not from a breakaway nation like the Ukraine or Belarus. He was born and raised in Murmansk, the largest city north of the Arctic Circle.

Igor was likable, but scary-tough. He was a combat sambo martial artist and former Soviet army paratrooper. Russian cops and soldiers as a rule were hard cases, and those who spent their youth in the frigid clime of the Arctic Circle were even tougher.

I thought I'd start the small talk while we waited to leave."So, how's the dog been?"

He gave me a confused look.

"You know," I said, "Pavlov's dog."

"I don't have a dog."

Okay, I was talking with the only Russian on the planet who had never heard of his namesake's dog. I made a note to remember to keep our conversations with Igor on less of an academic level in the future.

Our convoy departed for the Serb village, one of about twenty in south Kosovo. We arrived at a checkpoint one mile outside the village itself. The checkpoint was manned by Spanish NATO troops. It was heavily sandbagged and there was a large intimidating tank blocking the road. The troops all wore helmets and full combat gear. From a watch tower two soldiers covered us with a large machine gun.

Rick the Filipino was driving our armored car. Igor and I had been assigned as bodyguards because Jim figured the woman would be more relaxed with an American and a Russian together. Russians traditionally sided with the Serbs and many of the Serb villages were guarded by Russian parachutists. Igor explained to me that the Serb villages were typically surrounded by up to three hundred troops, ringed with wire fences and tanks to protect them from the rest of the population. They were essentially temporary military bases surrounding clusters of twenty to thirty homes.

I liked Igor from the start. He was simple, honest and direct almost to the point of naivety. While we waited, Igor offered a cautionary remark: "Mike, they will try to kill this woman today."

Stupid me, I figured he was trying to pump me up, since I was obviously bored with the many, successive, uneventful runs we'd been making. "Well," I replied, "the dentist should be okay. He has two studs, Hammer and Nails, guarding him."

Igor shook his head indicating a big *nyet*. "Germans are all show. You can't trust them. They don't like the Serbs and they don't like the Muslims. They don't like anybody but Germans. Everybody is beneath them. They are probably scaring the dentist so bad that his hands will be shaking when the lady comes."

Okay, so we had a Brit and an Irishman on the team who were at each other's throats, and now a Russian who couldn't stand Germans. Thinking myself in safe territory I said lightheartedly, "Well, at least Americans and Russians are getting along—detente and all."

Igor snorted another *nyet*. "Americans are soft like a baby's ass. They tell good stories and make good movies, but they are all pussies."

At least I no longer held any misgivings as to where I fit in Igor's cultural scheme of things.

When our operators called out the all clear and Bravo One gave the signal, Igor and I exited the armored car and practically ran into the local KPS substation. We surrounded the woman and hustled her into the backseat of the armored car. Igor had her from behind and I covered her side, so that no sniper could get a decent shot. Not that we feared it right there in the Serb village, but it was just the standard drill. Any slacking off would be a Christmas present to the bad guys.

The woman was sixty years old, but looked more like ninety, and she was frightened to death. Her extreme state of tension caused my own anxiety level to rise. Igor spoke with her in Russian which, like most Serbs, she could understand, and it seemed to calm her a bit.

Our convoy was escorted by NATO military vehicles and Spanish troops. It was turning into a real show, but not a good one. Off we sped toward Peja. My Peja. The Peja where everyone was always nice to me. The Peja where the Muslim residents waved and were friendly. The Peja where, if you dropped a wallet it would remain on the ground, untouched, money still inside, until you went back to the spot a day later to recover it. To me, the residents of Peja had proven to be honorable, peaceful and strict Muslims who did not take violations of the Koran lightly, especially those pertaining to the decent treatment of fellow people.

Ten minutes later, the convoy came to a screeching halt, the vehicles taking up defensive positions. Operators and soldiers poured from the cars and took defensive positions. Igor and I sat and looked at each other. We had heard no radio traffic from our men. We were locked in our armored car, with the primary target. At the moment, *we* had become "the package" everyone was so worried about.

The radio crackled with Jim Durfer's voice. "Bravo One. NATO found an IED up ahead. Stand by."

After ten gruesomely silent minutes, Jim crackled back on. "We are going to use an alternate route. Follow us."

After bouncing across a rocky pasture, the convoy rolled onto a small dirt path, that finally turned into a road, that eventually got us into Peja. We arrived at the dentist's street, one that I had walked peacefully down many times. Today it was an armed camp, locked down tight. Troops were everywhere, even on the rooftops, and armored cars blocked all street entrances including ours after we passed.

As Bravo Team deployed, Igor and I waited for the all clear signal. Igor, in a deadly serious voice, said, "Mike, I will take the rear position. They tried an IED, the next strike will be from a sniper. I will take the back, you the front. We need to get her in the building as fast as possible. If I take a hit from the sniper, you leave me and get the woman inside. You understand, leave me and protect the woman. Bravo Team will take care of me."

I wanted to say, "But what if he misses you and hits me?" but already knew the answer. Still, I couldn't believe that all our lives were suddenly on the line for a freaking loose filling. Igor was prepared to take a bullet for this old woman he didn't know and had never met. Despite all my training, I found myself wondering what the hell I was doing here. Nonetheless, I kept my eyes on Bravo One, waiting for the all clear hand signal. Then it came.

"Igor, we're on," I told him.

We exited the safe confines of the armored car and moved quickly toward the front door of the building. I had the woman by her clothes, pulling her along, while Igor pushed her from behind. We were manhandling her, but it was the only way to protect her. As I dragged her toward the door, I was unconsciously scrunching my shoulders and neck, waiting for the crack of a rifle.

The shot never came. Once inside, we both gave a "whoa" sigh of relief.

Hammer and Nails were in the dentist's office. Nails laughed and said, "You two guys looked like American football players carrying that woman like a football. What took you so long?"

I told them about the IED, and they said the dentist has been jumpy all morning. That was not good. Maybe he knew something.

Jim, Bravo One, came in and said that he did not like the situation. There were no protesters around as would normally be the case when a Serb came in to a Muslim city. He said to stay sharp, the street was too abandoned—too quiet.

The dentist almost but never completely finished his work. Towards the end, an alert came in, quick and urgent: A tenant across the street had gone to the Peja police station and reported that some men had put a bomb in his apartment during night. The apartment directly faced the dentist's office. The tenant did not care about the Serb woman, but he wasn't given the opportunity to remove all his property from the soon-to-be-destroyed apartment. He wanted to know if the KPS would help him move the rest of his things before it went off.

Bravo Team was on it instantly. "Bravo One! Evacuate now!"

With that, Hammer and Nails lifted the dentist off his feet and ran with him in their arms for the NATO vehicles. Igor and I picked the woman off the dentist chair and carried her, tubing still in her mouth, ripped from its connections. Igor carried her like a baby, cradled in his arms, while she screamed in fright. I led the way, in front of Igor, trying to make my body larger to cover the slight woman pressing against my back so that any sniper shot would hit me and not her.

We dove into the back seat of our armored car. As gently as he could, Igor pushed her to the floor. I lay on top of her for added protection. It was all standard bodyguard drill, but this time for real and it was scary. Rick had the armored car moving in formation with the rest of Bravo's cars before the doors were even closed.

I never got the whole story of why the explosives hadn't gone off, though a large bomb was found that had to be disarmed by explosives experts. All of that for a dental visit, and because the UN and the KLA each wanted to make a point. I learned that day that Kosovo was going to take a long time to heal—and UN police were going to have to be there a long time as well.

Blessed are the Peacekeepers

Chapter 14

Willy returned from his CTO refreshed and invigorated, and we both resettled into our daily routines. In early December, the winter cold, snow and ice arrived, making the high-risk escorts increasingly difficult. There were few snow plows in Peja region, and the Italian army only occasionally plowed the main roadways.

Our villa was heated by a wood stove and, when there was electricity, several electric heaters. It was like camping indoors. Most nights, we had no electricity so we slept in winter sleeping bags. In the morning, we made the long cold hallway trip in our woolen winter underwear to the bathroom. From there it was a cold wash and shave before breaking up the ice that had formed in the toilet.

Willy and I spent many a freezing night sleeping within arm's reach of the wood stove, so we could constantly feed the cast iron source of our warmth. We never sleep well. On the coldest nights we walked to the RHQ, started up one of Bravo Team's vehicles, cranked up the heater, and slept in the car. It was a miserable way to live, but we were toughened by then. We never complained or bitched about it to each other.

Jack, the RCMP deputy team leader, left for Canada as scheduled. Our German RPU Commander departed Kosovo on the same flight out of Pristina Airport, causing a minor political crisis within the RPU unit concerning who was going to fill their jobs.

The outgoing RPU Commander had created a problem: He had two teams, one comprised only of Germans that followed his every word to the letter. They had all belonged to the same national police department and any disobedience would have ramifications back home as well as in Kosovo. Alpha Team spoke only German on their escort runs. They worked as a single unit and were a well-honed machine. Then there was Bravo Team. To the Commander, we were the leftovers, a collection of mutts when compared with his pedigreed Germans.

Both teams were under the UN Spec-Op Command in Pristina, and did not answer to any orders from CIVPOL or Peja Regional authority. Our bosses were not all that happy that Peja RPU had been stocked and run as an extension of the GSG-9 system back in Germany and they wanted a change. Hence, Jim Durfer got promoted to RPU-Peja Unit Commander. It was a well-deserved promotion, as he was an outstanding leader. Captain Ernst, who had been groomed for the job by the former commander, accepted the move with dignity. I don't know how the rest of his team liked it, but I never heard a complaint.

Jim asked Ernst if he wanted to combine the teams and move people around. Ernst said no, his men really liked it the way it was. As a consolation, Jim said he would appoint a German as Bravo Team leader. The team leader is recommended to Pristina for approval, but before the appointment, the team must vote if they are willing to be led by the person.

As I thought, Willy was being groomed by Jim. It all made sense. Rick and I loved the idea. Hammer and Nails were totally on board to have him as the German team leader, and they no interest at all in changing their roles. D-Train backed me and my vote. All he wanted to do was drive his SUV like a madman.

Sandy went along because she knew Pristina would never appoint a woman to team leader in Spec-Ops. It just was not going to happen. Maybe in the UN patrol division, but not here, not with this crew of Type A crazy men. Besides, she and Willy got along just fine. The other Brit on the team, Billy "Bulldog" Davies from Aberdeen, Scotland, backed Sandy's vote.

Paddy Burke was probably the smartest guy on the team and would have made a strong candidate for the position, but he was too laid back and showed no sign of ambition to climb the ranks. He had no problem with Willy, and quickly gave his stamp of approval.

Mo, the Jordanian, knew he was going nowhere in the system. I found him to be intelligent and brave as well as humble. I liked many of the Arabs that I worked with, and Mo and I had many discussions, both political and military, concerning terrorism and war. He recognized the political end that Jim was trying to accomplish and gave his assent as well.

Igor, the independent Russian, just nodded and accepted the situation. He and I had talked about the impending leadership change several times while partnered up. I felt that Igor was beginning to like me and value my opinion.

That left only Rick, and there was no doubt about his support for Willy. So it became a done deal. Willy was the new Bravo One, at least for the next two months until he went home. It was a unanimous vote which satisfied Alpha Team that we still were in the fold and had nothing but love and respect for all things German.

Soon after the voting was over our new RPU Commander, Jim Durfer, and our new Bravo Team leader, Willy Steinhardt, dropped a bombshell: Jim unexpectedly announced, "Mike Granger will be appointed as Bravo Two, if he receives your vote. It has already been approved by Pristina."

There was no loud gasp in the squad room, but I could see some wide eyes and open mouths, and, to be honest, I was as shocked as anyone. I hadn't asked for it. I hadn't even wanted it, and it wasn't fair to the more experienced members of the team.

"Willy will only take the Bravo One position if Mike is his number two," explained Jim. "They have worked like this since they were deployed to Kosovo. I do not want to break up this combination and neither does Pristina. I have already asked Captain Ernst and his team and have their approval. I have already informally spoken to Hammer, Igor, Rick and Nails and I understand they will vote yes for Mike."

Well, that surprised me as well. I got along with them, but I did not think that was totally the reason they were on board with the promotion. I knew that Hammer and Nails would, like obedient Germans, go along with Willy, but Igor surprised me. There was no doubt that he would make a far better Bravo Two than me.

Jim called for a formal vote. Our team was down to twelve members because we lost two, but were only replacing one. Of the twelve, there were nine voting members on the team as Willy, Jim Durfer, and I did not get to vote, and Jack's replacement would not arrive until the next day.

Hammer, Nails, Igor, Rick and D-Train approved. That was five votes of confidence. The four other members: Sandy, Paddy, Mo the Jordanian, and Bulldog Davies all abstained. They did not vote yes or no. They just passed. I know how they felt. They did not know me well enough, and I am sure each of them probably deserved the Bravo Two position more than I did. Because of politics, and some backroom deals, they were being stuck with me as Bravo Two. It sucked.

Since the vote had come at the end of the day, we all went home right afterwards. I'm certain there was a lot of bitching that evening amongst team members, even some who voted for me. Even I knew that I didn't deserve the position, but there I was, Bravo Two. I would have some serious fence-mending ahead with some team members, and would do the best job I could. If I screwed up, they could just as easily demote me.

Willy and I talked about it that night, and he recounted all the wheeling and dealing that had been going on behind closed doors while I, blissfully unaware, worked my shifts. Willy, on the other hand, wasn't a backroom type of guy. "Mike," he said, "if I did not go along with Jim's plan, Bravo Team would have been broken up. I like Bravo Team and could not do that to them. Jim wanted you as number two. We will have to make this work."

Sure, I thought, *easy for you to say.*

I didn't get the chance to know RCMP officer Jack Kendrick well before he rotated home. I did get to know his replacement very quickly, though. His name was Jens "Arni" Knudson of the Danish National Police force. He was another stud. Arni was about six-foot-one and a solid, I mean titanium-solid, two hundred pounds. He was one of the leading martial arts instructors in Denmark, and had extensive experience in bodyguard protection techniques. On top of that, Arni had a reputation as a world-class rifle marksman. His lifelong "hobby" was the biathlon, and he had even been to the World Olympics where he came in fourth place.

Arni slid into the team as if he had been there since its inception. He made friends easily and instantly formed a close bond with our best handgun shooter, Igor. He joined the team within a day of me becoming Bravo Two, so I was assigned to train him. Arni had already completed the Spec-Op training in Kosovo, so when I asked how it went, he replied, "It was almost as good as the training I received in Denmark."

It takes most people several milk runs to understand the unique drill system that Bravo Team had developed, but Arni was proficient by the end of day one. I went to Willy and told him that the new guy needed no further assistance, that he was already good-to-go. I said that he could do anything we asked of him. Willy appeared to be slightly less impressed for some reason. I knew he was exceptionally good at finding chinks in people's armor, and I could tell that he had something on Arni.

"He sure can shoot," I said.

Willy shook his head. "That's not in question."

"He can break both of us in two while draining a beer and eating a bag of potato chips."

"Still, not in question."

I sighed. "Okay, maybe he can only leap *small* buildings in a single bound. Is that so bad?"

Willy smiled and said, "He can't drive."

"Ah...what do you mean he can't drive?"

"He can drive, of course. He's just not very good at keeping his vehicles in one piece. He would make a perfect Hollywood stunt driver doing chase scenes, but here, on my team, I'd rather he not get behind the wheel unless we are under fire. Then, I think I'd love to have him drive."

The worst thing we could find on Arni was that he was an aggressive driver? That didn't seem to me something of which to be ashamed.

"Well, we've got D-Train, Rick, and Mo," I said. "We'd have to pry the steering wheels from their cold dead hands before any of them would willingly accept being replaced."

Willy then gave Arni his ultimate compliment. "He is very good, though. He could be German."

The rest of Bravo Team quickly adapted to Willy's open

leadership style and readily accepted his position as Bravo One. Willy was easy-going, professional, and surprisingly flexible. It proved a simple transition from Jim Durfer to Willy, as the two were similar in so many ways.

I, on the other hand, felt like a fish out of water, and pretty much stayed under the radar as much as possible. For now, I was positioned on the team as "security;" I would only perform in a leadership role in Willy's absence. I thought it important that I try to connect with the four who had abstained from voting for me as Bravo Two before flaunting my authority. Paddy and Bulldog accepted my explanation that I had no part in the promotions and advancements. As a matter of fact, I found Paddy decidedly practical. He seemed to understand politics, and was not one to personalize such things. I got the feeling that his only concern was whether I would get the job done if Bravo One was incapacitated.

My conversation with Sandy was another thing entirely. Every interaction with her since the promotion felt like a challenge of my abilities—like I had to justify my mere presence on the team, never mind being second in command. I thought I understood where she was coming from, though. She was trying to prove herself and excel as part of an elite team whose main operating fuel was high octane testosterone—and she was running on a different kind of juice. Still, from what I could see, she was getting things done. I was mainly concerned that she might be unleashing her frustrations with the system, and maybe with men in general, on me, so I decided, in the end, to appeal to her sense of responsibility.

"Look, Sandy," I said, "I didn't ask for this job. But now that I've got it, I'm duty bound to do the best I can for the team. You wouldn't expect any less from me, would you?"

She replied, "No, but I hope that Willy stays healthy. You still don't have my vote."

I left her, thinking, *Okay, this is a work in progress.*

I went next to see Mo Mayoof, the Jordanian. He told me that he was thinking about returning to the patrol division where he had started his UN mission. I tried my good cop best to get him to rethink his inclination. "I worked patrol first, too, Mo," I said. "I loved it—but I have to say it would be a step backwards to return. You're with Spec-Ops because you are the best. Besides, where in Kosovo are you going to get the perks that we get with this job?"

Mo was a good, competent guy who had served in a previous UN mission in Bosnia. He was related to royalty back in Jordan, and he didn't have to do this shit. He didn't need the money or the adrenaline rush. Instead, he was putting his ass on the line every day to help people. Mo considered what I said, and, in his soft-spoken style replied, "You are right, Mike. I can not go back. I must finish my work in Kosovo with the team. My father would expect this of me."

I was relieved by his decision to stay—and happy that a good man was not going to leave either because of me or politics. I wasn't about to ask if him if he had rethought his vote. I just thanked him for listening and left.

In the morning, we had to escort the UN prosecutor to the Supreme Court Building in Pristina. This trip was to be a little different, though. The case before the UN tribunal was the Russian thug who had shot at Rick and me when we jumped the mule train during Operation White Mountains. Because the incident had happened in Peja, the prosecutor was the VIP that Alpha Team had been protecting.

I figured that the trip and the trial should both be quick and easy. The two main witnesses, Filipino Rick and I, were part of the escort team for the UN prosecutor, and KPS Officer Bekim was already stationed there in Pristina. He had only to go a short distance to the courthouse.

I was excited about getting the chance to see Bekim again and catch up on his life in Pristina in his new position. I suspected that he was in regular contact with Leo, and was curious if he had information on what that elusive spook was up to.

I hoped we'd have at least a few minutes to talk, as the case itself was expected to be little more than a formality. We had called out to the bad guys, identified ourselves, and the Russian kid had started shooting at us. One, two, three. We would return to Peja with a conviction for smuggling and assault. The Albanian Kosovar defendants had already pled guilty to smuggling, and walked away with thirty-day sentences, which they'd already completed. The Russian kid, however, had unloaded his AK-47 on us, so the UN prosecutor wanted a stiffer sentence. Even so, it was stil a slam dunk. They would have the testimony of three police officers against a low-level criminal.

Our entire team was scheduled go on the run. All the operators would spend the day in Pristina. During their relief periods, they would be able to shop at the UN PX—post exchange—store and later, eat in a real big city restaurant for a change.

Only one thing concerned me: The Intel brief stated the threat level on this run was heightened. Apparently, the Russian defendant was connected to some high-level Russian mobsters who had been financing the smuggling operation. UN Intel felt that, with the prosecutor and two witnesses in the same convoy, it presented a tempting target. That made sense to me.

To counter the threat, the entire team would be kept on alert. Willy, as commander, would lead the convoy with Rick behind the wheel of the armored car that carried the prosecutor. Rick loved driving, especially this type of high-end, high-risk driving. Igor, Arni and I, would ride ahead by twenty minutes to scout the road in a borrowed Toyota.

The run to Pristina went off without a hitch, except that the convoy got caught up in some heavy traffic just inside the city. My vehicle had left a few minutes earlier than the others, but we had to wait over an hour for them to arrive. While we waited, I used the down time to talk with Igor with Arni acting as security in the rear seat.

"Igor, I wanted to say how much I appreciate you casting your vote for me as Bravo Two. I know it wasn't easy."

"I vote for you because you are not German," he replied. "If I was offered Bravo Two, I vote for me." I'd forgotten that Igor lacked the normal diplomatic filter one would expect from someone in Spec Ops.

"Seems fair enough," I shrugged.

He put his hand on my shoulder. "Mike," he said. "You are pretty good guy. I like you. You don't talk too much on the escorts, and you followed my instructions on the dentist run. You treat people with respect, but you are still a pussy. It's not your fault. You are American."

I heard Arni snicker in the back.

"Ah, okay, Igor, but I'd rather you didn't call me a pussy. I served with the United States Marines, you know."

Undeterred, he replied, "In Russia, I trained to kill Marines."

It was time to change direction. "Okay, so what will it take for me to earn your respect?"

"Shoot a German."

Igor grinned. Arni broke out in uncontrolled laughter.

"Well, if the opportunity ever presents itself, I'll see what I can do," I said, and with that, gave up trying to mend any more damned fences related to the Bravo Two vote. I was just going to start acting like a leader. I'm sure it was what they expected from me all along.

As soon as the rest of the convoy arrived at the courthouse, we quickly unloaded and went inside. The trial had already started with the prosecutor presenting the case to three UN judges. Rick testified first, while Bekim and I waited in a small side room. I had the chance to catch up with my KPS friend, who was now in charge of a special unit that investigated serious crimes in the Pristina region. He told me that he was happy for the chance to live in the city, having been a country boy since birth.

Bekim then leaned towards me and said, "Officer Mike, I spoke with Leo yesterday. He said for me to tell you to be very careful today. He told me to watch your back, but I don't know how to do that." He looked genuinely puzzled.

"It's an American expression, Bekim. What he means is to be care…"

"Officer Granger," a court official called out. "Come now, please."

I was escorted directly to the witness stand. All the members of Bravo Team, except the drivers, were in the courtroom to hear Rick and me. My testimony was straightforward. I gave the facts, quick and direct. One of the three judges looked and sounded like he was asleep. Imagine a U.S. court where there is no jury and the judge is snoring away while you give testimony!

The defendant and two well-dressed attorneys sat in front of me while I spoke. In the row behind them, occasionally consulting with the attorneys and the defendant was a man with a shaved head—a mean looking, two hundred-twenty-pound Russian wearing a diamond earring.

Son-of-a-bitch, I said to myself. It's the same ugly bastard who stared me down at the French dress ball in Pristina months ago. But this time he was not just scrutinizing me, he was downright glaring at me. If looks could kill, my team would have been choosing flowers for my funeral instead of listening to court proceedings. He was definitely calling the shots with the defense attorneys. I had been face-to-face with a lot of bad guys over the years, but he was easily over the top of the badass list. There was no question in my mind that this guy had killed people, and would enjoy doing the same to me.

I had to struggle to keep my focus the rest trial. I kept saying, screw him, his guy had shot at us. What were we supposed to do, let him walk away with an "I'm sorry, it won't happen again" and nothing to prevent him from returning to his criminal ways? Nope. I didn't think so.

The Russian kid's lawyers claimed he didn't know we were the police, and that we shot at him first, so we were the aggressors. It was a stupid defense, but it was all they had.

When all the testimony was finished, the judges moved to another room to deliberate, leaving the courtroom audience to mill around and talk. The Russian boss kept staring at me from across the room. Igor slid up beside me and said, "Mike, be careful with that man over there. His name is Milosh Bukin, they call him 'KGB'. He's a real bad guy."

"KGB? I thought they went out of business."

"No. They are still in business—just they use a different name," and went on to explain that Bukin was a heavy-duty mobster, and nothing but bad news. His father was Russian and his mother Albanian, and both had worked for the old KGB. His nickname was honorary, but he had two brothers who were high up in the KGB's replacement, the FSB. Igor told me that even Spetsnaz gave him a wide berth because of his connections with the Russian state security service. "I am impressed that you have made an enemy of such a man," he said with a grin.

He might be amused, but now I was definitely concerned. I don't know why I did what I did, but I couldn't help myself. Something compelled me to walk over to Bukin, look him in the eye, and say, "Do I know you?"

He clenched his teeth, then relaxed. "I know you. I know that you are a policeman. Have you come over here to write me a ticket, policeman?"

"No," I said. "I think we are past the ticket stage. So you don't like policemen?"

He opened his arms wide in an exaggerated expression of confusion. "Why should I like policemen? They are robbers with badges and courts. I have policemen in many countries working for me. I don't like them, but I pay them. They are all assholes. I see you are with Igor Pavlov. Igor is an asshole."

The guy was more than creepy. His predator eyes made the hairs stand up on the back of my head. "If you don't like me, then why stare at me?" I asked.

"That boy on trial is my nephew. I want to remember you, and I want you to remember me."

The court officer called everyone to be seated. I nodded, then turned my back on Bukin, and went back to my chair.

The verdict came back guilty as charged, and the defendant was sentenced to one year in prison. Bukin started swearing and had to be hustled out of the courtroom by his attorneys. Igor, Arni, and I followed at a distance. It would be another hour before the UN prosecutor was ready to leave for Peja, so we decided to grab a bite to eat.

As we exited the room, Bukin hollered something in my direction from another end of the hall. I ignored him and left with the others. Once outside, though, I asked Igor what the man had said.

"He said that this is not the end."

When I arrived back in Peja, I found a bottle of vodka on my desk. One of the secretarial staff told me it was brought there by an unknown KPS officer. I examined it, and it was quality vodka imported from Russia. I figured it was a present from our Russian Regional Commander for a job well done. There was note in Russian attached, so I asked Igor to translate. It said simply, "To toast your passing."

We all knew then where it had come from. Bukin was trying to spook me, and it worked. For the next few days, the vodka bottle remained on my desk and on my mind. The team rallied behind me, though. Even Sandy came up, put her hand on my shoulder, and said, "Hey Mike, don't worry, Luv. The team has your back."

Hammer and Nails cornered me around the same time, also concerned about my safety. But their message was of a decidedly different sort than Sandy's. Hammer said simply, "Mike, if you want, we will drive to Pristina and kill that son-of-a-whore. Then you are done with this."

Tempting as it was, I knew he was saying it to make me feel more relaxed, or, I should say I *hoped* he was just saying it for that reason. I had found from experience that you never knew with these guys.

Arni and Igor made essentially the same offer a little later. I also told them not to, of course. And I did feel better knowing I had such willing and able back-up should I need it.

Chapter 15

Christmas was approaching and spending it in Kosovo would be a strange experience for me. Some disappointing life experiences had caused me to drift away from religion and religious celebrations. Divorce, disgust in the Catholic Church due to the child abuse scandals, and the many unjust things I had seen in police work put me in a fairly secular place where I have stayed since. The al-Qaeda terrorist attacks in September and three thousand dead Americans still weighted heavily on my mind. The shooting at Nashi, the face of the innocent victim of the honor killing, and the madness of the Junik riot left me feeling angry and frustrated. I didn't know what I believed in anymore.

Still, Christmas was coming, and it was hard to ignore. I might be four thousand miles away from home and living amongst Muslims, Hindus, Buddhists, Greek Orthodox Catholics, Orthodox Jews, pagans, and who knows what else, but it was still Christmas. Willy, born a Christian, considered himself agnostic, and lived by a personal code or set of mystical principles he called his *Weltanschauung*—his world outlook or point-of-view. It seemed that everyone believed in something but me. I was adrift.

I found the many beliefs and dogmas around me interesting from a cultural aspect. Besides our many political discussions, my friends and I often talked about religion. I found that a lot of them followed their faiths much more strictly, with more rigidity, than any of the people that I had known in America. I wasn't about to convert to someone else's belief system, of course, but those long, sincere conversations opened my eyes to the wide assortment of creeds in the world.

I would at least try to celebrate Christmas with some sort of observance. I was living in a Muslim country and had already celebrated the Muslim holiday of Ramadan with my friends, and now they wanted to share Christmas with me. It was not an easy thing, though, with so few Christmas reminders in the shops and stores around Peja.

Willy and I went out to the hillside near our villa, cut down a two-foot-high tree, and put it on our living room table. We decorated it with beer tabs, colored paper, and a string of nine millimeter shell casings. We topped it off with a combat glow stick that we planned to break and light up on Christmas Eve. The unique décor may not have been in complete harmony with the principles of the Season of Peace, but it was good enough for both of us.

We worked while a wild snow storm raged about us on Christmas Eve. At 9:00 p. m., the German UN judge, who by this time we all admired and adored, gave us each a present she had picked up while on CTO in Germany. They were small gifts, but thoughtful. Mine was a pair of brightly colored socks with toes in them. I held them up, laughed, and vowed that they were never going on my feet. "Imagine if I got shot and the medics in some NATO hospital pulled my boots off and saw these things," I said. "They would laugh their asses off and probably botch my surgery."

In fact, the socks were my only Christmas present that year. We received no "care packages," telephone calls or mail from home, and communicated with family and friends through sporadic emails. Those socks are, and will probably always be, the best Christmas gift I ever received.

Without all the commercial trappings of the season, I was left to think about what Christmas really meant to me. I focused on family, peace on earth and good will toward men—all that stuff—and it made me feel better.

One of my last runs that week had been a high-risk escort of a Greek Orthodox Christian priest from a monastery to say mass at several protected Serb villages. I guess someone was keen on establishing a new holiday tradition, because on the roadway to one village, we had a mortar round lobbed at us. It was off target, and we brushed it off with one of Arni's apt remarks: "Bunch of assholes."

Like I said, Christmas that year made me think and came into perspective for me for the first time in my life. More than anything else, I wished that people would stop hating and killing each other. The world was pretty fucked up. There was a war raging in Afghanistan, a vicious ongoing ethnic struggle in Kosovo, and terrorism everywhere. To me, everyone, no matter what their religion, needed to pray their asses off for peace on earth. It was that simple.

Scott Michaels, Billy Ray, Arni, Rick the Filipino, D-Train, and Igor dropped in for a few beers with Willy and me on Christmas Eve. We drank by candle light, since there was no electricity. We were warmed by the blazing wood stove and by the single green light-stick atop our odd-looking tree. The mood was somber, maybe a little sad. Everyone had someone back home who they cared about and missed. The visitors left by one o'clock in the morning and Willy wished me a final *"Frohe Weihnachten"*—Merry Christmas—before going to bed.

I stayed up. I had one more errand to run before I slept that night. Earlier in the evening, I had bribed the radio man at RHQ to give me a few minutes of satellite-phone time at two o'clock to call home and hear the voices of my family gathered for the holiday at my brother's house on Central Street in Manchester.

I had emailed them earlier to expect the call at 8:00 p.m. Eastern Standard Time, a six-hour time difference from Kosevo. I knew my large crazy family would all be there celebrating in grand style. I wanted to hear a friendly voice—to speak with my mom, wish her a Merry Christmas, and tell her how much I missed dad. I wanted to hear a real live voice from home. I figured if I got a whole ten minutes, I could talk quickly to at least twenty of them and hopefully hear some news about my sons in the Army and the Marines. I knew, sure as shit, they would be heading off to war before long, and I wanted to tell them that I loved them and to keep their heads down.

I walked to RHQ with my chin tucked against my chest while the blizzard snow froze my face and lips. When I got there, my face and jaw were so cold I could hardly talk. It didn't matter, though. The radio operator told me that the satellite phone was down. There was no signal because of the storm. I was stunned.

"Sorry officer," he said, shrugging helplessly. As I prepared to go back into the wintry night, he added, "Merry Christmas, anyway."

I managed a weak, "Yeah. Merry Kosovo Christmas."

The walk home was a new low for me. If I hadn't been so cold, I would have sat on the snow covered ground and cried. Instead, I reminded myself that I was tougher now. I had signed up for sacrifice. That was part of the deal, so I sucked it up and trudged home through the howling wind and snow. I just hoped to hell that *someone* at home in New Hampshire missed me as much as I missed them all.

Willy rotated home in January. Willy was my best friend, so I took about 800 Euros cash from savings, rented the biggest café in Peja and threw the best going-away party anyone in Peja had ever seen. I invited everyone and everyone came, because Willy was about the most popular and respected UN officer in Kosovo. Our KPS comrades, his German friends, and just about every UN person in Peja showed up.

The next day, I drove him to Pristina Airport. Before he got on the plane, I said, "Willy, I've got something for you."

He grinned. "Is it my Swiss watch?"

"Nope. It's something more valuable than that." I reached into my pocket and pulled out my Manchester Police detective shield. It was one of my most cherished possessions, and I knew he coveted it. I was losing my best friend, my only confidant, and my mentor. It was like getting divorced all over again. I handed it to him.

His renowned German stoicism cracked a bit under the strain of gratitude, and I saw the slightest amount of moisture collect in the corner of one eye.

"Mike," he said. "You will need this."

"Hey, if I make it back, then they'll give me another one."

"Of course, you'll make it back. Thank you. I will send you something as valuable when I get back to Germany."

I held out my hand and said, "Well, I guess this is the big 'auf Wiedersehen'."

He grasped my hand in both of his and held it for a long time. "Mike," he said, "you can trust everyone on the team, of course, but stay close to Arni and Igor. They will keep you safe. They will make sure that you get back home."

I tried to read his eyes. "Are you thinking about Bukin?"

He nodded. "There are always Bukins in this world. He will try something, I think. He must. It is in his nature. Just stay close to those two. Goodbye, Mike."

The airlines employee at the gate signaled Willy that it was his last chance to board. He picked up his bag and walked through the door and out onto the tarmac. I waited until the plane took off, then began my long lonely trip back to Peja.

Soon after Willy left, Billy Ray moved in with me, and so did Arni. Billy and I were good friends by then. He no longer wanted to stay alone in his cement UN apartment. Our villa was like a small mansion in comparison. Arni and I also became pretty tight. He was a wild man, a real warrior, but a decent guy. He claimed that he was the reincarnation of a tenth century Viking related to the Danish king, Harold Bluetooth. Of course, it was just a story, but then again, why would anyone want to wreck a good story with the truth?

Igor began spending time at our house. We swapped stories, made up new ones, and laughed at the antics of people we met on our runs. I began to wonder if Willy hadn't said something to Arni and Igor before he left about keeping an eye on me. I wouldn't ask them, though, and they wouldn't tell me if I did. Life turned fun again.

Things changed in the Regional Protection Unit as well. Like Willy, the burly Scot, Bulldog Davies, rotated home. I hadn't really gotten to know Davies well, and now he was gone. He seemed a good trooper, though. His main contribution to my education was to confirm that Sandy was gay. "A bleedin' dyke," was how he put it. Not that it was really a surprise.

Near the same time, Alpha Team lost a couple of its highly skilled Germans, and I know that Capt. Ernst missed them. Apparently, they had accomplished some good stuff on their special missions, but I wasn't privy to the details. Jim Durfer stayed in command of RPU, and recommended that I replace Willy as the leader of Bravo Team. The vote was quick and unanimous, though I learned later that Sandy was the last to agree. I still hadn't won her over yet. Without fanfare, I became Bravo One, and, despite the personnel losses (we didn't get any replacements from Spec-Op Command) we were still the same old team, just leaner and smarter.

The war with the Taliban in Afghanistan was pretty much wrapping up, and the UN and NATO were sending all available resources there to manage the peace. Kosovo was still dangerous, but winding down, at least from the United Nations' perspective. The big mission had become Afghanistan.

Bravo Team was down to ten operators, including me. I still had D-Train, Rick, and Mo the Jordanian as drivers. I had Hammer and Nails, the twin rocks, my team's bodyguards. And to complete things, I had four tough and deadly security shooters in Sandy, Paddy, Igor, and Arni.

I was now Bravo One, which meant I needed a Bravo Two. It was an easy decision, though I was aware of the political and personal pitfalls of field promotions. I picked Arni and he was approved unanimously. It helped that everyone on the team liked him, and the fact that he was the best shooter with a rifle and one of the toughest men any of us had ever met didn't hurt. From day one, he made friends with all the team members. With Igor's assistance, he patiently taught the rest of us advanced martial arts and improved our bodyguard skills. He was, as I said, a real warrior and on special missions his performance was always exceptional. Even Hammer and Nails looked up to him. More important, Jim Durfer had confidence in him.

Jim also seemed to have confidence in my leadership abilities, though I knew that he always retained some reservations based on my personal background. I had come from KPS patrol, had a questionable relationship with UCK, and connections within the State Department.

Jim hated politics and was a straight shooter; I would have to prove to him that I was deserving of his faith. I had always been a workhorse and learned early on that if I did my job at one hundred and ten percent, the only thing left for my superiors to snipe at was my off duty antics—unless, of course, I crossed that invisible line between having fun and "conduct un-becoming." From now on, I was determined to watch my step both on and off the field.

Chapter 16

January and February went by quickly, mostly routine, mostly cold and wet. I missed Willy's friendship and guidance, but had pretty much settled into my role as Bravo One.

At the start of March, Jim Durfer called me into his office. "Mike," he said, "I got word last night that the UN is investigating in Ratkovac a war crime mass grave. Tomorrow, the UN judge, in her investigatory role, will be going there to check out the situation. Bravo Team will be taking her. I think it is going to be a giant mess to tell you the truth. Send someone to scout ahead tonight and have your team down there as early as you can tomorrow."

I asked, "Any idea who the victims were—Albanians? Serbs?"

"Who the hell knows? Whoever they were, they lived in Kosovo."

I knew what he meant. Whenever a mass grave was discovered, everyone jumped to attention. The UN Police Missing Persons Unit in Pristina would have initial control of the area. Soon after, the Investigation Unit from The Hague's War Crimes Tribunal would arrive and take over. That meant VIPs, investigators, forensic scientists, and KFOR-NATO troops would be swarming all over the area. I figured that I had better send Arni and D-Train ahead that night, so they could fill me in on the sit-rep in the morning before our team took the UN judge there.

The whole war crimes stuff was a political hot potato, and such investigations were always fraught with controversy. I learned in training that between 1998 and 1999 about eleven thousand Kosovo Albanians were slaughtered by Serbs. As NATO Forces moved in, about twenty-three hundred Serbs were killed by the KLA revenge squads. When I first arrived in Peja, a mass grave of dead Serbs was found in Ishtok, a small town in northeast Peja Region. It was ugly business. I appreciated the need for an accounting of all the dead, but it was work that I did not care to get involved in if I could help it.

I had been to one war crimes trial in Prizren, about fifty miles south of Peja. Prizren was controlled by the German KFOR, and, as efficient as they were, every trip there was dangerous. The guy on trial was a Serb military reservist who operated a bulldozer used in the mass grave. His defense was that he thought that he was building an air raid trench to protect the villagers from NATO bombers. The prosecutor, whom Bravo Team was protecting, questioned why he had dug the hole one mile from the village. It seemed like a long way to run for shelter. He also asked if the bulldozer had filled in the hole after the entire population of the village was slaughtered and dumped into it. The Serb denied it, but he was screwed.

The trial itself was not the problem. It was the constant demonstrations, and the continued attempts to kill the defendant and his Serb defense attorney, both of whom had to be escorted in and out each day of the trial. In the middle of it all, Bravo Team was trying to slip in and out of Prizren with our package, the UN Prosecutor. We did it, but it was a mess. I hoped that this new mass grave investigation would not end up the same.

Ratkovac is about twenty-five miles south of Peja, so Bravo Team left very early and was about three miles away from the site by 0900 hours. It was a cool, bright and sunny day. I called on the radio to get Arni's sit-rep. "Bravo One, it's chaos here," he said. "Hundreds of civilians are trying to get up here. One hundred Spanish KFOR troops have blocked off the crime scene which is on a small hilltop. Fifty or so UN units are here, also."

"Arni, where should we park?"

"There is a parking area near the scene for official vehicles. I'll meet you on the road a kilometer away and guide you there."

We turned off the main road and took a secondary route into farm country before we came to the first KFOR checkpoint. The Spanish KFOR troops were unsuccessfully trying to deflect the flow of Kosovar Albanians from entering the area. We were passed through, and as we traveled the last five hundred yards on an old country path following the muddy tracks of the UN vehicles that arrived before us. On the way, we passed hundreds of villagers from all around the area ascending the hill alongside us.

Arni and D-Train met us and cleared a path to the crime scene. The Spanish military had done a better job there. The grass parking area was secured about seventy-five yards from the grave site. Soldiers in full battle dress ringed the entire area. The crowd, many carrying pictures and portraits of missing loved ones, stood silently watching as the forensic teams went about their work.

The troops kept the crowd about fifty yards from the hole. A hundred UN investigators, Pristina VIPS, and the UN prosecutor for the Peja region were crowded just inside the circle, many accompanied by their own personal security details. I noticed a number of my old friends from Spec-Ops school. The investigators stood nearest the edges of the dug up area, taking notes and doing the detective-type work I was glad to be away from this last year.

The real experts were inside the hole. These technicians were sifting through the mess of bones and rotted clothing for evidence while crime scene photographers at their sides documented the process. Forensic anthropologists were attempting to assemble and identify the bones to identify the victims. The forensic pathologists followed at their heels attempting to identify the manner of the victim's death. It was all very clinical, very efficient, and very sad.

Arni slipped next to me and said he'd overheard an investigator stating that the victims were Albanian. D-Train approached me a few minutes later, shaking his head. Pointing to a particular spot, he said, "Mike, nothing says war crime like the bones of an eight-year-old, with its wrists wired together and a bullet hole in the back of its head. Who could do such a thing?"

Thankfully, it was not be my job to find out.

After an hour or so, I walked to the command car to get a drink of water. I was glad to get away from the sickening smell rising from the upturned soil augmented by the heat of the morning sun. Igor joined me, pulled out his own tepid bottle, drained it, then elbowed me and pointed down the road. A white van was approaching. I knew instantly what it was—someone at headquarters had notified the press of the find.

The van pulled to a stop behind our cars and three men exited. Two hauled a camera and audio equipment out of the back and started marching uphill towards us. The other, wearing a suit, looked like a supervisor or manager. He wasn't hauling anything.

Then a fourth person exited. A female. She was medium height, and wore a tan military-style shirt with camouflage trousers and desert-style combat boots. She walked alongside the suit, gesturing and pointing out landmarks, I assumed, lining up background for the photo shoot. I tried, but couldn't see her face beneath the floppy wide brimmed hiking hat she was wearing though she was only a few meters away. When finally did, I instantly cracked a smile. It was Cara

Sanchez from the Grand Hotel party. "Well, hello," I said, walking over to her. "Good to see you again."

"Told you I'd be back," she said, turning to the suit. "Rupert, this is Officer Michael Granger. I am sure he's the one in charge here."

Igor turned his back, rolled his eyes, and left while I offered the pair a drink of water. The suit declined, saying, "Thanks but we've got our own in a cooler in the van."

I ignored the minor rebuff, and directed my attention back to Cara. "I suppose you are looking for the grave?"

"Yes, I was asked to do a story on it." She looked at the suit as if unsure how much she could say.

Without offering me a handshake, he said, "I'm Rupert Fullerton from CNN. We want to show a clip on TV tonight. It will be Cara's first time on screen, so we want to make sure everything is perfect."

Feeling that she was now free to open up, Cara said, "I'd like to interview you on camera, Mike. Very briefly. Is that okay?"

I'd done many interviews with news people back in the States, but this wasn't New Hampshire. "I'll have to contact headquarters about that, Cara. The public relations people will have to approve it. They're careful about these things," I replied.

"Why don't you contact them right now?" Fullerton snapped.

A lot of times, *how* something is said is way more important than *what* is actually said. The guy was not politely asking me if I would help him, he was ordering an insignificant civil servant to hop to it.

Cara read my face and immediately inserted herself in the middle. "Mike, could you do that for me? Pretty please? It would be so cool."

My attitude softened to the constituency of warm jello as it always did whenever a gorgeous woman put the words "pretty please" and "so cool" together using a sexy voice. "Yeah, sure," I replied. "I'll give it a shot. Not sure what they'll say, though."

Cara and Fullerton moved on to the site while I got on the radio to Peja RHQ. What they told me was, "No way!" The problem was this: the site we were at was unknown until the previous morning when a farmer chasing stray sheep tripped on a large bone that, because of the winter's erosion, was sticking out of the ground. He came back later with his sons, and they started digging to find more bones. He contacted the KPS and they notified the UN Initially, nobody knew for sure if the bones were animal or human. A little more digging and it was clear this was the site of a mass grave containing Kosovar Albanians killed by the Serbs, or Kosovar Serbs killed by the KLA. Both ethnic groups had scores of people missing and unaccounted for in the region. At the moment, it was a political hot potato that would soon be used by one side to brand the other as murderers. Until the all the facts were known, the UN command didn't want anybody saying anything to the press. That included me and my team.

I walked up to the gravesite and told Cara the bad news. She looked disappointed. The suit fumed and demanded I go over the head of whoever told me not to cooperate—now. Right away. Chop, chop!

By this time, I'd had enough of him. I made sure that the audio and cameras were not running, then whispered in his ear, "If you try to tell me what to do one more time, I will haul your ass out of here in handcuffs and charge you with interfering in a police matter. Got it?"

He turned beet red, but conceded with a curt nod. Cara had heard my threat, and I think she found the situation exciting: An egotistical news executive in an Armani suit versus a hot cop in a bullet-proof vest with a big gun. Who do you think she was rooting for—deep down?

Cara, though, pretended to ignore us both. Then she stepped a little too close to the edge of the excavation and her foot slipped on the soft earth. I grabbed her under the arms and pulled her back before she slid into the hole and upset the forensic evidence.

"Thanks," she said back on steady feet. "That was stupid of me."

"You might want to stay further back," I said, guiding her to a safer spot.

We watched one of the forensic cameramen below take still pictures from many angles. I never liked the crime scene photo process. I thought it kind of ghoulish. I figured that, whoever the victims, Albanian, Serb or some other Balkan tribe, they were entitled to their dignity, even if all that was left was a pile of bones.

It was a long day, and as the sun started to go down, the weather turned cold. The civilians drifted away, and the UN police and KFOR secured the area for work the next morning. The news people left as well, but not before Cara asked if I'd like to meet her for a drink that night. The memory of her in her black dress at the Grand Hotel party made up my mind for me in a heartbeat.

All the UN VIPs and the press went to Peja or Prizren for the night. Cara told me that she was staying in a secured villa in Peja. I told her I would meet her at her house and we could walk from there to a bar that I knew was safe. When I got back to my own villa, I cleaned up as best I could. No electricity, of course, and the water was freezing cold. I dressed and, before leaving, shared a warm beer with Arni. We discussed the events of the day, until, after an hour or so, I set off on foot for the center of Peja.

I had no problem finding Cara's villa. It was a nice place, lots of brick and stucco, larger than mine and a little older. It had its own electric generator and a security guard posted outside. I showed him my UN Police ID and told him that I was there to pick up Ms. Sanchez. He spoke by radio to someone inside and a minute later Cara appeared at the door.

She was wearing the same style dress that she wore at the party when we met—except this time it was bright red. I found it even sexier than the black. It was early March and there was a raw chill to the mountain air. She carried a thick sweater on her arm for a minute before putting it on. I think she was letting me view the contents of the package before covering it with wrapping.

It was twilight and the downtown streets were still busy with traffic. Couples were strolling by the stores and street vendor kiosks. This was the downtown block that shared electric generators, allowing the shops and restaurants to stay open a few hours after dark. The place I was taking her, a bar named "Black Stallion," was owned by a legitimate businessman. The KPS kept a close eye on the place to ensure that the criminal element stayed away, or at least behaved while there.

We went inside and I greeted the manager, a tough, former UCK fighter who I had come to know well. I'd not seen him since December, and he asked how Willy was doing. When I told him that Willy had left Kosovo for good, he looked sad.

I also said hello to the pudgy bouncer with a thick mustache who spent more time cleaning tables than bouncing, and asked about his wife and kids. He was one of the lucky ones in Kosovo. He had a good job: It paid well and was probably one the safest places in Peja. There were always KPS officers around, both inside and outside the establishment, if he needed backup.

We sat at a table with the view of the street. I ordered a beer and Cara red wine. The owner brought our drinks and signaled that they were on the house. Cara took a sip of wine and started laughing.

"What's so funny?"

"I'm remembering you from Pristina when you walked into the gala wearing your short sleeve shirt and Dockers. The French consul nearly had a heart attack."

"I guess it must have looked odd. I'm getting better at that sort of thing, though. I actually bought a tie and a new belt—one meant to hold up my pants. It takes a little longer to put on and get off than my gun belt."

She leaned forward and winked. "Well, practice makes perfect."

I took a long swig of beer and thought, *Now, that was certainly a fruitful exchange,* then decided to reduce the temperature a bit. "I have a question about that night, Cara. Do you remember a big Russian guy there? He was wearing a black tuxedo. We locked eyes for minute, and it turned into a sort of schoolyard stare down."

She nodded. "The bald guy with the earring."

"Yeah, that's him. What do you know about him?"

"Not much. He's a businessman, I guess. He came up to me after you left and asked who *you* were."

That got my attention. "So, what did you tell him?"

"That you were a police officer. That's all I knew about you, really."

"What did he do or say when you told him that?"

"He just sort of grunted. Then he left. It was kind of weird."

I figured it was time to let this go. The last thing I wanted on my mind that evening was KGB Bukin. "So, how did the TV clip go?"

She made an exaggerated pout. "They're not going to use it. The North Koreans decided today would be a good day to fire a missile over Japan. I can't tell you how irritated I am about that."

"North Korea, huh? Now, there's a wacky place. That's the thing about our jobs: you'll never run out of crazy stories to cover, and I'll never run out of bad guys to arrest." I lifted my glass. "Here's to job security."

She drained her wine, and I asked the owner to bring her another.

Then she leaned forward in her chair. "So, tell me about Mike Granger. The last time we talked, I think I told you my entire life story. It's your turn."

I've never been comfortable divulging information about myself to women. It always seemed to get me into trouble. Besides, my strength was my natural ability to get others to talk about themselves. Even so, I knew I had to say something, so I offered her the condensed version: "Not much to tell, Cara. I come from an average city in a small state. I believe in the New Hampshire motto, 'Live Free or Die.' I went to college and studied political science, but discovered I hate politics. I'm a registered independent, but rarely vote. I love Italian and I hate Chinese food. I preferred Hispanic women, until I discovered a natural fondness for blondes as well. I love being a cop."

The look she gave to me said, *Is that it?* She took another sip of wine. "That was an excellent police report—succinct and to the point. And you carefully avoided all the very important personal stuff, like, are you married? Divorced? Engaged? Have children? Spoken for?"

"Ah, you're right. I should have mentioned some of that. I *am* divorced *and* I recently broke up with my girlfriend. How's that for a pretty poor official record?"

"How recently?"

"The divorce or the breakup?"

"The breakup."

"The night I met you—the day that I graduated from training. You could say I'm on the rebound, I suppose."

She said she was sorry, but I could tell she wasn't really. She finished her second glass of wine, and I asked if she wanted another. She shook her head, no. "I think I'd like to go back to the house, but you'll have to escort me there, of course."

Cara knew as I did that in this deeply Muslim part of Kosovo a

194

woman walking alone, especially at night, was strongly frowned upon. When I didn't respond quickly enough she sweetened the pot. "It has electricity and other amenities if you want to come inside."

The invitation had real potential, but I decided to ratchet things up a notch just to be sure I was reading her correctly. "It's very tempting, Cara. My electricity is out again. Do you know what I miss most?"

"What?"

"A hot shower—a long hot shower."

She smiled, reached over, and touched my hand. "Well, you're in luck, Officer Granger. That happens to be one of the amenities."

It turned out to be the best shower ever. Cara made sure of it. From there, we went straight to her bed. In bed together, I suddenly felt a sudden lack of confidence. I think it the fact that she'd been married to an NFL quarterback. The subconscious question of how I would measure up in performance kept popping into the back of my mind. She figured it out quickly enough, though. While resting in my arms after our first go at it, she said, "Did you know my ex-husband was cut from his football team? He's out of a job. Not even second string anymore."

I kissed her neck and ear and said, "That's tough. I hear it's a bad time to be unemployed back in the States."

She put her arms behind her head and arched her back, stretching out her fabulous naked body in front of me."Well, I've got a job for *you* if you're interested, and it might just take the whole night."

I kissed her tight, Pilates-hardened stomach.

"You're in luck, Cara. For some jobs, I take whatever time is necessary."

Blessed are the Peacekeepers

Chapter 17

When April came to Kosovo, there was more than a change of weather. Change itself was in the wind. For example, the civilian telephone landline infrastructure had been pretty much destroyed during the war. Though attempts to fix it were in the works, availability of service was sporadic. An American company arrived during the winter and erected cell phone towers everywhere. The youth of Kosovo were thirsty for the technology, and within two months everyone who was anyone carried a cell phone. Most of my team members jumped on the bandwagon and were suddenly exchanging numbers and "connecting" socially. I was older, more set in my ways, more stubborn and more resistant to technological change, so, of course, I refused to get one.

First, I would have had to go to Pristina to sign up, and it just seemed too much of a hassle to go there. Second, I liked the idea of getting *away* from cell phones. I had been tied to them at my job back home.

Unlike New Hampshire, true spring weather starts early in the Balkans. It seemed premature to see farmers tilling the land in March, but by April I understood. With the onset of spring, the birds reappeared, especially the blackbirds that had spent the winter months tucked away in nests in the nooks and crannies of heated buildings. The young people of Peja, who loved American fashions, also appeared and started walking the roadways and city blocks again.

In Peja, only a small percentage of the population had cars. With the huge influx of foreign humanitarian aid, the people of Kosovo began to eat well and cheap. It was a clean, healthy environment as long as you didn't get shot or blown up. Unfortunately, spring was also the time when the bad guys started up their shit again, digging out the hidden weapon caches that had been stored for the winter and preparing to settle old scores. The uptick in violence included domestic assaults, gangland assassinations, and attacks on Serb enclaves. Even foreigners who were there to help the nation recover weren't safe.

One day, Peja Station received a cell phone call from an isolated village on the outskirts of the city. The caller was an elderly sister who ran a combination Christian school and home for war orphans. Someone had apparently attacked the place with hand grenades, and the caller was pleading for help. Then the phone went dead.

All RHQ knew was that someone needed to go there fast. The UN Police and KPS tried driving there, but had to turn back because the roads had been washed out. Consequently, the UN Police in Peja asked for a Spec-Op team to get out there immediately. The team would be relieved the following day by the Italian military.

It was around 1000 hours and my team was on standby. I was on the computer, reading my emails at the time. The one occupying my attention was from Lieutenant Law, my commander from the Manchester Police Department. It said that the court unit that assists the District Attorney's Office had an opening for a detective. Lt. Law wanted to know if I wanted to transfer to that unit when I returned in September, as I had both priority and seniority. It was a good job, but a desk job, and I was a street cop. He knew it, so the fact that it was being offered bothered me. Bottom line, I was being asked to go out to pasture. I had been gone from the department for a long time, and there had been changes, and I was out of sight and probably out of mind. I wasn't mad, just upset that they viewed me as ready for retirement when here in Kosovo I was leading a Spec-Op team, rappelling from helicopters and quelling riots with officers half my age.

I emailed a buddy on the force who gave me the background story: Seems a couple of the young eager-beaver patrol cops had been filling in for me and were jockeying for my job, which I'd been assured was being held for me upon my return. I can't blame them really, because a detective job is the best one in the force, and the ultimate end-goal for many good street cops.

I had just printed a copy of the email and stuffed it in my pocket when Jim Durfer dashed in and gave me the word on the crisis at the orphanage. "Mike," he said. "Get your team together. Leave your three drivers behind. Briefing in five minutes."

The briefing was quick. It was little more than a map check and sit-rep: Bravo Team would off-load at the end of the roadway. From there, it was a two mile hike to the village. We would approach the village from behind so that any bad guys planning a rude reception would be thrown off-guard. It would be me and my choice of six operators in full combat load, with the green light to go in as hard as necessary. We were to secure the orphanage, and wait for relief the next morning. Anyone who got in our way or interfered with the mission was to be terminated.

Terminated? I thought. *Not arrested or neutralized, but terminated!* That got my attention. I would have to rush to assemble my team and get them there before anything further happened.

The good news was that a NATO helicopter flyover, just before the weather got bad, showed nothing amiss in the village. They even saw kids playing in the school courtyard, according to Durfer, so maybe it was a hoax call, or a set up? Either way, it didn't matter to me or my team. Our job was to be prepared for the worst, and execute the mission quickly and efficiently as we were trained to do.

Within a half hour, we were loaded and almost to the drop-off point. I left Mo and D-Train behind, as they were drivers, but I had Rick with me as my point man for the overland approach.

I decided to leave Sandy, our temporary driver, with the vehicle and stand radio watch. To be honest, despite all her toughness, she was still a woman to me. I know it's old fashioned and wrong, but as a father with sons who were nearly her age, she was a young woman who hadn't yet had the opportunity of having children of her own. I didn't want to have to meet her parents at a funeral and try to explain why I placed their daughter in harm's way. If this is sexist reasoning by an out-of-touch dinosaur, then so be it. She could hate me or love me for leaving her behind, but I had made up my mind. I told her I needed Rick, so she would stay. Sandy knew that Rick and I had a history going back to the firefight up in the mountains, so she swallowed her pride and accepted the order. At least she appeared to. This time in front of the others, she acted like a trooper.

It was a warm day with a light drizzle, perfect for inserting a team without being detected. We were ready for anything. As I looked the team over, including Igor who was quietly sharpening a Spetsnaz combat knife, I actually felt bad for anyone who decided to mess with us. With Rick at the point and Arni as Bravo Two right behind him, we moved into the forested hills single file. Igor was third. I figured to use Igor and Arni to eliminate any bad sentry guards, if necessary. I was in the command middle with Paddy covering me. Hammer and Nails took up the rear.

We took our time, skirting the obvious trails and any usual

approaches to the village. We were quiet, invisible, and methodical. The misty overcast weather covered our approach, and kept us from getting too hot. We arrived at the far side of the village and scanned the twenty-five or so small houses. The school complex was easy to spot. It consisted of a two-story building with a smaller cement schoolhouse, an attached dormitory, and another structure that looked like a garage. In the small courtyard was a white Range Rover with a blue dove painted on the door.

The facility was surrounded by an eight-foot-high whitewashed cement wall, with a ten-foot iron gate at the entrance. The village seemed peaceful but deserted. Most likely the people were indoors because of the light rain. I couldn't see inside the walls of the school, but didn't observe any obvious damage from an attack. Then, I saw a young woman lead a group of children from the school house to the main house as if on a Sunday morning stroll.

Arni scooted next to me. "Mike, are you sure we're at the right place? It looks like nothing is wrong here."

I shrugged. "We're on target. Let's find out what's going on."

I made a simple plan on the fly. Hammer and Nails would stake out the back side of the walled compound. Igor, Paddy, and I would approach by the front gate. Arni and Rick would slip over the wall on the west side of the compound and open the gate for us. We would enter as a team, gather all the occupants into the main house, and then figure out the situation. It sounded simple enough but my hackles suddenly rose, and I gave a quick warning. "Be careful. No bloodshed unless necessary. Get ready to move."

Before we went in, Arni asked me what else was on my mind. He said it seemed like something was bothering me. Though it did not seem the proper time or place, I showed him the email from my lieutenant in the States. Here I was, all set to enter into who knew what kind of danger, dressed to kill, with my team of elite cops who had just humped two miles through reportedly bad guy territory.

"They want to put me out to pasture back home," I told him.

Arni buried his head in his sleeve to stifle his laughter.

Six minutes later, we were through the gate and hustling the occupants of the school buildings into the living room of the main house. While Hammer and Nails cleared all the outer buildings of any threat, and Igor and Arni swept the second floor, I surveyed the group in front of me: one gray-haired woman, about seventy years old who was the spitting image of a postcard Mrs. Santa Claus right down to the smile and jolly red cheeks; a dozen frightened kids under the age of ten; five young women, all about twenty years old who looked at us with disdain, maybe even loathing.

I looked at my team. We had black-painted faces, dark stocking watch caps, and were bristling with weapons. We were caked in mud and must have looked extremely frightening. We had invaded a peaceful orphanage with stunning speed and efficiency, and were scaring the shit out of everyone, except, apparently, Mrs. Claus.

She spoke first. Looking me directly in the eyes, she said in proper British English, "That was a wonderful rescue effort, Captain. You scared the girls and children a little bit, but I am very impressed. You can have your men relax now, as the situation here is no longer dangerous." She turned to the children and teachers assembled behind her and announced, "Children, these nice soldiers have come to help us. Please thank them for putting on such a good show for us."

As she started clapping, the children relaxed, and clapped right along, finally bowing as a sign of greeting and respect. The woman then turned to the teachers.

"Ladies, would you please take the children back to the school house and have them continue with their studies. The captain and I need to talk."

With that, four of the teachers led the children outside. I ordered Bravo team to stand down, but posted Rick and Paddy outside as perimeter security with Igor at the front gate just in case.

One teacher stayed. Rick, of course, did his instant switch from soldier to paramour, making eyes at the young teachers as they departed the house. I explained to the two remaining woman that we were not soldiers, but a Spec-Op team from the UN Police, responding to a cell phone call for help. Our orders were to secure the compound until the next morning. Mrs. Santa Claus' eyes twinkled and she nodded that she understood completely. Then held out her hand to me.

"I am Sister Margaret from the Anglican Church of England. Our missionary work often takes us into war zones to establish safe havens for war orphans. My helpers, including Sarah here, are college students who volunteer for a six-month sabbatical from school and receive teaching credit for their work."

I checked out Sarah. She looked really cute with her reddish hair and freckles. She was thin and wore a light sweater, white cotton slacks, and running shoes. She had a nice smile.

"I'm Officer Mike Granger," I said to the two women, "and this is Arni Knudsen, my second in command."

"Wonderful! An American and a Dane—it's a pleasure to meet you both," said Sister Margaret. "This is this group of ladies' first charity work, and they are not used to seeing such displays of military precision. Several come from backgrounds that are not particularly police or military friendly. I will address this matter over dinner. You will be staying with us for dinner? But, yes, of course you will: Your mission requires that you stay until tomorrow. We will serve breakfast to you as well."

I was dumbstruck. This affable woman had clearly been around soldiers and danger before, yet she didn't seem nervous or concerned about us. All I could manage in reply was, "That will be fine, Ma'am."

"Brilliant!" she concluded, sitting, and, with a sweeping gesture of her arm, inviting us to do the same. "Now, here's what happened. This morning a young chap threw an explosive over the wall into the courtyard and it rolled under our Range Rover out there. It blew out all the tires, but the girls and I have already changed them with spares. Whenever I set up a new place, I always have the locals weld a steel plate on the bottom of the Rover, and collect as many replacement tires as I can. It helps in case of rough terrain or land mines. I learned that trick long ago in Vietnam."

Arni, Hammer, Nails, and I sat awestruck by this plump old British woman who seemed to know more about the craft of self-protection than we did. I also noticed Arni and Sarah smiling at each other. *Good, he's safely switched off*, I thought.

"The village lad had apparently become smitten with one of my young ladies, and became angry when she didn't return his interest. The village men at this very moment have him secured until the local constable arrives to speak with him. So you can see that it really is all safe now, Captain. May I call you Mike?"

"Of course, Sister," I replied. "Since we will be staying for the night, could you make a place for the men to sleep?"

"Oh, that won't be a problem. No problem at all. We have lots of space and plenty of blankets."

"Good," I said. "Now, can you tell me where the suspect is being held?"

"The lad is at the village headman's hut. Down the road a bit. Do you want to see him?"

"Yes, I do. I won't be long."

I asked Arni if he wanted to come with me, but he declined. "I think Bravo Two should stay here, Mike," he said, "so I can make sure that your orders are followed." He said it with a serious voice, but his eyes were solidly locked on Sarah, who was preening her long red hair.

I whispered to him, "Pay attention to the rooftops, not the sidewalks." In other words, do your job and stop being distracted.

He just grinned back at me. I could see I was wasting my breath.

I told him to order Bravo Team at ease, but to keep at least two men on watch at all times. Then Igor and I washed our faces clean of the black face paint and donned our blue berets.

Along the way to the headman's hut, Igor volunteered, "Mike, it's going to be a long night. There are seven of us men and five pretty young women. We must be careful."

"Five? You left out Sister Margaret."

"Oh, she is for you. After all, you're the one in charge."

After serving us tea, the village headman led us into a back room where we found the teenager in question sitting on a bed. He was being watched by an unarmed middle-aged farmer. The villagers had obviously given him a beating, and it looked like they might have broken his right hand in the process.

"He will stay with us until the Kosovo police take him," the elder said. "There will be no more problem. Sister Margaret said that she will not press charges."

Satisfied that local justice was being served, Igor and I walked back to the teacher's compound. It was now about four o'clock in the evening and the rain had stopped. Arni and the rest of the team were looking very smart and professional, all cleaned up, wearing their blue berets—and definitely trying to flirt with the young teachers.

The girls were rebuffing any small talk, but at least were no longer glaring at my men like before. The only one of my guys who looked totally at ease was Rick. He was playing with the children while, at the same time, slowly shifting ever closer to one dark-haired teacher of Asian descent. I didn't bother to reprimand Rick because the kids were having such a great time and I could see no harm in a little flirtation. I just wondered if and when I was going to have to start drawing lines.

Igor and I went inside and sat with Sister Margaret, who had prepared afternoon tea, English style, and was awaiting our return. "And how is the lad?" she asked.

"Well, I think he's going to need some medical attention. It looks like he resisted arrest."

"Oh, dear," she said. "Should I go and see?"

"I think the villagers have it under control. They seem to like you. Maybe you should let them resolve this for you—to keep face."

She thought awhile, then said, "Yes. Yes, that would be the sensible thing."

We sipped our tea while she recounted for us some of her previous missions and experiences. Igor and I were nothing less than fascinated. She told us she had started her missionary orphan work in the 1960's in Vietnam, then was sent to Cambodia and later, Laos. From there, she had gone to Africa—all the rough places there like Angola, the Congo, Zimbabwe, and Sierra Leone. After that, it was South and Central America for seven years. Now she was here in Kosovo. She went into each place either during the fighting or right afterwards with troops from the peacekeeping forces. She and her many Range Rovers had been everywhere, she told us. Her only breaks in service, were when she went back to England to meet with her church superiors, report on successes and failures, and recruit new college girls.

Sister Margaret, I discovered later, had become a legend. She'd been bombed, beaten, and, once, even kidnapped and held for ransom by Columbian guerillas. Widowed at thirty and without any children, she spent the next forty years of her life doing humanitarian work in war zones. She spoke of the many wonderful orphans she'd had the pleasure of helping over the years, and how some had become quite financially successful and were now helping fund her missions. She also spoke with fondness of the brave college kids who volunteered to go on missions with her, going unarmed into some of the worst hell-holes on earth. She said nothing of her own sacrifice and charity, though.

Igor got up from the table and whispered to me, "This woman is an angel," and, stifling a sniffle, went outside to compose himself.

I thought, *Christ, if Igor is choked up, then this lady must really be special.*

Relaxed, tea cup and saucer in hand, she talked more about her work. I have always been fascinated by military operations, but had never really given much thought to the roles of the NGOs—non-governmental organizations—that served the world's war-torn populations. We had our role, and it was important in the big picture, but they made a difference in the lives of individuals. Then suddenly, Sister Margaret switched gears on me."Mike, you and I may have some close supervision to do tonight. Your team is made up of handsome strong men and my girls are young and beautiful. They have not encountered Western men for many months, and I would imagine that your men have also been occupied with work. Do you understand what I'm saying?"

I certainly did. I assured her that my men were professional police officers, and wondered if it was a sin to lie to a nun by saying that that I could keep them all in line.

"Mike, I think you've misunderstood me. I don't want you to be shepherd to your men, and I've no plans to lock the girls away in a

207

room. What I meant was that I think you and I should…let things take their natural course. Within reason."

I nodded, more than a little concerned at what that course might turn out to be.

"I am just an old lady, but my assistants have a lot of life yet to experience. They deserve some harmless attention. Now we shall have a communal dinner, and I hope that you will agree to share some of the fine local wine with us."

Six of the children went home to their extended families. Six others ate dinner, then were marched up to the second floor bedroom before the teachers and my team sat down to a full home-made meal complete with red wine. Only Arni was missing. He had volunteered to stand guard outside in the compound courtyard while we ate. He was soon joined by Sarah, the lead teacher, who thoughtfully brought Arni a dish of lamb and salad greens.

Sister Margaret stood to address the remaining teachers and my team. "We welcome these young men into our home to share our food and hospitality," she said. "We must thank God for the presence of these peacekeepers and the other members of the police and military who risk their lives to protect us. Without their help, we would not be able to do our work. They pave the way for our Christian ministry and make the path safe for us to help the poor little children who suffer so much in war."

Then she did something I will never forget. She requested that each of her teachers personally thank us for becoming a peacekeeper and coming that day to their orphanage to help. They did as instructed and maybe for the first time understood that we were the good guys.

The last girl to speak, a tall brown-haired British lass, raised her wine glass and said, simply, "God bless the peacekeepers."

We all clinked our glasses together and drank up.

Sister Margaret then asked me to say something on behalf of my team. I thanked the teachers for preparing the meal for us and told them that we admired their charity work. With glass filled again, I stood up and said, "Bravo Team, please rise." I waited while they stood to attention, wine glass in hand.

"To Sister Margaret," I toasted. "Your kindness and forty years of good work is an inspiration to my team and me. I know you're modest and humble, but you're also the bravest person I've ever met."

She tried to wave me off, but I was not having any of it. I finished with, "Sister, it has been my honor to meet you. You are truly one of God's angels."

Paddy said, "Hear. Hear," and we all drained our glasses.

I meant every word I said. If there is a heaven, then that woman and the too few others out there like her deserve a seat at the head table.

The meal finished, my next challenge was to keep a lid on things. I took my guys aside and told everyone to behave. Of course, nobody listened. It was about as effective as a father lecturing a teenage son before a date—nothing there but deaf ears, and my guys didn't even bother to *pretend* to hear me.

At ten o'clock or so, we all settled in on couches and cots that had been prepared with sheets and pillows by the girls. I set up a schedule to have two men on watch throughout the night on two hour shifts. One operator would be on the second floor front room balcony, the other in the kitchen watching the back area of the compound. Both positions had excellent views. I slept on a couch next to the balcony and would stand watch there from midnight until two.

Sister Margaret said she would wake us at 0600 hours for breakfast. I went to sleep immediately, leaving Arni to keep watch on the balcony. I slept fully clothed with my gear within arm's reach.

At midnight, Arni woke me and said it was time for my watch. As I got up and he left the room, I saw Sarah standing in the doorway. I figured, okay, they were both adults. While I stood watch on the balcony, I saw Rick and his new friend sneak out of the school house and hustle into the first floor of the main house directly underneath.

What was I supposed to do? I didn't want to make a scene and wake up Sister Margaret. "For crying out loud," I said aloud, noticing one of my men and a teacher in the back seat of the Range Rover. I gave up, and pretended not to see. At 0200 hours, I went back to bed after Igor relieved me on the balcony.

As I tried to go back to sleep, I heard bare feet all over the house, and tried to convince myself that it was just the ladies visiting my men on guard duty, talking with them to help them stay awake. By three o'clock, I finally fell asleep.

The next morning, we ate breakfast together at the large table. It was very quiet at first, and I waited for the reprimand that I thought was sure to come from the woman I so greatly admired.

Sister Margaret broke the ice. "Well," she said, "I hope we all got some sleep last night. The poor little children must have been so excited about seeing the soldiers yesterday. I could hear them running pitter patter to the bathroom all night long." She said it with a twinkle in her eye while all her young teachers stared at their plates and tried not to giggle, while my men hid their own grins behind napkins.

Then she offered a prayer. "Dear Lord, thank you for our food this morning, and for this much needed visit from our new friends on Bravo Team."

I almost choked on my toast. I said my own silent prayer that everyone involved used common sense and protection. A little later the KPS cavalry arrived in three muddy patrol cars, escorted by a pair of Italian KFOR vehicles. Bravo Team returned to Peja, and back to our "normal" routine.

Blessed are the Peacekeepers

Chapter 18

Spring was in full bloom; the weather was consistently balmy and beautiful. The hills around Peja glowed a deep summery green, and the fields were teeming with brightly colored wildflowers. My only concern was that the early warm spell was likely a harbinger of a hotter than usual summer.

Bravo Team was busy working our regularly assigned escort and bodyguard missions. Arni started teaching martial arts classes on his radio watch days, and his first students were three of the young women from the orphanage, including his new friend, Sarah.

As a result, our once-quiet villa began to take on the character of a college frat house. On the warmer nights, we borrowed a generator to power up the place and hosted cookouts with music from a mobile karaoke system that the Filipino officers had brought with them. It was their most cherished possession, and Rick made us treat it like it was a Stradivari violin, which was difficult since the people who handled the microphone were usually hammered.

Billy Ray and his friends, the six-man Filipino contingent, Arni and his trio of budding warrior women, Jim Durfer, Alpha Team, most of Bravo Team, and the UN judge's female staff, all became regulars at our villa. After-work hours were becoming one big party. Life was good.

Just when it seemed like the final third leg of my mission in

Kosovo might be one of ease, routine, and relaxation, Jim Durfer called me into his office, signaling me to shut the door after I entered. As I sat down, Jim leaned back in his chair and clasped his hands behind his head. "Mike," he said, "RHQ is planning a big operation in Djakovica. Three Spec-Op teams will be assisting the local police. Looks like we're in, though I'm not at liberty to share the details."

I was thrilled to have a break from the routine. "When will we know?"

He could see I was excited and frustrated. He leaned forward and glanced over my shoulders as if he was about to tell me a secret he didn't want anybody else to hear. "There will be a special briefing with NATO and UN reps in two days. You will be asked to attend. Everything is being played close to the vest for now, so don't tell anyone on your team anything."

"What? Are we going to take down the Mafia?" I joked.

Jim didn't laugh. "I'll just let you know when and where the briefing will be when it's time," he said.

I went back to my office, took out my map, and tried to recall everything I knew about Djacovica. I had passed through it many times on high escort runs to Prizren. There was a two-lane main road from Peja to the Prizren province capital that ran for about fifty mostly straight miles. The industrial city of Djacovica was at the midway point. Intel consistently designated that area as a red zone. It had a long history of KLA bad guy activity.

Djacovica was a short five miles from the Albanian border, and during the Serbian War, was a major hub of guerilla warfare. KLA headquarters was located in this area, and some of the worst of the KLA bad guys had sprung from there. The men there were a mixture of big healthy farm boys, and tough factory workers.

After the war, some of the Djacovica-based KLA turned to the dark side and became local Albanian Mafia bosses. They ran the criminal end of the post-war activity including drug smuggling, weapons smuggling, and the newest post-war enterprise, the white slave trade: forced female and child prostitution. It was a place that regularly needed cleaning up.

Two nights later, after everyone had left for the night, I reported as instructed earlier that day for the briefing. I passed through a security checkpoint on the top floor and was directed to a large office. When I entered, I saw a large map on the center conference table. The room was filled with high ranking UN and military officers. The lowest ranking officers in the room were the three Spec Ops team captains, one of which was me. We three introduced ourselves to each other and sat quietly in a corner listening until summoned for our part of the briefings.

Colonel Alexi, the UN Peja Regional Police Commander started the briefing flanked by a NATO military colonel and a lesser UN Police official. With barely a trace of a Russian accent, he began: "Djacovica is overrun with criminal activity. It is time to take back control. At 2100 hours tomorrow night, we intend to lock down the entire city. Specialized teams will simultaneously raid key mafia and KLA strongholds. Though we hope to stop all criminal activity, we are specifically targeting weapons depots and suspected slave trader locations."

After some additional instructions including the need for secrecy, he turned the briefing over to the Intel Specialists from Pristina. They told us that the KPS were not going to be informed of the raids until one hour before the start time and only after all their cell phones had been confiscated. The large scale operation would involve close to a thousand men and women. It was going to be a major show.

A half hour was spent giving us the latest intel on the explosive growth of the white slave trade throughout Kosovo. We were told that the bad guys who ran the forced prostitution operations were exceedingly violent and would be well armed. Two hours into the briefing, the commanders of the involved units were dismissed, with the exception of a few top commanders, an intelligence specialist, and the three Spec-Op team leaders. We were given a separate briefing. A more detailed map of the city was produced. There were nine high priority targets. Each team would be assigned three to hit, one after another.

Each team would consist of at least ten men backed by a specialized military unit to provide additional firepower. Bravo Team would be backed up by forty Russian Spetsnaz commandoes attached to Military Intelligence—the GRU. This specialized unit would be under the command of a Russian major whom I would meet at our first staging point.

Bravo's targets for the raid would include a weapons cache, a boarding house where trafficked women were thought to be held captive, and a combination restaurant-brothel that was the headquarters of the local Albanian Mafia kingpin. The Intel Specialist warned us that the prostitutes would likely include young children.

The intelligence specialist then handed me a profile packet on the kingpin my team was targeting. He headed the drug and human trafficking part of the Djacovica mob. His name was Luftar Abazi, forty-two years old, six-foot-two, and a hefty two-hundred-fifty pounds. Included in the file was an Albanian police photo that showed him with a hostile expression, predator eyes, close-cropped hair and a trim goatee. I'd seen a million mug-shots over the years and his screamed out that he was one mean dangerous bastard.

An Intel guy saw me studying Abazi's features and said, "He's a ruthless pimp and murderer. Pure scum."

"Yeah, I picked up on that," I replied distantly.

I scanned the Intel packet text and found a very interesting paragraph near the end. It said that Albanian and Russian mobs were involved in an increasingly nasty post-war power struggle in northern Kosovo. And it mentioned a name that caught my attention. It said that Abazi's main competitor was a new arrival on the scene, a Russian-Albanian mobster named Milosh Bukin, a.k.a KGB.

I pointed out his name to the Intel officer.

"What do you know about this guy?"

He shrugged. "Not a lot, yet," he said. "He keeps his hands clean, but there are a lot of stories. Some say he's worse than Abazi."

I read on. It seemed the competition was heating up, and that dead bodies were piling up from both camps, some of them headless, a Luftar Abazi trademark. I thought that maybe this Abazi guy wasn't so bad if he hates a guy wo would like to see me dead. The enemy of my enemy, right?

As I read on, however, I found that Abazi was not only a bona fide killer, but probably insane as well. He was a rabid football fan and a big supporter of the Albanian national team. The report recounted a story that had been circulating regarding a beef with another mobster who made a denigrating remark about the Albanian team. According to the story, a couple days later, Abazi allegedly sliced off the guy's head and personally kicked it like a soccer ball into a net goal at a city playground. Abazi's part in the story was never proven, though, a severed head was found in exactly the spot indicated.

I could care less if Abazi was nuts or not. The Djakovica operation sounded exciting, and I was going to get the chance to work with Russian elite commandoes. I wrote myself a note to remember to bring my camera. If I was lucky, maybe I could get a group picture of the Spetsnaz unit and Bravo Team. I thought it would help to spice up the scrapbook.

The mission briefing continued late into the night. I went home and filled in Arni, my Bravo Two. My other roommate, Billy Ray, was already asleep which was good because I was not allowed to discuss the mission with him, anyway. Arni and I spoke briefly and decided that all of Bravo Team should take part in this one. No exceptions. By no exception, I was, of course, referring to Sandy. The only question remaining was how much of a grudge she might be carrying over my slight on the orphanage mission. She didn't seem to be the forgetful or forgiving type.

Early the next day, Bravo Team assembled in our squad bay. While the others waited, Arni and I met a final time with Jim Durfer in his office. I relayed all the data I had received the previous night and presented him my game plan. Jim reviewed the plans and gave his immediate approval, adding that he would obtain a sledge hammer and bolt cutter for use that night. He ordered me to send everyone home after I briefed Bravo Team. He wanted no leaks, and for us to rest up and be sharp for the night operation. Jim's only regret was that he couldn't come with us. Command obligations in Peja took precedence.

Arni and I returned to the room where the rest of the team had gathered. I planned on a quick half-hour briefing, sending everyone home afterwards as Commander Durfer had instructed. What I didn't expect was for the briefing to turn into a leadership challenge.

I had come to like everyone on the team to varying degrees, but easily the most likable for me was Paddy Burke. He was totally dependable in any situation. He was quiet, humble and laid-back almost to the point of appearing lazy. Paddy was thoughtful, the kind of guy who would hold the door open for the whole group, and always remembered to wish everyone a good day or evening. He was a please and thank you sort of guy who spoke with a soft, pleasant Irish brogue and never picked a fight, except, it seemed, whenever Sandy Wright got in his face—which seemed to be happening more and more often.

Sandy was a talented cop. She was attractive, tough, athletic and blonde as well. She had passed the special operations training course falling somewhere in the middle of all the male candidates—and she did it legitimately. The only concern I had with Sandy was her disdain for authority figures. She had supreme confidence in herself, and was not very accepting of criticism, hence the moniker, "Sandy Wright— Can Never be Wrong," that followed wherever she went. Like I said, she was a good cop, and I was always glad to have her around in a pinch, but, unfortunately, at this moment, I happened to be an authority figure.

Paddy Burke wasn't an authority figure. However, his being Irish, super-intelligent, and soft-spoken, and her being British, brash and overtly aggressive made for a caustic mix. Sandy began to openly critique the plan I had devised and had just been accepted by my boss. Then she pushed aggressively for her own which she thought was a better one. In her frank assessment, my plan was a "cock-up," the British equivalent of our FUBAR—Fucked Up Beyond All Reason.

Paddy, who must have reached his Sandy saturation point early that day, cut her off in mid-sentence. "Sure, then," he said, "it must be true what I heard: that the Queen of England has abdicated the throne, and they've anointed a certain London police matron in her place."

"Shut your bloody mouth, you sorry Mick," Sandy spat back at him.

Paddy smiled, unmoved, and replied, "Now, it's true enough that I'm sorrier than most, but you haven't answered the question, Sandra. Have you accepted the position yet, or are you planning on a bit of diplomacy training first?"

I watched her face redden as she glared at Paddy. I expected her to erupt in a loud cursing tantrum, but she bit her tongue for the moment, and turned on me. "You're supposed to be in charge here. Why can't you keep these briefings under control?"

I shrugged, but could see out of the corners of my eyes amused or curious looks on the faces of the rest of the team members as they waited for me to respond.

"Sandy," I said, "You're right, I *am* in charge. And we are going to use the plan I developed and our boss has approved. I thank you for your input, though," and turned to Paddy. "One change, though. Paddy, I'd like you to be first in the doors of targets one and two tonight. The success of this plan requires perfect timing. You're the best we have in that department. I'll be first in at target three. Are you okay with that?"

Paddy grinned and nodded in the affirmative. "That I am, Captain," he said.

"Good."

I then turned to my two German teammates who looked confused. "Hammer, you to take out the doors with the sledgehammer as usual. Nails will back you up with the bolt cutter, if needed."

Turning to Rick, I said, "I'd like you to take Paddy's original position, okay?" It had been next to Sandy.

Rick shrugged. He'd been the first one in so many times, he had nothing to prove. At first, Hammer seemed a little uneasy when I revised the original plan, but I knew that he had confidence in Paddy and everything would be okay. The others either wore the awed look of someone watching a budding King Solomon in action, or were sensing that I was in full no bullshit mode.

I looked over at the testy Brit and asked her, "You okay with the plan, Sandy?"

I could see the wheels turning in her head. I thought she might be calculating that she'd pushed too far this time, or maybe that if Paddy took one in the face during the raid she would be responsible. She may dislike him, but she surely didn't want him dead. What could she say? Poker-faced, she acquiesced.

I told everyone to head home, review their roles, and get some rest. I wasn't finished with Sandy, though, and asked her to stay behind. After everyone but the two of us had departed, I closed the door, took my seat, and faced her directly. She had a challenging look on her face, as always. I offered her a cigarette and she accepted. I lit hers, then mine, and we settled in for what I suspected would be a tense ten minutes.

"Sandy, we've got a problem." I finally said. "I get that you think you could do this job better than me." It was both a statement and a challenge.

"Yes, I do," she replied flatly.

"You could have thought about your answer for a moment first."

"I didn't have to."

"Okay, here's my problem. I have ten Alpha males on this team. Now, I don't know what I am exactly, but I'm pretty sure that it's somewhere a bit further back in the Greek alphabet. Then, I have you acting like Wonder Woman with PMS. You're a good cop, maybe a great cop, but you can't question everything I do in front of the whole team. It just isn't right."

I could see from her frown that she was not going to give any ground. "If you don't like being challenged by a woman, maybe you need to grow a bigger set..."

"Okay, let's not make this personal," I said, cutting her off.

While she took a long drag on her cigarette, I asked myself what Commander Tony would do in this situation. He'd probably smile and let her know that she was appreciated, then in a very subtle way indicate that she should work at improving her people skills.

But, I wasn't Tony.

"Sandy, you can be part of this team, or you can move on," I said. "It's up to you. I'll support either choice, but if you choose to stay, you'll have to respect my position. It's that simple."

She stared at me in silence. I couldn't tell if she was about to reach over and strangle me or cry, so I persisted. "Which is it? What do you want to do?"

"Stay."

"Do you agree to save your criticism for the appropriate time? I'll always listen to what's on your mind, but you can't cut me up in front of the others."

Silence.

"Well?" I asked.

"Yes, I agree."

I extended a hand. "Good. I really want you on my team, Sandy. You're one of the best cops I've ever known. And I mean that."

She gave my hand a limp squeeze. I could see she was starting to tear up. "For what it's worth, I don't really think this mission will be a cock-up," she said. "I just thought it could be done better."

"We'll see," I replied, and repeated with resolve, "We'll see."

The confrontation with Sandy made me to go over the entire plan in my mind several times more just in case I'd really missed something. The operation was simple in design, but, of course, would be more difficult in the execution. At predesignated assembly points five miles outside Djakovica, the military units would gather and prepare. To an observer, it would look like another of the many maneuvers that occur in the area with regularity. At quarter to nine, the military units would surround the city and block all exit and entry points. KPS units would join the military at roadblocks to assist with language issues, searches, and arrests.

While this military ring was being placed around the city, UN Police and KPS units would patrol the streets, and establish checkpoints within the city, stopping any suspicious vehicles. Simultaneously, the three special operations teams, with their military backup units would hit their pre-established targets. Bravo Team would assemble inside the city at a secret location and join with Russian support as well as one undercover UN Intel vehicle. Two UN agents and an Albanian informer would be inside the UN Intel car. They would point out the target building and do a drive-by to further assess the situation.

If we received the clear sign, Bravo Team, a block away, would exit our three vehicles and approach the location on foot in single file. Hammer and Nails would breach the doorway, and while they covered the door, the rest of the team with Paddy in the lead would enter and secure the location. The Russian commander would be watching our entry. Once we were inside, his men would surround the building and standby in case we needed help. After the entire location, inside and out, was secured the UN investigators would arrive and conduct the arrests. That was Plan A, and as anyone who has done this kind of thing before knows, Plan A never goes right, and most of the time Plan B goes to shit as well. Plan C usually works because Plan C is to just wing it, after the other plans go haywire. I had been on raids where nobody told us about the canal between us and the building, where we hit the wrong building entirely, and where we hit the right building but couldn't breach the door. Like Murphy's Law says, anything can go wrong, and at least half the time, it does.

In our case, timing was critical. As soon as the raids started, word would spread and the guilty would begin to flee. We had three locations to hit. I wanted to hit the restaurant/brothel first, but was overruled by the UN command. If we were going to catch anyone in the third site, we would have to hustle through the first two. I felt our chances of catching anyone at the last stop were zero to none, but I vowed to pull out all stops to try. After all, that was where the big prize, Luftar Abazi, was.

Our ride to Djakovica, highlighted by a splendid Balkan sunset, was uneventful. At dusk, we met the Russians and UN Intel team in an abandoned factory near the city center. Igor couldn't keep still. He was utterly thrilled to be working with his countrymen again, and especially a Spetsnaz team. He was pumped up. I figured it was like me getting to work on a mission with a U.S. Navy SEAL team.

The Russian Spetsnaz unit was everything I imaged: All of them were fit warriors, wolf-like and emotionless. After formal greetings and introductions, we got right down to business. Arni and I, the Spetsnaz major and his second-in-command, and the Intel team set our maps side-by-side to get oriented. At kick off time, we would race like hell, convoy style, to the first target. The Russians and my team would dismount, while the UN team did their drive by. Then we would go in.

The only change to the plan came when the Russian commander demanded that two of his best go in with my entry team. One would keep in radio contact with the commander. In broken English and Russian told his two men that I was "the boss." He slapped me on the chest as he spoke so they would understand who he meant. The slap practically knocked the wind out of me. When I got my breath back, I shook my head to let the major know I was not at all happy about having those guys go in with us. They were an unknown to me and had not practiced entries with us. I thought it could be dangerous.

Igor stepped up and said he would stay near them so that there would be no problems. He went on to quickly instruct them on our drill protocols. I could tell that they were fast learners and soon felt a little better about it. We stood down and watched the clock tick off the minutes. I was excited and anxious, mostly that I would screw up somewhere, or forget something important. I kept thinking of Sandy and wondering whether she was right as we double-checked our gear, mounted up our vehicles, and waited for the signal. At 2100 hours sharp, D-Train pulled out of the parking lot and the convoy sped the five blocks to our first target, the weapons cache. It was an old wooden boathouse on a river bank. The raid went off without a hitch. We were inside and done securing the place in less than ten minutes. No bad guys, no lookouts, and as far as I could tell no weapons, either.

We waited impatiently for the UN Police and KPS investigators to arrive to conduct a more thorough search and examination as planned. After five minutes, I grabbed the UN Intel guy and asked, "Where the hell are the UN cops? I'm not waiting here another minute. Time is ticking by. I wanted to be at the next target by now."

The Russian major overheard me. He said he would leave a squad of his men to hold the fort so we should move on to target number two. The vote was two to one against the UN Intel guy who wanted to wait, so we mounted back up and drove like madmen to the next objective.

Plan A was still sort of working. The second target was the boarding house for prostitutes. It was actually two connected apartments right in the downtown center, on the second floor of an old Communist-style apartment building. We hit it fast and hard, and found the place as empty as a church on Super Bowl Sunday. Nobody was inside, though outside the streets were pandemonium. Our military-like strike had stirred up the entire neighborhood and over a hundred on-lookers lined the sidewalks.

Arni, Igor and the Russian major came up to me. Igor said, "Mike, they were probably tipped off. If not, they will be now, for sure." Amidst all the chaos, the UN Police showed up. I checked my watch. We were forty minutes into the raids. A quick look inside the apartments revealed that at least ten young girls had been living squeezed together into one small room. We jumped into our cars and sped to target three, the restaurant-brothel headquarters of Abazi. Plan A was still on track, though, so far, we hadn't found a single criminal to arrest.

I had given myself a one hour window for the first two hits, and it was now five minutes to ten. I really didn't want to go back to the RHQ empty-handed, especially if the other two teams were meeting with success elsewhere. We raced to target three and parked in the darkness down the street while the UN undercover car did its drive by. We couldn't see the restaurant from our location. I sat in the car next to D-Train with my fingers crossed, waiting for the word to move out.

The radio suddenly came alive with the Intel guy's voice. "Bravo One, the place is full and lit up. I can hear music inside. The front door looks locked. You have the green light."

"Son-of-a-bitch! There is no way that Plan A could come together this easy," D-Train whispered.

I had the same thought.

We exited the vehicles and I had Igor give the word to the Russian major, who grinned and slapped me this time on the back. I checked my team a final time and gave the command: "Let's move out!"

We moved at a slow trot, staying in the shadows of the darkened street. Hammer and Nails worked their way in front of me to take the door, leaving me next in line. I was going to enter first this time, the privilege of command. In the U.S.A., back in the old days, the detective who signed the search warrant was always the first in the door. It was payoff for all his hard work, and I was a believer in tradition. We reached the target and lined up on either side of the door. I gave the nod to Hammer and Nails. Like Thor reincarnated, Hammer lifted his battering tool and swung. The flimsy locked door exploded.

Inside, I could make out six round tables, all filled with wide-eyed men. As I entered, my MP5 raised, I noticed four women near the bar, and another three walking between tables. No threat. The men at the tables were farmers. Again, no threat. In the far right corner, however, there was a booth with about six hard-core-looking dudes wearing black leather jackets. Definite threat.

I swung my weapon at the leather jackets and shouted, "Everyone on the floor! Now, now, now!"

On the far side of the small bar was a squat, muscular bartender. Another threat. I pointed my weapon at him. And yelled again.

From the corner of my eye I saw Paddy charge the bartender, so I pointed my pistol back at the six bad guys in the corner. I could only see some of their hands. *Shit,* I thought, *they're going for their guns!*

My mind raced. I yelled out, "Gun, gun, gun!" and ran full speed for the table. With Arni at my right shoulder and Igor at my back, we crashed it, smashing the men against the wall. Two men continued struggling to get a grip on their handguns.

"Don't move, you fucks!" we screamed in unison. With three automatic weapons leveled only inches from their faces, they wisely froze.

I turned and did a quick scan behind me while keeping one eye on the booth guys. Paddy had cold-cocked the bartender unconscious and was dragging him from behind the bar. Hammer and Nails were pushing the bar patrons onto the floor. We stunned the crowd, and that had allowed us to secure the area without injury. We had noise, movement and overwhelming firepower on our side. Son-of-a-gun, it seemed like, for once, Plan A had actually worked!

The two Russian commandoes were helping Hammer and Nails pat down patrons. Sandy was searching the girls for weapons with Mo

227

protecting her back. Arni and Igor disarmed the six gangsters and had them lean against the wall with their legs spread so they could be searched head to toe. D-Train covered us all with his MP5 from the door. Rick, the normally animated Filipino, was standing near the foot of the bar staring at the floor like he was in a trance.

Across the room, Paddy held up the bartender and a shotgun. "Mike, he was reaching for this behind the bar," he yelled.

"Bring the asshole over here with the other gangsters," I shouted back. "Keep everyone separated. Don't allow any of them to talk."

I looked over at Rick. He was still staring at the floor. Worried, I shouted, "Hey, Rick. Snap out of it!"

Arni recovered four handguns from the men secured against the wall. The rest of my crew appeared to have everything under control. Except for Rick who was still out of sync. If it wasn't for whatever was going on with him, I would have called the all clear to the UN Intel guys outside.

Rick suddenly bent over and appeared to collapse. I said, "Oh, shit," thinking that a bullet or the stress had got him. After all he'd gone through, Major Rick, the hardened South Asian warrior, had cashed it in on a simple brothel raid. As his hands hit the floor, he turned and looked over at me with a big toothy grin. In one swift motion, he lifted a trap door to a hidden basement.

"Mike," he yelled, "more bad guys," and he jumped into the hole and disappeared. One second he was there, the next second he was gone. Arni and I ran to the spot where Rick had been. The room light was just bright enough to see a the top of a stair type ladder. Down in the hole, it was all darkness, and from there was coming the unmistakable sounds of a fight. I had no time to think. I jumped into the dark hole and crashed onto the floor. Arni landed almost on top of me a half-second later.

In the darkness in front of me, shadowy figures came at me with clubs, fists, and boots. I was crouching and could sense to my right that Rick was being swarmed as well. Arni and I disentangled. In a heartbeat, the two of us were squatting back-to-back.

Arni screamed, "Knives, now!"

He was right. We couldn't shoot blindly into darkness as there might be innocents there, too. With one quick practiced motion we had our fighting blades out. Rick, upon hearing the command, pulled out his knife and crouched down same as us.

I stabbed and slashed at anything that came near me from out of the darkness. I slashed and stabbed for anything flesh-like, just as I had been taught. The darkness about us immediately erupted into a cacophony of stereophonic screams.

From our crouching positions, the attackers couldn't approach us without suffering major damage. My hands were dripping wet, and I smelled the tang of fresh blood. The next moment, there was a bright shock of light and two bodies hit the floor behind us. The two Russian commandoes had jumped straight down into the cellar while members of my team climbed down the steep wooden stair ladder. The Spetsnaz operators had tossed glow sticks ahead of them as they dropped. It was an impressive entry.

In the sudden light, I could see that the basement I was crouching in was quite large. A number of men stood frozen against the far wall while others squirmed on the ground trying to stop their bleeding. Four young girls, two half-naked, who looked about twelve years old, stared wide-eyed at us.

Sandy found the light switch and flipped it on. Then we rounded everyone up and began to search them, somewhat reluctantly giving first aid to the wounded. Rick had apparently found the brothel part of the restaurant. Half the fifteen or so creeps were patrons, the other half looked like professional bad guys.

Rick's lip was slashed and bleeding. "Mike, what took you so long?" he asked me with a bloody grin.

"I'm not as fast as I used to be," I said. "Arni had to push me into the hole."

Rick smiled wider, winced, and pumped his fist in the air, shouting, "Killing machines! Yeah!"

The cavalry had arrived while we fought for our lives in the basement, so I climbed up the ladder to sort out the situation. Everyone was trying to separate patrons from bad guys. The UN bigwigs would arrive soon, as well as the female KPS to take care of the adult prostitutes. Some UN organization or NGO would take the children and hopefully return them to wherever they had been kidnapped from.

None of that, of course, was my business. I was the SWAT team commander and would soon have to step out of the way, to let the investigators and UN cops who set up the operation take all the credit and publicity. While I was gathering my team, I spotted Abazi against the wall. He was one of the guys in the booth, but at the time I didn't recognize him. He and the others were being handcuffed by the UN investigators.

The raid was a success by any standard—twelve or more bad guys hauled away in handcuffs, ten possibly enslaved women or girls freed, and no major injuries in spite of the life and death struggle in the basement. The KPS took Abazi and his crew to jail, and Arni took most of my team back to base. Sandy, D-Train and I remained behind to await the arrival of the team that would process the girls and determine if they had been victims of illegal international trafficking of women.

While we waited, the girls sat at a table in a corner and talked in whispers. Sitting with them was a middle-aged woman, quite plump and unattractive, who had been found with the others downstairs. She was in control from what I could see, and I suspected that she was trying to coerce them into fabricating a story. I had Sandy remove her from the group. As the woman was being escorted past me she turned and asked to speak to me alone. Thinking that maybe she might want to provide us with some helpful information, I took her over to a table away from everyone else and we both sat down.

"What is it?" I asked, trying to keep her from noticing that just having to talk to her made my skin crawl.

She said in poor English, "These girls. Don't want get trouble. If you let us to go, they will..."

She smiled, displaying her nicotine-stained teeth, and made a crude gesture with her hand and mouth. I glanced over at the girls and saw two of them watching to see if they might be summoned to my side to do some work. Both looked no more than thirteen. One of them, a bone-thin waif with a mop of sandy brown hair ran her tongue along her lips and wet them as if on cue.

I was incensed. I turned back to the ugly bitch and hissed, "You will stay here and not signal or speak one word to those girls or to me. If you do, I will shoot you! Here! Now! Do you understand? I will shoot you right between the eyes!"

I got up and went over to D-Train who was at a window keeping watch on a group of inebriated young men loitering in the street outside the bar.

"Do you know what she just said to me?" I asked him.

He didn't turn to look at me, but continued to gaze outside. "Sure," he replied. "She offered you free sex. What did you expect her to say? That's what these people do."

I was so angry, I had to calm myself. It wasn't easy, though. I looked again at the bevy of young girls and found myself wondering how the hell some people could treat others, especially innocent kids, like that? Some of them would be in the eighth grade back at home. Then my eyes met those of one of the older girls. She was thin, long-limbed and had long stringy red hair draped over a short faded-yellow dress. She had bruises on her face and arms that indicated she been repeatedly beaten. She raised a shaking finger as if she wanted to talk. I huffed, once out of exasperation, a second time out of pity, and approached her. She was pretty enough, but it clearly didn't matter.

"What?"

"Can we talk?"

I said, "I've just been through that with her over there. There is no way…"

"I can tell you things."

I took a deep breath. "Okay, what kind of things."

"Of a kill. I saw a kill."

The other girls were staring at her in horror as was the madam. That was good enough for me. I knew instantly that this was more than just a bid to get away. I shielded her from the eyes of the madam, and escorted her through a door into a back room. The place was cluttered with several filthy mattresses on the floor where the girls took their customers for quick jobs. The room had a disagreeable odor, a mix, I think, of nicotine, ultra-cheap perfume and dried bodily fluids. There was a single chair, and I indicated for her to sit down. I called Sandy to stand in the doorway as a witness just in case I was later accused of any improper action. I still was not sure of the girl's real intent. Then I asked her to find a KPS interpreter so the girl could tell her story in Albanian.

With Sandy manning the doorway, and the interpreter at my side, I asked her, "What do you mean? Are you saying you saw a murder?"

"Yes. Luftar, the one who beats me. He killed my friend last

232

week. He threw her away."

The detective in me quickly took over. I would have to turn her over to the HQ investigators, but I wanted to know more first.

"What is your name?"

"Luana," she replied.

"Hello, Luana. I'm Team Captain Granger of the UN Police. Please tell me what happened."

The gist of it was this: A week earlier, Abazi had a problem with a girl from Moldova who had suddenly stopped producing for him. The friend had confided to Luana that she was pregnant and did not want to hurt the baby. Abazi did what any good pimp would do in that situation and beat the poor girl. He whipped her with a heavy belt, then encouraged his goons to rape her all night. Luana and the other girls heard her scream for hours.

Early the next morning, the girls were put into a van and driven out into the countryside. A sedan followed close behind. When they reached a high bridge over a swollen river, the vehicles stopped and girls were forced to stand out in the cold while two of Abazi's men opened the trunk of the sedan, lifted out a black body bag, and dropped it on the ground.

Trembling, Luana recounted that there was someone inside the bag, struggling to get out. Abazi, wearing steel-tipped work boots, kicked and stomped the bag from top to bottom until all movement inside stopped. Then he unzipped the bag to show the girls the smashed and bloodied face of the pregnant Moldovan girl. Luana recalled that the trapped girl had duct tape wrapped around her mouth.

The girls, of course, were terrified. Luana said she nearly fainted. She thought she saw her friend's eyes open in horror just before Abazi zipped the bag back up, but didn't know for sure if the girl was really conscious at that point. She told me that Abazi's men wrapped the bag in a heavy iron chain they took from the trunk, then, all three men lifted the bag and tossed the poor girl over the side of the bridge into the water. The black bag disappeared beneath the surface in an instant.

Luana said that she particularly remembered the words that Abazi spoke right afterwards. He told the girls, "You work for me. If you want to leave Luftar, this is the way you leave. You feed the fish." He and the other men laughed at the joke while they pushed the stunned girls back into the van. Luana was in tears by the time she finished telling her story.

I was more emotionally impacted by the crime than Sandy who had listened at the door. I remember telling her afterwards that I sincerely regretted not shooting the man when I had my gun trained on his face a little earlier. Sandy shrugged and told me I might still get the chance. I doubted that, but looked forward to doing my part to make sure that the prick was tried and convicted for murder.

Chapter 19

For several days after the Djakovica raid, Bravo Team was in high spirits. Everyone had participated and everyone had a story to tell. We had come together as a team. The rescue of the trafficked underage girls had made the news in Europe and the U.S., and the role of the Special Operations units was mentioned in several of the press stories. There was no mention of the Spetsnaz contribution to our success, though, but I suppose that was normal for military Spec-Ops.

When I finished with my reports and debriefings, I thought it was time for the team to have some fun. We had all had enough of Arni and Igor arguing about which was the best shooter. I decided that it was time to put them to the test. They could both hit the bull's-eyes in paper targets all day long so I devised something a little different. It was based on a simple shooting game that I played with my brothers in the New Hampshire woods during hunting season.

We set the date, May 20th, and the location, a field outside Peja bordered by a steep rising, treeless hill that acted as a perfect bullet backstop. We often went there to practice with our sidearms, shotguns and MP5s. It was a perfect spot for shooting—no neighbors in the area to complain about noise, and no chance of a stray bullet causing any damage to people or property. We played it up big. D-Train created some signs and put them up in the Peja offices to alert interested UN police officers and KPS. The posters gave the time, date, and location with "RPU SHOOTOUT: THE MURMANSK KID VS. ARNI OAKLEY" printed in big block letters at the bottom.

We described the event to UNMIK management as a combination training and PR stunt to show the skills of Special-Ops and then crossed our fingers that they wouldn't stop it. They didn't. Side bets, of course, were kept quiet. When the time came, all the members of Bravo Team gathered along with twenty curious observers at the indicated site. It was a sunny day with barely a puff of wind—perfect weather for a shooting event.

Twelve empty soft drink cans were in random spots all within a fifty yard radius. Some were on the ground, others on rocks or logs. Three dangled at the end of long strings in the branches of a small tree.

There would be no time to warm up, and the one who could hit all the cans in the quickest time with the fewest misses would be the winner. Igor chose two handguns, twin Berettas, and Arni, the champion biathlon competitor, his MP5 in single-shot semiautomatic mode.

After a short introductory speech, I signaled to Igor and stepped out of the way. The unpredictable Russian was very focused and intense. I wasn't sure what to expect from him when I took out my stopwatch.

"Ready, Kid?"

Teeth tightly clenched, he gave a curt nod.

"Go," I shouted, and started the timer.

Igor sprinted across the field, attacking the cans like they were Nazi storm-troopers invading the Motherland. Firing with both hands, he made the cans dance. It was awesome to watch. Every can had been hit in just 9.5 seconds. He only missed twice. When he finished, he smiled and pretended to blow imaginary smoke from the barrels of his weapons. I just stared at him, hardly believing what I had witnessed.

Several team members replaced the cans while Igor stood to the side accepting compliments and backslaps from his many fans. Arni quietly took his place at the starting position, neither looking at Igor nor acknowledging the man's amazing feat. When everyone was safely gathered back away from the shooting area, I reset the stopwatch and gave Arni the go.

Arni didn't charge the targets. He simply raised his weapon to his shoulder and squeezed off twelve aimed shots. A can exploded with each crack of the rifle. I looked at the time. It read 9.25 seconds. I was completely amazed—it seemed impossible. I walked right past a grinning Arni, who I could tell already knew he'd won and showed the time to Igor.

I expected Igor to go into one of his Russian fits, but he just gritted his teeth and nodded. Then he went over to Arni, gave him a bear hug, then took hold of Arni's right arm and raised it Rocky-style over Arni's head in a sign of victory. It was great sportsmanship.

I announced to the crowd, "Nine point two-five seconds. No misses. Arni is the winner."

While everyone celebrated, I moved next to Paddy Burke. "Do you freaking believe that?" I asked.

Paddy rubbed his chin for a few seconds then put on his staple wry grin. "Impressive, at that," he said. "But, then again, the cans were not shooting back at them."

How the hell was I supposed to get these folks to look up to me when they were all so much better than me at, well, just about everything? After we picked up the expended brass, Igor pulled me aside and showed me a small object that he always kept tucked in his boot. It looked like a metal ball-point pen, though a bit thicker. He knelt down, pointed the tip down at the grass, and squeezed a hidden trigger. With a snap no louder than a toy cap, the pen-gun fired a .22

long rifle bullet into the ground. He stood, blew the last of the smoke from the tip, and grinned. "It is a last resort in a life-and-death struggle. A single shot at close range into the head or heart and the fight is over. Standard FSB issue."

Sneaky Russian bastards, I thought. But, though a cool spy weapon, I couldn't imagine it proving very practical for a cop—even a Russian one.

The day after the shootout, Jim Durfer stopped me in a hallway at RHQ. I wasn't sure what his take on the event was going to be, but I knew that he had a strong appreciation for elite marksmanship skills and assumed he'd be as amazed as I was. He surprised me by talking about something else entirely. For a week, he had been gushing over the successful Djakovica raid, saying many times how much he regretted not being there. "Mike," he said, "I need you to go to Pristina tomorrow to talk with investigators. It's about the arrests. I guess they want to prosecute these guys as soon as possible and they will need your help."

"Be happy to," I replied. "What kind of help?"

Like always, he couldn't tell me anything more for the moment.

That evening, I had dinner with Mo at a nearby café. He told me again about his mixed feelings about America since the invasion of Afghanistan. Though he liked me and considered me a friend, his problem was serving under an American commander while my country was busy killing Muslims in another part of the world. I tried to tell him that just like in Kosovo, we Americans were working against "bad" Muslims, the Taliban. I reminded him of the Gulf War where we helped get rid of the bad Muslims to free Kuwait, but he wasn't buying it. He was depressed, and that, in turn, depressed me.

Later that evening, I was driving in my UN car through Peja, thinking about Mo, worrying that he might leave Spec Ops. I was so distracted by the thought of losing a good colleague and friend, I turned down the wrong street and ended up a few feet from Paddy Burke's apartment. I needed to talk to someone, and, of all the guys on the team, Paddy was the best listener—and one of the few who could afterwards serve up a dose of semi-coherent and even logical advice.

As a rule, I never went to a team member's home in Kosovo unannounced, but tonight was different. I had arrived by dumb luck. Serendipity. It was a matter of circumstance, and I really needed to talk. Besides, I was in no mood to follow rules, any rules, even my own. I knocked on the door and, after a minute, heard Paddy's calm voice inquire, "Who's there?"

"It's me, Mike Granger. Can I come in for minute, Paddy?"

There was a long silence. I was about to excuse myself and go when the door opened. He was wearing a dark tee shirt, sweatpants, and flip-flops. He had a sheepish look on his face that made me even more uncomfortable. I had clearly intruded on his personal time. He was courteous, though, and invited me to come in and take a seat.

"Beer, Captain?"

"As long as it's cold."

"It is that. We've had electricity for three days—a record."

While he went to the refrigerator, I noticed his uniform tossed on the floor, which I thought was odd since the rest of the apartment was compulsively neat. Then I noticed that there were actually *two* of everything in the heap—two men's trousers, two shirts, two pairs of combat boots. I also noticed that the boots weren't the same size. Suddenly things shot way past awkward to overtly disturbing. I had stumbled upon something that could prove embarrassing to both of us, to say the least. And I could think of no easy way to deal with it, so I tried to pretend I didn't notice anything unusual.

Paddy returned with a Beck's in each hand and read my face in an instant. His eyes darted to the discarded clothing, then back to me. "Well, Michael," he said as he handed me my beer. "I suspect you have a question or two."

I sighed. "Paddy, I think I'm just going to take my beer and leave, and when I wake up in the morning, I'm going to tell myself this was a dream. Yep, that's what I plan to do."

He turned his head towards the closed bedroom door. "Come on out, Luv," he said. "It seems that the captain's imagination is playing tricks on him, so we better bring him back down to earth."

The door opened with a squeak and my jaw nearly dropped. Standing there in a tight red tee shirt and nothing else was Sandy Wright—Can't Ever Be Wrong. Her eyes glared at me, like always, but her lips were curled up into what I could only describe as an amused smirk. "Well, Captain?" she asked, standing there defiantly.

"Sandy," I replied grasping for words. "Well…this is unexpected." I turned back to Paddy. "So…you two, ah…actually *like* each other after all?"

Paddy took a sip from his bottle, placed it on the coffee table, then said, "Well, *like* is a strong word, wouldn't you agree, Luv? I would categorize our relationship as more along the lines that we *understand* each other."

I couldn't help myself and blurted out, "But I thought Sandy was…"

"A dyke?" she offered as she plopped herself onto the couch next to Paddy. She picked his beer up from the table and took a long draught. Then, wiping her wet lips on the back of her arm, she took a cigarette from an open pack on the table and, lighting it, blew out a long stream of smoke. "That Bulldog is a royal shite. But what he said about me does serve a purpose: It helps to keep all the ugly male flies away—and there are swarms of them in Kosovo. It gave me the space

I needed to choose who *I* want to be with."

It was getting a bit surreal for me. I had never seen an inch of Sandy's legs before and there they were in front of me, bare from painted toenails to the top of her shapely thighs—not at all the manly, muscular limbs that I had imagined. I must have stared at them a bit too long, as Paddy put a arm around her and gave her a squeeze. "And to think she chose me over the rest of you muscle-bound, testosterone-ridden stallions," he said. "It must have something to do with my native charm, or maybe the tender and fragile soul beneath my tough cop exterior."

Sandy gave me a rare, probably final, glimpse at her soft side when she said, "Paddy is both sober and sensitive. I like those traits in a man."

"And Sandra is neither of those things," he added, "but I've come to see the value of that, Michael. The English, you see, have a need to dominate—to always be on top. And I think you can imagine the obvious advantage in this case."

She turned and punched him in the shoulder.

I'd had enough. I drained my beer and set the empty on the table. "I need to be going," I declared.

Paddy protested, "But, you wanted to ask me something, Captain?"

"It can wait."

"Are you planning to report us?" asked Sandy, always the direct one.

I thought about that for a minute. I couldn't recall offhand the fraternization rules, and, frankly, I didn't care. They were both consenting adults. My take was that at least two of the people on my team whom I had worried might one day shoot each other, were clearly unlikely to do it any time soon. That was a good thing. "Well, as your commander," I said, "consider yourselves self-reported. As far as I'm concerned, it won't go any further than this room. Just be on time in the morning."

I was formally ordered to Pristina the next morning to meet with a senior UN commander—the meeting Durfer had mentioned briefly yesterday. The UN commander was a Frenchman named Henri something-or-other. He told me that I was there to provide personal protection for a witness in an Albanian Mafia case. I was to coordinate with two CPU—Close Protection Unit—officers. A little irked and confused, I asked why a regional special operations captain would be asked to do the job of a Pristina CPU team leader. It didn't make sense.

"This is outside standard operating procedure, Captain Granger. You see," he explained, "the witness in this case is very nervous about testifying against one of these bad men. She is close to having a breakdown. She asked for you by name. She said she trusts only you."

"A red-haired girl, right?"

He looked puzzled for a moment then continued, ignoring my question. "Her name is Luana Gjoni. You rescued her during the operation in Djakovica last week."

"Yeah, I remember," I said. "Is she going to testify against Abazi?"

"*Oui*, for murder. The trial is going to be held in your area—in the Italian sector. A lot of people high in the UNMIK administration want to see this man go to prison. The woman is everything to this case. None of the others who were rescued will say a word about him. And why would they? These guys have a long reach. No?"

"Well," I said. "I'm paid to follow orders, sir. What exactly do you want me to do?"

"She's here, now, in an office down the hallway. Please talk with her. See if you can help calm her. Tonight, we will send her in a convoy back to Peja. You will accompany her to a safe place we are setting up. You may choose some of your own trusted men to work with you—five or six."

"For how long?"

"Everyone wants this to be prosecuted and concluded quickly. The UN judge has been notified. The trial should begin in two days and shouldn't take long. We ask that you keep this girl alive for that long."

I looked at him with surprise at the way he put it. "I would hope she'll live a lot longer than that, Commander."

I walked down the hallway to the room where I was told Luana was waiting and knocked. A female UN officer answered, looked me over, smiled, let me in, and closed the door as she left. A frail young woman with dark hair and nervous eyes was sitting on a cushioned chair biting a fingernail. I had been expecting a redhead with heavy make-up, so I must have appeared confused.

"Are you Luana?" I asked pointing to her hair.

She smiled wanly. "Oh. I wear...for work," she stammered.

"A wig?"

"Yes, wig."

"Well, I like you better without it. How are things, Luana?"

"Here, I am good."

"Is the food okay?"

Her smile was a little stronger this time. "Yes, good. I eat a lot. I get fat."

I took out a pack of cigarettes and offered her one. She took one. I lit hers and then my own, and we smoked quietly for a minute.

"Okay, well, why did you ask to see me?" I asked, finally.

"I afraid of Luftar."

"You don't have to be. There are a lot of fine officers here with guns. Why are you afraid?"

She looked down at the floor. "I just afraid."

I took the seat opposite her chair. It was hard not to feel sorry for her. She had nothing and nobody. The only people she had known the last two years wanted only to kill her. To the justice system, she was a tool to get at a very bad character. Once finished, what would happen to her? I'd seen this before, and it rarely ended well.

"Luana. That's a pretty name." I said. "Is it Albanian?"

She laughed then raised her hand and made a playful clawing motion. "A lion woman."

"Ah, it means lioness. I see. My name doesn't mean anything special. It is Mike, for Michael—after Michael the Archangel in the Bible."

She shook her head and said, "All names mean something. Yours means, 'Like God'."

I must have looked surprised. "I didn't know that," I muttered. "How do you know that?"

"I talk to many men. One day I just start to ask what means their names. It is just something I do. I know many names. One man give to me a book with names for babies. I learn them all."

At first I thought it a creative way for a call girl to break the ice with a customer. Then I thought, *Who uses their real name with a prostitute?* Still, I'd learned that Luana wasn't simple-minded. And she was speaking English better with me now than I recalled from our first meeting.

We talked a bit longer, then I left her with the female KPS guard and went to an office on a higher floor of the building. There was someone there I had to visit. Leo had left me a message in Peja that he would be in the capital for a few days, and he'd like me to drop by for a chat when I got there. Of course, I told him I would.

As I surveyed the area looking for the room where he'd instructed me to go, I began to suspect all this wasn't a coincidence. Why would Leo be in Kosovo at this particular moment? How did he know I would be traveling to Pristina? What was he up to with Bekim? I began to wonder if *he* had something to do with my being assigned to guard Luana. *What the hell?* I thought. *Even if he did, he wouldn't tell me. Damned government spooks.*

I approached the KPS guard sitting at a small desk outside the correct door. He looked up at me and asked right away, "Captain Granger?"

I nodded and he raised his index finger, picked up the phone, and said, "He's here, sir."

Ten seconds later, the door opened. Leo greeted me with a broad smile and vigorous handshake. "Mikey, good, you've made it," he said. Leo was dressed in a yellow tee shirt, jeans and running shoes. Nothing about him indicated that he was anything other than a tourist, except there were few tourists in Kosovo at this time.

"You're a hard guy to get hold of lately, Leo, but an even harder one to miss."

"Yeah, I know. I got your messages, but with the time I've been spending between here, Afghanistan, and Washington, I don't know if I'm coming or going. I made time for you today, though. Come on in."

I followed him through the door and down another corridor lined on either side with nondescript rooms identified only by numbers. He stopped at one and we went inside. It turned out to be a large office with a desk, several chairs, a small sofa and several IBM computers. He sat in a black leather chair and motioned for me to sit on the sofa.

"Beer?" he asked.

"I'm on duty."

"So, will a Beck's be okay."

"Sure."

He retrieved two beers from a small ice chest beneath an end table next to his chair. We popped the tabs on the cans at the exact same moment and laughed.

"It's amazing that we're so in sync with each other," he said.

I saw my opening. "Are we?"

"What do you mean?"

"In sync. On the same page. Of the same mind."

"I don't follow."

"Leo, do you know what we call Pristina back in Peja?"

"What?"

"We call it the Emerald City in the Land of Oz. Something tells me that I might just happen to be talking to the guy behind the curtain."

He laughed. "You give me too much credit. I'm just a civil…"

"We both know that's bullshit."

He stopped laughing. "What is it you want to know, Mike?"

"Why do they want Abazi so badly? He's a scumbag, but there are thousands of scumbags in Kosovo. I've never seen a trial move forward so fast."

He took a long sip, then placed his beer on the end table.

"That's something the justice system controls, Mike. I'm just here to represent the State Department. My guess is that with all the publicity about the white slavery bust, UNMIK wants to be seen as acting with dispatch to get justice for the victims. Good work on the raid by the way."

"Yeah, right. Tell me straight, Leo: Are you behind all this?"

"I guess you didn't hear me."

I was getting exasperated. "Leo, I've spent years interviewing some of the biggest lying bastards ever to walk the planet. Do you think that I can't smell a setup?"

He actually looked embarrassed for a second, but recovered quickly. "Mike, we're on the same side. Just take good care of that girl. You're here because I trust you. I need you to trust *me*."

After more fruitless conversation, we finished our beers and shook hands. It felt like the end of a formal business meeting at which nothing at all had been concluded, and I left feeling more confused and distressed. Leo, a guy I'd known for close to three decades, had asked me to trust him. If there was one thing I'd learned over the course of my career, it was that if someone had to ask to trust them, then they couldn't be trusted. I had a sad feeling our relationship as I had known it up to now was over.

The safe place turned out to be a house located on a secluded street on the outskirts of the eastern edge of Peja. The convoy trip had been uneventful. No mortar shells bursting near us, no exploding road mines, no sudden sniping. We arrived at the safe house in the evening around 2100 hours. It was located on a cul-de-sac with only one way in and out. The other houses on the street were vacant, and in various stages of destruction or repair.

A KPS-manned patrol car was parked on the street, keeping an eye out for any suspicious activity. I had five team members in the house with me: Arni, Sandy, Rick, Mo and Nails. I positioned them in separate rooms to guard every possible entry point and keep an eye on any activity through the windows. There was one unfurnished room, a second story bedroom facing the street, that I didn't want Luana or anyone else to enter because I thought its exposed position made it an easy and obvious target. Few times in my life have I been so far-sighted.

Luana was exhausted, totally worn down, her nerves stretched to the breaking point. She fell instantly asleep next to me on a couch in the downstairs living room. She was snoring softly. The room was otherwise silent, as it should be that time of night.

I had a book of New York Times crossword puzzles in my hands, and was in the midst of trying to figure out a nine-letter word for "animus" when an explosion lifted me out of my seat and tossed me and the book onto the floor. Pieces of the plaster ceiling crashed onto my head. I could smell smoke.

Someone had fired a rocket into the window of the vacant bedroom above us. Mo came running into the room from the rear of the house and I shouted, "Stay where you are! It could be a diversion!"

I picked my radio off the floor and ordered a check in. "Anyone hurt? Sandy?"

"No," came her response.

"Mo?"

"No."

"Rick?"

"Okay."

"Arni?"

"Alright here."

"Nails?"

Silence.

"Nails, are you okay?"

More silence.

I'd stationed Rick on the second floor nearest Nails. "Rick, check on Nails—and the smoke."

Rick replied, "Got it."

The smoke was getting thicker. I radioed the command center and told them to send the fire department and an ambulance pronto.

Luana was curled up in a ball on the floor next to the couch, eyes wide, frozen in panic mode. I could hear her whimpering like a frightened animal. I wanted to comfort her, but didn't have time. A bunch of Albanian thugs could come crashing through the door any second.

I shouted into the radio, "Rick, report status!"

He didn't have to. I saw him work his way down the stairs supporting a dazed Nails who was babbling incoherently in German. I ran to the stairs to gave Rick a hand. When we reached the bottom stair, I called out for the others. Surrounding Luana, we moved her to the bathroom, and I left them to check the KPS officers who had been parked on the street, the threat of a mass frontal assault having passed. I was worried, however, as I stepped onto the street, that I might be in the crosshairs of someone's rifle scope. I searched the car using it for cover, for the two officers. They were missing.

Then I saw them jog out of the darkness, short of breath. I had requested English-speaking officers, and asked the closest one, "What happened?"

He pointed at a thick cluster of evergreen brush about forty meters away and said, "We heard nothing until we saw the rocket fire. We chased after them, but they had too great a lead. They left this."

He handed me a pair of night vision goggles. Expensive ones. Not something someone would leave behind on purpose. Whoever dropped them had left in a hurry. The KPS had done their job from what I could see. Nobody could have spotted the attackers in the darkness, on this moonless night, with such heavy cover to hide in. I told them both "thanks" and "good job," then instructed them to move their car out of the way, as I could hear fire trucks and ambulances approaching.

I got on the radio and told the team to once again form a protective shield around Luana and take her outside to the command car we had parked across the street. Then I scanned the windows and roofs of the houses in the neighborhood with the gift left by our attackers. I was still worried about a possible sniper, but what could I do? The second floor of the house was ablaze, and I had to get Luana and my team out now. I had no choice, but to take the chance.

The fire spread to the attic and roof, as the team rushed out the door, Luana being carried between them like a log riding a white-water current. When they reached the command car, they pushed her inside, face down, on the backseat floor with Sandy on top of her. I zigzagged in a crouch over to the car and checked Nails. He'd been badly stunned by the rocket blast, but I didn't see blood anywhere. His eyes appeared clear. He knew my name and the day of the week. I could tell that his head hurt, though. Rubbing the back of his head, he said, "Captain, what are your orders?"

I thought, *Germans, you gotta love 'em.*

Once I determined that Nails was really okay, we executed the appropriate maneuver for the circumstances, and got the hell out of Dodge.

Rick drove while I got on the radio to Pristina and screamed for someone to wake up the French commander. He answered several minutes later with a bad attitude about having been disturbed, which got me even more pissed off.

"Whose idea of a safe house was this?" I shouted into the radio handset.

"It-it-it was always safe in the past."

I didn't give him the courtesy of a further comment. "I just have one other question?"

"*Oui?*"

"Who leaked our location to Luftar Abazi's men?"

He hesitated for a moment."We don't know that," he said. "This may have been a random event. Kosovo is a very dangerous place, as you know."

"Random, my ass," I said. "You've got yourself a security leak at headquarters. This time, I'm taking the girl to a safe place of my choosing."

"Where?"

"My villa. I'll contact you from there in the morning."

I had lied, of course. We drove straight to Sandy's flat. It was located on the second floor of an apartment complex in a built-up neighborhood. The private houses on the quiet street were all occupied by families. The access road was paved and wide, and there were clear lines of sight from her second-story front balcony and rear windows. There was no heavy brush anywhere. Sandy, Rick and I ushered Luana inside the building and waited in the apartment for the others.

It was two in the morning, and we were all tired. Sandy found a blanket for Luana and made her some tea. We set up much the same way we had at the not-so-safe house, with Luana on the couch in the main living room and me on a chair nearby. The rest of the team went off to different rooms to cover the windows. I kept an eye on the only door to the apartment.

I was dozing off at around 0400 hours when I felt a hand touch my knee. "Luana?" I asked sleepily.

She murmured, "Can you hold me?"

"What?"

"I'm afraid. Can you hold me?"

Now, as a professional I knew that I shouldn't do it. My job was to get her safely to the courthouse, not ease her emotional trauma. As a man, I was worried that if I did do it I might easily step over the line. After all, it was dark and she was twenty-years-old and sexy and very vulnerable. Even so, as a parent and a decent human being, I knew that

I could not just ignore her cry for help. I moved over to the couch and sat next to her. She immediately put her head on my chest and her arms around my neck like a small girl would do with her father. She was shivering. I pulled a blanket over us and put my arms around her shoulders. In a minute she was sound asleep.

At daybreak, the smells of coffee, toast and scrambled powdered eggs filled the apartment. Sandy was cooking. Mo showed up while we were eating together, and reported that there'd been no activity during the night—and nobody appeared to be watching my place. I hadn't expected Abazi's crew to react that fast, even if they were tipped off again in Pristina, but I thought it worthwhile to be cautious.

Throughout the morning, I was in contact with Tony at Peja police headquarters, Jim at RHQ and the Frenchman in Pristina. I did not reveal my location to any of them. I just asked Tony and Jim to have some reinforcements on alert in case we needed them in a hurry. We all stank from sweat and smoke so Sandy allowed each team member and Luana to use her shower. There was nothing that we could do about our dirty clothes, but the showers made us all feel better as we waited for instructions.

I asked the guys in Pristina several times to make up their minds about what to do next. The answer finally came back in the early evening: Return the package to the capital. I asked them to repeat, but their instructions were the same.

Now I was really pissed. What the fuck? We had risked a convoy, come under rocket attack, and now they wanted us to turn around and go back? What about the trial in Peja in a day or two? Were we going to end up turning around in a few hours to do it all over again?

My team needed time to stand down and get cleaned up, so Jim Durfer had the Germans of Alpha Team saddle up to convoy Luana and me back to the capital. Once we arrived at headquarters, she was immediately taken to a secure room. I asked to speak with Leo, but was told that he had left Kosovo. I called his direct number, but got no answer. I didn't bother to leave a message. He knew it was me calling.

I was asked to meet with the Frenchman and two other senior UN commanders. One of them was British, the other Spanish. We sat in a room around a large conference table. They went out of their way to appear friendly—too friendly—and I immediately began to sense that something was not right. I told them so, diplomatically, of course.

Henri cleared his throat. "I am sorry about the attack at the safe house, Captain Granger. You have done excellent work for us keeping our key witness unharmed. However, we no longer require your assistance on this case."

I had mixed emotions. I wanted badly to get home but I felt compelled to make sure that Luana remained protected.

"What's changed?" I asked. "What about Abazi's trial?"

The British commander was next to clear his throat. He was a bone-thin Field Marshal Bernard Montgomery look-alike who until then had been sitting back in his chair, casually smoking a pipe.

"Captain Granger," he said, "all we can tell you is that there will likely be no trial. The suspect has cooperated with us on important criminal matters and we have reached an agreement. We do thank you for your efforts, my good man."

I was stunned. I took a deep breath and stopped to think before I spoke. These guys were my boss's bosses and I had to be careful.

"Sir," I said, "Are you telling me that Abazi has cut some sort of deal and will walk?"

The British commander appeared embarrassed. "Ah, well—do you mean will he be released? Well, yes, at least for now, I'm afraid. At least until the charges are more thoroughly investigated. Then, we may indict him."

"Oh, that's just great," I replied sarcastically. "A revengeful murderer and rapist back out on the streets."

None of them responded. They all just looked at me as if to say,"It's a pity the poor fellow doesn't get it." Unfortunately for them, I got it.

"What about the girl, Luana?" I persisted. "If Abazi is freed, then she will be in grave danger. What are you going to do about that?"

The Spanish commander spoke for the first time. He appeared sterner than the other two, and impatient to end the meeting. "We will make certain she is returned to her family. She has some relations in the Peja region and others in Albania where it is perhaps safer. Either way, it is not your problem anymore, *Capitan*. You are not to involve yourself any further with these people or this case. Thank you."

He was more than rude in his delivery, but he was also right. It was their show, and the girl's safety was their problem. I had no way of knowing if Albania would be any safer for her than Kosovo. But then, there was the old rule of creating distance from bad guys—the farther away the better. It had to be at least a little safer there.

I was dismissed and went to find Alpha Team for the midnight ride back to Peja. The whole thing had left a bad taste in my mouth. The trip back took several hours, but in my head it felt like several days. Alpha Team drove me to my villa gate, and Captain Ernst asked if I needed to be tucked into bed. I told him to fuck off. He laughed and ordered his men back to headquarters.

It was 0330 when I finally crawled into the sack. I couldn't sleep, though. Luana and Abazi were on my mind. I knew that back in the States it was common to cut deals with criminals for information. I was disappointed, though, that a dirtbag like Abazi might walk away from all his crimes. I wondered what the hell he had to offer to get them to drop such serious charges. I knew, however, that they were never going to tell me.

Blessed are the Peacekeepers

Chapter 20

The next morning, I called Leo several times and left messages each time for him to call me back. He didn't. We had a scheduled milk run to Prizren to drop off a key witness in a revenge murder. It was rated low risk. Normally, I would take my place in the command car, but that day I was bone-tired, having barely slept the past two days. I was still willing to go, but Jim Durfer suggested that I let Arni, my Bravo Two, handle the run for the experience. I was scheduled to leave Kosovo in two months, and Jim wanted Arni fully prepped to take over.

That was fine with me.

The first couple hours into the run, I shuffled papers and surfed the internet. D-Train was on radio watch, and used my proximity as an opportunity to berate my eating, smoking, and other bad health habits. He said I could change my life through a combination of yoga, meditation, and moderation in all things. With his help, I would become a new and happy man, if I would just let him. I told him to go screw himself and left to smoke a cigarette.

At quarter to noon, the radio suddenly came alive with hectic chatter. D-Train yelled for me to come to him fast.

"What's going on?" I demanded. The voices on the airwaves sounded frantic.

Paddy's voice called out over the speaker, "We need ambulance assistance immediately! The lead car has been hit!"

I told D-Train to send both ambulance and fire assistance to the location pronto, and went to the next room to alert Jim Durfer. Jim immediately dispatched Alpha Team which was in a helicopter returning from another mission. I returned with Jim and we huddled with D-Train around the radio.

"Paddy," I said. "Give us a sit-rep."

"It was an IED. They hid it in one of a dozen haystacks alongside the road, a direct charge, aimed at the side of the passing vehicles."

I knew that Arni and Igor had been together in the Command car.

"What about casualties?"

"We got them out," Paddy replied. "Both are conscious. Arni is all bloodied up. He's in the worst shape. Igor may have a broken arm, but he's up and about directing traffic."

Jim took the microphone. "Durfer, here, how bad is Arni?"

"Don't know, Commander. Paramedics are just arriving. Italian KFOR is right behind them. Here comes a chopper."

While we waited for an update, Jim turned to me and said, "Looks like you picked a good day not to ride."

"I feel bad enough as it is, Jim," I said.

"Yeah, sorry, Mike. That was stupid of me. Well, at least the blast hit the side of the hard-skin Toyota. The added armor must have helped."

Alpha Team broke in on the radio. Their helicopter had arrived on the scene. A few minutes later, Captain Ernst gave an update and said his men were doing a sweep of the area. They found the spot where the bombers had been hiding in a thicket about a hundred meters away, but there was nobody still around, of course. Alpha had followed their tracks to a sunken road where a vehicle had been waiting to take them away.

Sandy notified us that Arni and Igor were being airlifted to the Italian base for emergency medical care, so Jim and I took a car to meet them there.

When we got the base hospital, we found that Igor had indeed broken his left arm, but was otherwise fine—just a few minor wounds, cuts, and contusions. The surgeon had his staff take some x-rays. Then he set the bone and cleared him for release.

Arni had taken the brunt of the blast. He had a concussion and was banged up on his left side with a shattered radius and ulna. He also had a damaged eardrum and small pieces of glass embedded in his face and left eye that would require surgery by a specialist.

The vehicle was totaled, but it could have been worse. I thanked God that there was no fire. Both my guys were alive, and that was the only thing that mattered. The pragmatist in me, however, could not help note that I had just lost my two best shooters. Arni was airlifted within hours to a hospital in Germany, and I barely had time to say goodbye and wish him luck. Igor was escorted by Alpha Team back to his residence. He knew his time in Kosovo had ended that day as well. It was a downcast team of survivors that returned that night to RHQ. I stayed on into the night to collect my thoughts and figure out what to say to what was left of Bravo Team in the morning.

It was around nine o'clock and getting dark outside, and, as I gathered my things to leave, an officer at the security check notified me that someone wanted to talk with me. When I asked who, the guard put the guy on the phone. I instantly recognized Bekim's voice.

"Officer Mike, I need to talk with you."

"Come on up, Bekim."

"No, Officer Mike. Can you come down? I need to protect my privacy. I can drive you home. I'll wait."

I finished gathering my things and proceeded to the first floor.

Bekim was wearing a white dress shirt, tan slacks, and an outdated striped tie. The KLA leader turned KPS investigator was starting to look quite the Kosovo professional.

We shook hands, climbed into his KPS car, and he drove off towards my villa. The traffic lights were out, so the driving was slow. He stopped at an intersection bottleneck and said, "Mike, I'm sorry about your guys. Everyone in the KPS is angry."

I asked Bekim, if he knew who planted the bomb. Was it the Mafia? The KLA?

"Officer Mike, that's why I am here, our intelligence in Pristina thinks it was a Russian gangster named Bukin. The one who hates you for arresting his nephew. We think he was trying to kill *you*."

I thought of the vodka bottle Bukin had sent to intimidate me, but I never figured he would actually try to have me killed. "So, you're telling me that the attack that nearly killed Arni and Igor was meant for me?"

"Yes, and that now you are in even graver danger."

"Fuck that. Where is Bukin?"

"We are looking for him," Bekim assured me.

I knew almost nothing about Bukin, except that we had stared each other down twice and I testified against his nephew in court—and that he was feuding with Abazi. I asked Bekim what he would do in my place.

His face turned serious. "If I were you, I would kill Bukin."

I shook my head. "I can't just kill him."

He looked surprised. "Why not, Officer Mike? He tried to kill *you*."

That night, my mind was besieged with thoughts about tracking down and shooting Bukin. It was a fantasy, though. Sure, on paper I was a well-trained "killing machine," but it just wasn't in my makeup to become an assassin. Bukin would have the same chance I would give any bad guy. Perhaps Igor was right, and deep down I was an American pussy.

I speculated for a moment on how the others on my team would act in my situation. Hammer, Nails, and Rick would probably take the man out. D-Train? No, he was a straight arrow. Paddy? I think he would eliminate Bukin, but he'd make it look like an accident. Sandy, I couldn't say. Mo? It would be against his religious beliefs. The two guys who would have taken on Bukin in a heartbeat, Arni and Igor, had been taken out by him first.

Bukin might be gunning strictly for me, but by remaining in Kosovo, I was putting all my team in harm's way. I thought about leaving. I could go to Jim, and say that I was scared for my life and wanted out, and he couldn't really do anything to stop me—at best, he could have me sued for breach of contract. Such an act would negate all the good I'd accomplished in Kosovo, though, and Jim most likely would let me go without making problems. That would leave everyone in Kosovo who knew me to remember me as the vampire guy who turned tail and ran when the going got tough. In short, I couldn't have Bukin wacked, and I couldn't leave the country, so the only thing left was to stay focused and play out my hand. I wanted to get Bukin for what he'd done to Arni and Igor. There was no doubt about that. I just needed to be patient and wait for the right moment.

In the morning, the faxed medical report on Igor arrived on my desk. He had a fractured elbow and badly torn ligaments. There was no way that those injuries could heal before the end of his remaining two-month term.

I gave him the bad news over the phone. Igor would be going home to Russia on a medical discharge. He was due some R&R time, however, and chose to stay a while longer in Kosovo.

Actually, I believe that he was hoping against hope for a miracle that would allow him to stay on with the team. He argued that he could still shoot better with just one hand than anyone else on the team, which was true, but unrealistic. I felt responsible for his situation, but there was nothing I could do. I was going to miss him.

It turned into a quiet day. We had no protection runs scheduled, just a planned recce near the Macedonian border for a future mission. After a short briefing, in which I mainly updated the team on Arni's and Igor's conditions, I sent Mo and Hammer for the ride to southern Kosovo. I told the others to chill out and find something to do, then locked myself in my office to think.

What I thought about was Luana. I needed to know that she was safe. Safe back in Albania "with relations" as promised. I called a friend at headquarters and asked if she had left yet. What I was told made me instantly fume: Luana had been released—in Pristina. No one knew where she went after that.

I was now more afraid for her safety than ever. How could they leave her out hanging in the breeze like that? Luana had risked her life attempting to bring a very bad guy to justice, and no one seemed to care any more about her. Well, I did. I felt responsible and I wasn't going to let Abazi find her and stuff her into a sack and toss her into the river—or worse.

It took me most of the morning and a dozen phone calls to finally locate her. Bekim and my other KPS friends finally came through for me. They exercised some proper arm-twisting with an informant who hung out with someone in Abazi's crew. The informant said he had heard that Luana was staying on a remote farm some twenty miles northeast of Peja. I wrote the location given me by the KPS in my notebook. All I could think about the rest of that afternoon was the rest of what the informant had told my KPS contact: "Abazi plans to get his revenge very soon."

That evening, I skipped my usual dinner at the café, and quietly slipped into my UN car. I didn't tell anybody where I was going. I needed to check on her. I knew I shouldn't go alone, but I didn't want to get any of my teammates in trouble. I had been given a direct order from Pristina to stand down from anything concerning Abazi or Luana. I also didn't want my action to taint the reputation of my team. Before leaving the parking lot, though, I looked over the map I'd brought with me one more time. My KPS contact had been somewhat vague about her exact location, and I wasn't confident which route to take.

There was a young KPS guarding the lot entrance who I'd seen a few times, but didn't know well. I pulled up next to him and said, "Good evening."

He smiled, probably unused to receiving such pleasantries from a Spec-Ops guy.

"Hello, sir," he replied. "Do you need something?"

He spoke English. Good. I showed him the map and pointed at the general area I wished to visit.

"Do you know this place at all?"

"Oh, yes, sir. I have many family there."

I focused his attention on a specific sector. "This spot, here. I'm told that there is a farm here about a quarter mile off the main road. How would you get there from here?"

He leaned in the window and traced the route with his finger, identifying the several secondary roadways.

"Be careful at this place, sir," he said. "One road will take you far away into the mountains. The one with a long high rock on the left side is the good one."

I thanked him and drove off. It was a warm clear evening. I drove with the windows open for nearly two hours through rolling farmland over increasingly deteriorating roads until I found the one with the long boulder on the left just as the KPS guard had described. That final length of dirt road was actually a cart path packed down over the decades to where it could support the weight and width of my car.

I soon spotted the farm in the distance. I turned down an even smaller rocky pathway that got me to within fifty meters of the place before ending at an uneven grassy patch of land. There were no cars or trucks parked within sight. That was not unusual for Kosovo at that time since few private citizens had motor vehicles. There was a small barn next to the house where, I assumed, a cart and maybe a donkey were kept inside. On the opposite side, there was a narrow decrepit outhouse with rotting wood at the base.

I parked next to a large haystack and walked the rest of the way to the farmhouse. It was a single-floor white plaster and stone cottage with an aging rust-colored tile roof. The door opened even before I got close enough to announce my presence. Luana stood in the opening wearing a thin summer dress covered with tiny blue print flowers. Her feet were bare and dirt-stained with fading pink paint on the nails. No wig, no make-up—she had made a very quick, unlikely transition from weathered prostitute to innocent-looking farm girl. Few hookers could have pulled that off, but she had somehow managed it.

I smiled, but she did not return it. She still had the sad eyes.

"Hello, Luana," I said when I reached her. "Are you okay?"

She replied, "Okay," nodding, showing no emotion.

"You probably want to know why I'm here."

"Yes."

"Would it be okay to come inside?"

She hesitated, but then nodded. I followed her into the house. It was small but neat with white walls decorated with old black and white photographs. There was a tall multilevel stand against a wall with several arranged green plants. I detected a musty odor mixed with a faint smell of garlic and what I figured was pipe tobacco smoke. She led me to chair in the kitchen area. The chairs and a heavy table had obviously been hand-crafted some years prior by a talented carpenter. She sat on a chair opposite me.

I heard a noise come from another room that sounded like a man coughing and clearing his throat.

"My grandfather," she said. "He is very sick."

"Too bad," I replied. "Is your grandmother here?"

She shook her head.

"She died. One month. He has no one else."

"Sorry."

"Okay. I'm to take care of him."

I looked into the main room and noticed what looked like a bolt-action Italian Carcano rifle resting above the stone fireplace on a pair of thick wooden pegs. The stock was scratched, chipped, and weatherworn like it had seen heavy use in the past.

I pointed to it and asked, "Did your grandfather fight in a war?"

"Long ago, he fight with the Albanians and the Germans against Serbs. Then, he fight with the Serbs against the Germans. That is Kosovo. Everyone fights everyone else."

I sighed. That is Kosovo. How many times had I heard those words uttered in the same resigned way the past nine months?

I had planned on convincing Luana to return with me to Peja where I could keep an eye on her, but she had just thrown a big monkey wrench into that idea by telling me that she was caring for her grandfather. I decided to just tell her what I knew.

"Luana, I think you are in danger here. I have heard that Abazi knows where you are and will seek revenge soon."

She shook her head slowly. "Did you think that Luftar would let me live? I always know that he would find me. It's up to God to decide when."

That kind of thinking wasn't going to cut it with me.

"I can help you. I can take you to someplace safe."

Her eyes darkened. "Where were you when I needed the police to help me? You took me to Pristina and told me that everything would be okay. They were going to send me to Albania, to my mother's house. But they drive me to the middle of the city and tell me that I am free. I say to them what do you mean free? I don't want to be free. They laugh and drive away. Where were you, Granger?"

I was so angry at the three commanders who had promised to protect her I could barely speak.

"I didn't know about that, Luana," I said. "I would have intervened. I would have done something."

I didn't know if she heard me.

"I walk for three days and nights to get here," she said. "I hide in the woods to not get hurt by men. I am here now and I will stay. My grandfather needs me."

Maybe she saw in my face that I was sincere. Maybe she was just played out. She reached over and touched my hand then held it. "I'm sorry, Granger. You have been kind to me. I think you would have done something."

I held her hand for a moment, then got up and started to leave. She stood and kissed me, on the cheek, much like a young girl would kiss a brother.

"Thank you. I will remember you always," she said.

I left the house and crossed the field to my car. When I got there, I just sat and tried to think. What could I do? I had offered my help and she had refused it. I couldn't take her by force. I couldn't assign my team to protect her because she was no longer a witness. I remembered how the KPS that had camped out in front of my villa after 9/11. I was irked by the thought that while I had not needed protection, how much I appreciated their loyalty. If they were in my car, now, instead of me, they certainly wouldn't just drive away.

As I was going over my options, I realized that I was there for a reason. Things like this had happened to me before. I'd get a feeling that I could not explain, that turned out to be a forewarning of something big headed my way. My mother was a believer in horoscopes, and told me when I was young that it was just the Pisces in me. That zodiac sign dictated that I should be deeply intuitive and sensitive to the psychic energies all around. I had no reason to doubt her theory—she usually was right and it did seem to always play out that way.

It began to get dark. I watched a light appear in the window of the house, and saw Luana move to close the shade, looking out towards me several times. Maybe I was freaking her out. I had just decided to leave when the door to the house opened, and Luana began walking towards me carrying an antiquated oil lamp like a Balkan spirit. She skimmed through the ankle-high grass until she reached my car. I thought she was going to blast me for acting like such a damned stalker.

"You do not leave?" she said, peering into the car.

"I want to stay here in the car until morning," I replied. "Then I'll have to go to work, but I feel like I have to stay tonight."

She shivered as there was now a marked chill in the air.

"It's cold," she said. "Come back inside and be warmed by the fire."

Back in the house, I found the grandfather sitting in a rocking chair next to the fire with a woolen blanket covering his lap and legs. He wore a white wool Albanian cap on his head. He had a white

Turkish-style mustache, turned up at the ends, but no beard. Luana probably shaved his cheeks and chin every day. When he saw me, he bent forward and gestured with his hand over his heart. I did the same in return.

Luana asked if I wanted to take off my gun belt, and I did, placing it on the floor in a corner, and took a seat near the old man. He watched me with rapt curiosity.

"The fire makes the house very warm," I said to him. "Did you build this place?"

He looked at me blankly and turned to Luana. "He speaks only Albanian. He does not understand what you say," she explained.

She translated, and he told me he built the farm with his own hands sixty years ago. He had been an apprentice woodworker by trade when young. He also made all the furniture. He asked me if I was a soldier, and I told him that I was an American with the UN Police. He did not seem to understand the concept, but I suppose that as long as I was not a Serb it was okay with him.

I pointed at the rifle. Antique firearms were a hobby of mine. I smiled and maybe I looked like a kid who wanted to touch a toy. He got what I was trying to convey and lifted his hands, motioning for me to take it down. I took it off the pegs and felt its weight. I tried to imagine this small old man as a young man lugging the eight pound weapon up and down the mountains day and night for years. The MP5, by comparison, weighed only five pounds. I put it on my shoulder and pretended to buckle under its weight and he laughed. It was probably the best laugh that he had had in a long time.

I carefully put it back and sat down again.

With Luana interpreting, he started to tell me of a time and place of which I had little knowledge. Like a lot of old men who could not tell you what they had for breakfast an hour ago, he remembered every detail of days almost sixty years past. When the Germans came and allied with the Albanians, he had thought it an opportunity to resist Serb oppression in Kosovo. He had no problem killing Serbs in battle, but had a change of heart when the Albanian SS Division began to commit vicious atrocities on the Serbian civilian population. He said it was so bad that even the Nazis were embarrassed by the level of their brutality.

Luana's grandfather deserted his Albanian cousins and survived a scary two weeks with a company of Serbian Chetniks who, it turned out, were as bad as the SS. They were killing Germans and Albanians while at the same time acting as guides for other Germans and Albanians who paid them to help set up ambushes against communist-led partisans. He ran off again with his rifle, and found a home with the partisans under the Marxist leader, Tito. The old man told me that his best friend during his two years with the partisans was a Serb. The man saved his life twice. His friend was later murdered by a gang of Kosovar Albanian nationalists. It was just as Luana had said earlier: Everyone fights everyone else in Kosovo.

With a tear in his eye, the old man said that Tito promised them a free Yugoslavia where Albanians, Serbs, and all the other ethnic groups that made up the former Serbian nation could live together in equality and peace. According to him, Marshal Tito delivered on that promise—at least for a while.

After an hour or so he began to drift off and Luana helped him to his bed. When she returned, she sat in the rocking chair. "He likes you," she said.

"Is that unusual for him?"

"Oh, yes. He is sometimes hard. Not with me. He loves me. My other grandfather was much meaner, but he is dead."

For some reason I thought about the young farm girl victim of the honor killing a few months back. Before I could stop myself I had asked Luana, "Does he know about what you did for work in Djakovica?"

She looked embarrassed and turned her eyes away from me. "He suspects some things," she replied. "He is not like other men here in Kosovo, other Albanian men. He has seen many sad things and does not judge. All he wants now is for me to stay here until he dies so he can be buried next to this house with my grandmother."

I felt guilty for making her feel uncomfortable, so I tried to make her forget by starting to tell her about my trip to Zurich in the fall. I asked if she would like to go to Switzerland someday.

She just shook her head and said, "My place is here."

There was no electricity in the house, of course, just the oil lamps, and oil was limited and precious. She put out the lights until only the fireplace glowed. We talked a while longer and sipped tea, but we were both sleeping in our chairs when the last flames disappeared.

Just like at the not-so-safe house in Peja, a sudden explosion rocked us from our dreams. It was total darkness inside the house, but I felt my way to the window and looked out to see through a fog what appeared to be a raging bonfire about fifty meters from the house— exactly where I had parked my UN vehicle. After a few seconds, I saw the flashes of weapons firing and heard the pops, cracks and thuds as bullets from automatic weapons raked the house. I dropped as fast as I could and dragged Luana down with me.

As we lay hugging the floor, the bedroom door opened and we could hear a shuffling movement across the dark room behind us. A moment later the front door opened, and I could see the silhouette of Luana's grandfather exiting the house with his old rifle in his hands. There was a flurry of gunfire from out the fog and he moaned and crumbled to the ground.

Luana cried out, "Grandpa!" as I scurried across the floor, feeling around for my gun belt. Still in complete darkness, I felt for my radio and tried to contact my base. There was no response. Our handheld radios didn't always work in the more remote areas. The one in my car would have, but I was sure that it had already gone up in flames. There was a lull in the firing after the old man was shot. I crawled out the door and tried to drag him inside, but it was clear to me that I was working with dead weight. The firing started up again and I retreated, slamming the door as bullets splintered the wood no more than a few feet above our heads.

"Luana," I said. "I don't how many of them are out there, but they will try to surround us. We have to get out of here. Fast."

She squeezed my arm tight and we crawled along the floor to a small exit on the side of house that led to the outhouse. The fog masked our escape past the outhouse into a wide grassy pasture in the rear. Dawn was being stymied by a thick cloud covering. We ran until we came to a small rock-filled ravine, crossed over it, dashed across a flat field and into a small copse of tall pine trees and dense brush.

Luana had no shoes and ran barefoot over the rocks, tree roots and fallen branches. Her feet were soon lacerated and bleeding. She complained of the pain, but what could I do? Our lives were on the line, not just our comfort. We rested at the edge of a wooded area while I watched for any movement in the fog. A few seconds later, I saw beams from two flashlights cut like searchlights through the fog. They were following our footprints we'd left in the dew and were heading right for us.

I had to slow them down. I inhaled and exhaled deeply several times to calm myself. Then, I took my Beretta and aimed six inches above one of the bobbing lights. I squeezed off a shot. The light fell to the ground, and the second beam shut off a second later. I heard angry shouting.

"What happened?" whispered Luana.

"I think I hit one of them," I said. An instant later fire from half a dozen weapons began raking the trees around us. We ducked. Luckily, the shots were not aimed. Whoever was out there was reacting out of anger. My lucky shot had halted their advance, but only for awhile.

The sky was starting to lighten, but the low mist kept us invisible. I guessed that, being one less, they would choose to wait for better light, and for more of the fog to burn off. Then, they would fan apart, move forward, and attempt to flush us out.

I tried the radio again, but still no signal. I took Luana's hand, and dragged her deeper into the trees thinking that if the woods were deep enough we could elude our pursuers. It did not turn out as I had hoped, though. The trees were barely thirty meters deep and at the back of the copse was a steep rising hill. If we tried to climb it, we would probably be spotted and dead within minutes. The pine thicket was no more than one hundred meters wide as well; six or eight men could sweep it in ten minutes or less, and I figured it was their plan to do just that.

I heard a rough voice erupt from out of the mist. It was Abazi. He was calling something out in Albanian. I recognized Luana's name a part of it. "What did he say?" I asked.

Her face paled in the dim morning light. Voice shaking, she said, "He said he forgives me. He said come out and he will buy me a red dress. He said he does not want to hurt me."

"You know that he's lying, don't you?"

"I don't want him to catch me. If he will catch me, I want you to shoot me first."

I was getting nervous, but I wasn't yet ready to give up hope. I still had my weapon and I was good with it. I felt I stood a fair chance of hitting at least two more of them before they got too close. If there were six of them or less, I was sure that fifty percent casualties would be enough to make anyone, even these crazy Albanians, stop and think.

Also, if I could just get the damned radio to work, I could call in help, maybe in minutes. I tried it again, but got nothing except a low-battery signal. All I could do was move around to different spots in my small wooded hideout, hoping to pick up a signal.

After five minutes of frustration, I finally got it. I heard someone on the other end answer, "Kosovo Police Service."

I said, "I'm UN Captain Granger of police special operations. I need immediate assistance. I am under fire and need help. Please send..."

There was beep, then nothing. I stared at the handset in disbelief. The freaking battery had died! My lifeline had been severed by...fate, I guess. Luana covered her face with her hands and groaned. The only object that could have saved us was now useless.

It was getting lighter out and I could see forms maybe sixty meters ahead in the dissipating mist. As the minutes passed, I found myself mindlessly fiddling with the useless radio as if it might somehow come magically back to life and save us at the last moment. It didn't, of course.

I dropped the useless handset and looked ahead. I could see new movement in the field, so I focused and got my weapon ready. They were starting to spread out, advancing slowly. Behind them, I caught sight of something on the road in the distance. It looked like two vehicles racing towards the field. My nerves were popping like a bag of Mexican jumping beans. Was it cavalry to the rescue, or was it Abazi reinforcements and with them the loss of any chance that I had of shooting our way out?

I watched the two civilian cars stop, and a group of armed men pour out of each. They clearly weren't UN, KPS, or KFOR. They were civilians carrying hand guns and assault weapons. I heard shouting, and watched the two group form into one, and approach Abazi and his men. I figured it was over, that Luana and I had at most only a few minutes left to live. If I had been the religious sort, it would have been an appropriate moment to start praying my ass off.

Then, I noticed something strange. The new guys and Abazi's men were not shouting greetings, as I had first thought. They were exchanging what sounded more like angry threats. I took Luana's arm and dragged her to a spot near the edge of the wood, closer to the shouting men—now maybe thirty meters away. They were close enough to hear their voices clearly.

My jaw must have dropped when I recognized the leader of the new bunch was none other than KGB Bukin. He and Abazi were screaming insults at each other, pointing fingers, performing what we in law enforcement called the "monkey dance." It was the name for a primal impulse handed down to us by our ape ancestors, involving a litany of exaggerated posturing, yelling and intimidation that was often the prelude to a fight.

Bukin's and Abazi's men formed into two lines facing each other and began brandishing their weapons at each other. I didn't know what they were saying. Everything was in Albanian, and Luana was too terrified think about translating. I assumed the two chief bad guys were arguing over who was going get to keep my head for a trophy after they lopped it off. Luana was now fully despondent. Overwhelmed by everything she was seeing and hearing, I could see she had given up.

"They are going to kill us, Mike Granger," she said. She lowered her head and said in a whisper, "Please shoot me. Now. Please."

My mind was racing. Kill the two of *us?* It looked to me more like they were getting ready to kill each other first. Either way, I guessed Luana was right. In the end, whoever was left would surely take us out.

I could think of only one option left, and decided to go for it. I pointed my weapon and fired it twice...into the ground. An instant later a nervous trigger finger in the field must have twitched at the sound. A shot rang out, and a millisecond later all the bad guys were blasting away at each other, leaving us to duck and cover our ears. We hugged the earth and each other, watched in fascination as the OK Corral meets Lexington Green played out in front of us. Nobody out there in the now chaotic field at that moment cared a whit about the two of us. Men were screaming and killing each other.

I saw Luftar Abazi tumble to the ground and watched KGB Bukin follow a moment later. Four or five of the thugs emptied their weapons, then ran off into the mist. After less than a minute of raging, ear-splitting violence, the field was again calm. No shouting, no moaning—complete, utter quiet.

The silence, however, lasted only a few seconds. Thousands of blackbirds, frightened by the racket, had begun swirling in the sky over our heads, shrieking warnings to the rest of their flocks. Luana looked at me, clearly surprised she was still alive—that the two shots she had heard and thought were meant for her never hit home.

I was tempted to check the field, but I stopped short. There were likely wounded men out there, holding onto their weapons. I wasn't going to let myself get shot by a guy who might be only minutes away from greeting his maker. I had seen too many old war movies to make that mistake. After a minute, I heard someone moan. I still waited. If I had to wait for hours I would have—but, as it turned out, I didn't have to.

The huge flock of birds suddenly veered away, and in the distance I could see, then hear, the reason. A white helicopter with black UN lettering hovered for a few seconds over my burning UN

Toyota, then approached us low from the east, hovering momentarily over the field, and finally touching down. From the doors exited the members of my team, fully dressed and fully armed. Out came Paddy, Hammer, Nails, Rick, Mo, Sandy, and D-Train. The last one out was Igor, the Murmansk Kid, with one arm in a cast and a Beretta in his other.

I watched with pride as Bravo Team rushed to the scene and secured it like the pros they were. Normally laid-back Paddy Burke was in the lead, barking out orders in an atypically animated fashion. They were gathering up the weapons and starting to give medical aid to the living wounded when I yelled out, "Paddy, it's me, Mike! I'm coming out!"

When he spotted and recognized me, he ordered everyone to lower their weapons and waved me on. Luana then stood up shakily beside me, and we walked over to them. Paddy smiled and pointed to the bodies lying all around. "Captain," he said, "I knew that you were a fair hand with a sidearm but this…"

D-Train cut him off. "What the hell happened here, Mike?"

"Do you want the official story or the real story?" I asked, relieved to be among friendlies again.

"Take your pick, but tell us," D-Train piped up.

"In good time, Dee. In good time," was all I was able to say.

Hammer called to me, "Mike, come here. Someone wants to speak with you."

I walked over to where he was standing. He had his MP5 trained on a figure lying at his feet, bleeding from wounds to his arms and legs. It was KGB Bukin. None of the wounds appeared mortal, but they had kept him from crawling away.

He looked up at me and sneered. "Is the God-damned pimp dead?" he demanded.

276

I glanced at Paddy and he nodded. "Yeah, Abazi is dead. Happy?"

Bukin gritted his teeth. "Not yet," he replied. Then he looked me in the eye and said something in Russian. The tone was enough to indicate to me that gratitude for keeping him alive was not the core of his remarks. I shrugged and instructed Hammer to take care of his wounds. A KFOR helicopter appeared on the horizon on its way with a medic.

Bukin had barely finished speaking when another chopper flew in causing a God-awful racket about forty meters away. Before it even hit ground, a score of Italian paratroopers poured out, looking for something to shoot. I thought, shit, here we go again, and asked Paddy deal with the officer in charge. I was too tired to talk. I stepped away from Hammer and Bukin, and pulled out a cigarette. As I searched for my lighter, Igor appeared at my side with a pocket Zippo and flicked it. I bent over as he lit my cigarette, and took a deep drag.

"Thanks," I said. "I thought you would be safely back in Mother Russia by now."

"Today. I am to leave today," he said.

"Couldn't resist one last mission with me, huh?"

"Yes. This is a good mission. You are okay."

He leaned forward and whispered, "Captain Mike, you must listen to what I say."

"Sure, Igor, what is it?"

"What he told you, in Russian. He said that you and Abazi will soon sleep in the same grave."

"Well, that doesn't seem very likely now."

"What he means, Kosovo will be your grave. He will heal and will have you killed."

"He's already tried that. Why should I be worried?"

Igor lifted his cast. "Don't underestimate him. Maybe you have been lucky."

I was too beat to even think about that. "Igor, my friend," I said. "I'll worry about Bukin later when the time comes."

I saw Luana sitting inside the UN helicopter with Sandy. I thanked Igor for his concern, and headed over to the aircraft, stepped inside, and sat down on a bench next to Sandy. She had Luana's lacerated feet on her lap and was treating them with antibacterial ointment.

"They look sore," I said.

"She'll be fine with a few days of rest."

"Thanks, Sandy."

"For what?"

"For sticking it out with me. I know I'm a piss-poor boss."

She smirked and didn't argue with me for once.

From the helicopter, I watched Igor talk to one of the Italian medics. He had his good arm wrapped around the medic's shoulder. I saw the medic nod and run back to his helicopter. Igor then knelt down beside Bukin and talked to him. Despite the bad angle of sight, I saw Bukin's leg's twitch, then relax, and figured Igor had given him some morphine for his pain. The medic returned to Bukin's side with a stretcher and looked confused. Igor seemed to be explaining something, then the medic shrugged, and with the help of another soldier, transferred Bukin to the stretcher and took him to the helicopter.

Igor hurried away. Something seemed odd.

I exited my helicopter and walked to where Bukin had been. There were dozens of shells littering the grass. While I stood there, Paddy came to tell me that the Italian KFOR platoon had received orders over the radio to take over the scene until the KPS and UN patrol officers arrived. I was fine with that. I left Paddy and Mo with

278

the Italians. The rest of us climbed into our chopper and I asked the pilot take us to Peja.

Blessed are the Peacekeepers

Chapter 21

When we arrived at Peja, I left Luana with Sandy, and told the others to stand down and wait for instructions. Though I was still dressed in muddy, torn BDUs, I went directly to the Peja police station to meet with Tony before going to RHQ. He was happier than I had ever seen him to find that I was safe. I knew he was chomping at the bit to get the details of what had happened, but I had questions that couldn't wait.

"Tony," I said, "I reached the KPS this morning looking for help, but my radio died on me before I could give the details. I still got the help. What happened?"

His face turned serious. I could see he was formulating a careful response. "The officer who got the call contacted me and told me that you appeared to be in trouble," he said. "When I heard it was you, I got in touch with Bekim. He knew that you had gone out to the girl's farmhouse. The guard at the gate told him and all of the rest of the KPS. I contacted Patrick Burke, and he was able to get your team together in a very short time. He found you."

I was impressed. Tony was good. Paddy was good. They were all damn good. I felt, though, that he was holding something back. "Thanks, Tony," I replied. "Something else is bothering me: Bukin showed up before the rescue team did. How did *he* know that I was there?"

Tony looked embarrassed, as if he hoped I would never ask that question. He sighed. "Like I said, Michael, all the KPS knew you were looking for the girl. One of them probably tipped him off for a reward. We are investigating that. Maybe Bukin thought it was a good opportunity to deal with both you and Abazi at the same time. Anyway, he found you as well."

The phone rang, and Tony took the call. He mostly just listened to the person on the other end and said "yes" numerous times before hanging up. He looked over at me and said, "That was a report from an officer at Peja hospital. Two of the wounded men are on their way to surgery. They think that they should recover. Bukin is dead."

My head jerked up. Dead? I didn't think he was that bad off. Dead? "No kidding?" I exclaimed.

"They do not do autopsies at the hospital, so we may never know what killed him," Tony explained. "He was dead upon arrival. I don't think you'll miss him."

"No. I sure won't."

Something about Bukin's demise did not pass the smell test, though.

"Is Igor still in country?"

"He's at the airport. Why? Do you want us to get in touch with him?"

I thought about that for a minute. I wanted answers, but sometimes there were answers that I'd be better off not knowing. I said, "No. Well, yes. Could you get a message to him? Please tell him I said thanks for everything, and that I will always appreciate his loyalty."

"Is that all?"

"And tell him I said to have a safe trip back to Russia."

"I'll call it in now."

While Tony was at the radio contacting an officer at the airport, I tried to recall the half-minute scene with Igor and Bukin together while the Italian medic was away. I won't pretend to know what happened. How could I? I only knew that Igor had personal score to settle for Arni and he was not the kind of guy to allow Bukin to make a comeback and eventually get to me.

I had been a detective long enough to be able to put two and two together. If it added up to five this one time, then I could live with it. For now, it was Bukin who would be buried in the same grave as Abazi. Many in Kosovo would consider that justice.

Early in the afternoon, Commander Durfer returned from a meeting and told me to go home, get cleaned up, and start working on my incident report which he was dying to read. I'm sure that, after he read my official version, he would insist on hearing the real story. I had to think about how much I could tell him without getting into trouble.

There was at least one thing I was not going to mention. My friend, Dr. Meski, at Peja hospital had called me a few minutes earlier. He told me that while examining one of the shooting victims, he had found something odd. He said one of them had been shot in the heart, and when he dug out the slug, it was a .22 caliber bullet. He thought it odd that mobsters would carry such a weak weapon. I then recalled seeing Igor's hand rest on the top of his boot for a moment as he hovered over Bukin on the field. I remembered, too, what he kept there. I could have asked more questions, but told Dr. Meski to forget about it, the UN does not request any autopsies, and we know how they died.

Even before I'd wrirtten the first word of my report, the rumor mill was spinning out of control. I was happy that I didn't have a cell phone on my person, or a land phone in my villa. Instead, D-Train,

Paddy and Rick dropped by for a few minutes to update me. The most fantastic KPS story had me crossing an open field like a modern day Wyatt Earp and drawing down on the bad guys, killing all thirteen of them—or was it thirty?—without suffering a scratch.

I was still experiencing a bad case of writer's block when I heard another knock on the door. It was too early for my remaining roommate, Billy Ray, to be back from work. Besides, he'd just use the key. I figured it was someone from Bravo Team again. Still, being cautious, I picked up my Beretta and slipped off the safety and held it to my side as I opened the door. Standing there, like the fresh cherry on top of a melted ice cream sundae was my ex-friend, Leo. He was grinning.

"Well, let me in for Christ's sake…"

I opened the door, but checked first that he was alone. I saw his car parked near the gate with a guy wearing dark sunglasses behind the wheel. I let Leo in, then locked the door behind him.

"I could use a cold one," he said.

"The beers are warm as piss. No electricity today."

"Never mind, then."

He went and sat on the couch and I sat on a chair opposite him.

"I didn't know you were back in Kosovo," I said.

"I just got in this morning and heard what happened. I just wanted to check to see if you were okay."

We made small talk for a few minutes, and then before leaving he said, "Your tour here in Kosovo is almost up, Mike. You just took two really bad guys off the street and saved the life of a poor lost soul at the same time. Not a bad day's work. I could use that kind of production on my team. I'm off to check on another post-war situation tonight, and while I'm gone, I want you to chew on something: If you like this kind of work and you're interested in joining my team, call me. I really want you to think about it."

I did think about Leo's job offer over the course of the next few days. I figured it was not meant to be, though. I was too damned tired and I just wanted to go home. Back to the States. I was tired of cold showers, chicken and rice, unpaved roads, no electricity, barking war dogs, dead bodies, and working every day. I desperately wanted hot showers, electricity, cable TV, cold American beer, green grass, friends and family.

Sure, I would miss the comradeship and the excitement, but war and peacekeeping are young men's games. Middle-aged men need not apply. In the summer of 2002, things were heating up all over the world. There was even talk about going to war in Iraq again. I wanted to go back to the States and see my two sons, Scott and Sean, before they were shipped out, as they most certainly would be. They were part of the new "greatest generation" of young men and women being groomed to march into harm's way.

Me, I was plain old tired.

Bravo Team underwent further change after Arni and Igor left. Mo left us, and went back to the patrol division as a team leader. We parted friends. He even gave me a headscarf from the Jordanian Royal family as a gift before leaving. In the end, he just couldn't work for an American, not even me.

I nominated Paddy Burke for Bravo Two, and he was unanimously approved by the team. On the side, I got Paddy's commitment to elevate Sandy to the Bravo Two slot when he was made Bravo One. She deserved it and I hoped it would shake up the system a bit.

Hammer and Nails moved to Alpha Team. They had wanted to be part of the all-German group from the beginning, so it was nothing personal. D-Train was happy just to drive lead car, and Rick just

285

wanted to have fun. We got five new operators fresh out of Spec-Ops school, new "killing machines" to be broken in by Paddy and Sandy. Me? I chilled out and spent a lot of time thinking about my next step in life.

The days leading up to the end of my tour were unusually hot and busy. It hadn't taken long for the competing Albanian and Russian mobs to replace Abazi and Bukin, and the crime rate quickly returned to normal. The difference this time was that none of them wanted anything to do with Mike Granger or his crew, and that was fine by me.

I decided I wanted to see Cara Sanchez one more time. Our romance, if you could call it that, was more the product of two lonely people in an exotic location, with helicopters, guns and danger all about. We were genuinely attracted to each other, for sure, but it was a mutual unspoken understanding that the relationship wouldn't work back in the States. I called her and we made a last date in Pristina. The long goodbye took all night. I told her to look me up the next war. She laughed. So did I. I think we both felt we would run into each other again someday.

The Monday of my last week in Kosovo I got to my office early and logged onto the computer. There was an email from my police chief. He said he had held the investigator position in the DA's office open for me, and wanted me to confirm my acceptance so he could get the transfer paperwork started. So...I *was* going to be put out to pasture after all.

Then I thought about it. Maybe it wouldn't be so bad. I would walk files around the courthouse every day for the next few years. Then, I would pull my retirement papers, and retire with a pretty good monthly paycheck. I could sell the house in Manchester and move into my lakeside cottage year-round. I would grow a small pot belly, start balding, wear reading glasses, watch all the world conflicts on the military history TV channels, and grow happily old. Maybe I could even learn how to garden.

I re-read the email again. *Shit*, I thought, *who am I kidding? I still have something left in me, and there's a whole lot of world out there yet to see.* I replied to the chief that we could talk about it when I got back. Then, I picked up the phone and called Leo's number. It went right to his voice mail.

"Leo, you son-of-a-bitch," I said. "Give me thirty days in the States to re-charge my batteries, and I'm all yours."

About the Authors

Tom Donnelly has a background that includes work as a U.S. Customs officer, business intelligence analyst and trade compliance professional. He is working on several more novels currently in various stages of development. A graduate of Northeastern University, Tom lives with his wife, Judi, near Boston, Massachusetts.

ABOUT THE AUTHOR

After graduating summa cum laude with a degree in pure and applied math in Britain, Alec Sharp moved to Boulder, Colorado. He has worked as a programmer or project lead since 1979, in a variety of languages, and on many different applications. In particular, Sharp has used Smalltalk in applications ranging from GUI-intensive configuration modeling to headless, multithreaded robotics control.

Sharp is the author of *Software Quality and Productivity*, and of several articles on Smalltalk published in *The Smalltalk Reporter*.

Sharp is also president of Spiral Software Solutions, a company providing consulting and training in Object technologies. He can be reached at asharp@spiralsoft.com.

Printed in Great Britain
by Amazon